Greening Wheat

Greening Wheat:

Fifteen Mormon Short Stories

Edited by Levi S. Peterson

Midvale, Utah
1983

© Copyright 1983 by Orion Books
All rights reserved
ISBN 0-941214-12-5
Printed in the United States of America

Distributed by Signature Books, Midvale, Utah

Contents

Introduction

Good stories are appearing among the Mormons, greening like wheat in a Utah spring. This collection is intended as a sampling of them. As the acknowledgements will show, most of these stories have appeared recently in magazines or journals; a few of them appear here for the first time. It is possible that they will gratify readers desiring escape and amusement through the simple drift of a plot. But I hope that they will also prove rewarding to those who read intensely. I hope that readers will find in them a skillful exercise of the conventions of modern fiction: economical, expressive sentences; diction within the modern idiom; carefully controlled point of view; conflicts ripening organically into climaxes. I hope moreover that readers will find something fresh and original: unusual metaphors giving old ideas and conflicts a new and compelling significance or ingenious manipulations of structure or puns and poetic extensions creating unheard-of connections between words.

Hopefully these stories will appeal to Gentile as well as to Mormon readers. In one sense their Mormonness gives them a unique character. The Latter-day Saints have derived from their frontier experience the idea that as a new people they are to create a new civilization in all its aspects. Their profound, insistent identity compels them to fashion it as nearly as possible in unique Mormon terms. Most of these stories therefore reveal the visible Mormon apparatus of missionaries, home teachers, prayers, sacrament meetings, and so on. Fundamentally, however, they do not fall into a singular species of fiction. Mormon fiction belongs to a large and venerable literature featuring the conflict between orthodoxy and the world at large. These stories have much in common with stories by Jews or almost any other writers having a cohesive, closely defined religious identity. In particular, the tensions of a timeless Christianity underlie these stories. Exacting and unrelenting, the Mormon ethos invites opposition and creates conflict, which inevitably attracts the makers of fiction.

A major tension of Mormon fiction arises in the possibility of wrong behavior. Like all who take sainthood seriously, Mormons live in a perpetual ambivalence, pulled between the commandments and an intractable human nature. Many find themselves beset by unfed appetites and stifled aspirations; they are tempted to misspend the Sabbath, to neglect their tithes, to wax promiscuous, to free their egos from the impossible quest of an absolute perfection. Even the best intentioned and the most abstemious can err through misperception. "Everncere" presents a mother who worries that her son lacks due reverence and conscientiousness; events show her that it is not the boy's devotion to the gospel but merely his style of expressing it that differs from hers, and she is both grateful and ashamed of herself. "The Age-Old Problem of Who" depicts the impropriety of Mormon ethnocentricity; a youth working on an Alaskan fire crew comes to recognize that his Gentile comrades are persons of full, rich spirit. In "Original Sin" a girl preserves her chastity by breaking off with a boy but suffers from the denial of her love for him.

A similar tension arises in the question of believing or not believing. For Mormons, as for centuries of other Christians, belief is an ultimate imperative and disbelief an ultimate perversity. The faith of the Latter-day Saints survives and even flourishes in a scientific age, its adherents protected by invisible walls of doctrine and attitude against the unbelieving among whom they live and work. Yet many of them are susceptible to dissonance; in the secular world or in their own perverse psyche they find opposition to their faith. As one might expect, some of the stories in this collection amplify one side or the other of this conflict. For example, "A Song for One Still Voice" depicts a man enlarged by his faith; touched by God's presence, he overbrims with beatitude. "Counterpoint" features a cynical, uncommitted youth who finds in a hostile setting the catalyst for affirming his neglected faith. "Low Tide" presents a couple at the melancholy point of stepping from the warm, domesticated structure of the Christian world into the forbidding expanse of a strictly natural universe. Appearing at this late moment in the twentieth century, these stories make a new sweep over the old battleground in the human mind between faith and doubt, myth and science, revelation and reason.

A closely related tension arises from the failure of the promises. Mormons typically cannot accept tragedy as a part of the authentic Christian life. They do not esteem the books of Job and Ecclesiastes, and they mistrust traditional Christian art depicting the tragic themes of Christ's passion and death. They believe fervently that the commandments are a blueprint for happiness and that God is bound when human beings prove faithful and will shower upon them temporal as well as heavenly blessings. So imperative is this belief that it sometimes amounts to a psychological defense. Like other kinds of people, Mormons do more than simply control and discipline disorderly impulses and emotions; they tend to deny and repress them, to interpret them as absent from their experience. This psychological proscription extends not only to anger and sexual impulse but to despair and grief as well. Among its many functions, the gospel serves as a defense against the traumas of mortality, as a tightly woven fence encircling the fearsome thickets of the unconscious mind.

Writers, however, are led irresistibly into this forbidden territory. At the heart of a number of the stories in this collection is the failure of the promises. "Yellow Dust" depicts a young missionary in Latin America who awakens to the horror of mortality at a funeral; the doctrine of a remote resurrection cannot mitigate his instinctive fear of death. In "Answer to Prayer" a married man prays successfully for relief from adulterous impulses. However, his prayer has not given him an easy power over temptation. The fractious sexual desire which is integral to his personality will recur and he will again have to struggle against it. "Four Walls and an Empty Door" features a girl whose untimely love for a quadriplegic boy underscores the ironic futility of the boy's unwavering faith in his eventual recovery.

These stories and others give a fresh articulation to the old Christian perplexity about the existence of evil in a universe ruled by a benign God. They suggest that for even a Christian life can be tragic and can offer more problems than solutions. They also raise the question of how one is to find salvation in a Freudian age. Christians too can exist in a state of defenselessness. Their repressive devices and mental protections fail, and they are compelled to confront the puzzling, unwarranted contents of the unconscious mind. They are pilgrims on their way to Heavenly City with an enormous bag of psychic burdens on their back.

A final point: the stories in this collection fulfill the criteria for moral literature not through exhortations and messages but through dramatic probabilities and patterns of experience. Literature has a duty to be moral as well as beautiful; ultimately, it ought to enhance life rather than to depress it. However, its moral purposes are served, not by censorship and exclusion of the problematic or violent or forbidden but rather by the achievement of breadth, balance, and proportion. An explicit treatment of sex, violence, or other disorderly impulse is not of itself immoral. Immorality exists—pornography exists—wherever these qualities are given in such unrelieved, completely amassed detail that they become the single large effect of a work. But when any of them is balanced proportionately with other qualities and appears as a part, rather than the entirety, of experience, it is valuable and appropriate. Nothing human should be excluded from literature; neither should any single aspect of experience—cheerful or dark—monopolize it. A health comes to human beings when they acknowledge in their philosophy and celebrate in their art a broad range of experience, manifesting thus that they are appreciative of life's fulfillments and beauties and toughened to its hardships and deprivations. Moral art has been served if a grouping of stories such as this collection reflects an abundant sampling of experience—comedy and tragedy, ecstasy and disillusionment, restraint and sensuality, heroism, and failure, romance and defiance.

—Levi S. Peterson
Weber State College

A Song for One Still Voice

Bruce W. Jorgensen

He is awake, and knows the time. In its reliable way that he does not yet trust, his mind has waked him just before the alarm should go off. His side of their bed, in the small room, must be jammed close to the wall, so he leans across his sleeping wife to reach the nightstand and press down the button. He has set it early to have time to dress, get his shovel, and make his way through the block to the headgate, so he has maybe twenty minutes, and he half-wishes to wake her. With the children, there is little time when they are entirely alone, in quiet like this. But she was up till almost eleven settling the girls, and when he finally held her she turned, snuggled her backside against him, tucked his arm under hers, his hand spread on her chest, and mumbled into her pillow, "Let me go to sleep like this." He did, lay listening to random snapping and easing of joists, cyclic rumble and hush of heater, long past the time when his fingers told him she slept, till he turned over to find his separate sleep. He knows she still needs this placidity that he senses with his whole body. Touched, her skin would lie still as water without a breath of air moving on it.

But he slides out of the covers and scoots himself down his side, the lightstring from the ceiling brushing his scalp so the hair on his neck rises and he thinks for an instant: spider. Bugs are one problem of this old house; winter drives them in, and as spring swells into summer they will propagate madly. He has taught the girls to stomp on the slightest suspicion of a black widow.

Cold is another problem: their northwest corner room is farthest from the heater, which is central only in having been built into the wall between kitchen and living room so it blows both ways; to keep the girls' northeast corner room warm they must prop kitchen and bedroom doors at angles calculated to guide an optimal airflow. In winter, one of them will rise at least once each night to check and re-tuck blankets. Not quite twenty-six, he has begun to understand why some old people, his grandmother, brag of lasting out the winter. One night this past January he spent almost eight hours with a propane torch trying to thaw the water line; he'd come in for five minutes or so in every hour, sit at the kitchen table to drink hot chocolate, both hands on the mug, shoes off so warmed air would blow across his feet. Under the house, gloved hand gripping the pipe to feel when the water would start, he knew his first terror of the simple elemental world. And in this rented house, far more than in three years of apartments at school, he has felt on himself and on Lea the entire weight of their needs of shelter, heat, food, clothes.

He stands at the foot of the bed, thankful for carpet even if it is cool. And it is spring now, the worst of the cold past, and if there is no late frost, the lilacs may all bloom—first time in years if it happens, the old residents say. But the hawthorn came through anyway last year, and will again, a thick, monumental bouquet of red and green he is glad to have lived to see on a front lawn, even if not his own. A sort of stewardship. Just out that blinded window he could see the hawthorn if it were day, a few knots of bloom already open. He remembers coming into the room one afternoon last August to a moment's stunned joy at the pear-yellow light flooding through the drawn blind. He has been happier here this past year than anywhere or anytime else.

From the dresser mirror his clownish ghost shimmers back at him as he stoops with knees spread to hold his pants up while he reaches his shirt. He wonders if anything has been left on the floor between here and the door to trip him going out, but the way is clear, and he carries his shoes to the added-on porch that he and a colleague wired and plumbed for washer and dryer and he and his wife papered with yellow stripes—their first try and not a bad job. The door to the kitchen closed, he opens the back porch door and sits on the steps to pull on the heavy steeltoed shoes he bought years ago to work in the sheetrock plant, the summer before he met Lea. The stiff shoes pinch and bunch his toes.

Standing again to take his hat and gloves from the hooks below the back porch window, he remembers coming home early one afternoon last week, quiet to surprise them, walking through the house, then opening the door to the porch and seeing them blurred and pastelled through waterspotted glass and screen: sitting under the blossoming apple trees, petals strewn thick around them on the grass, the little girls calling to make it rain again, and she shaking a low branch to shower more on them. He stood and watched, drowned in delight that he could find no words for, hardly daring to go on out because his coming might be less to them than what they already had. Later he walked them to the corner and across the highway for soft ice cream.

Picking up the shovel he stood last night by the step, he crosses the yard to the southeast corner, climbs the fence at the solid post there, pulls his shovel through, and makes his way along the ditch that runs through his neighbor's deep back yard—a good man and kind to them, though Carl does not more than mildly like him yet and so feels undeserving of even shared surplus corn or broccoli.

He stumbles and almost falls over a short tree stump that he knows well enough to avoid, and chides himself again for not buying flashlight batteries. His shovel striking the ground has waked the dog, who comes dragging his chain from his house under a honeylocust, sniffing and starting to growl, then wagging his tail when he catches Carl's approved scent. Carl squats to stroke the dog and scratch his ears, trying to recall his name. He hasn't had a dog since high school, and it pleases him to make friends; he wouldn't mind just staying here and patting and talking to this one, but it is time to start the turn and he whispers, "Go back to sleep, boy, it's o.k.," and walks up through the driveway to the headgate in the cement ditch running north on the east side of the block. They don't have a dog because the fur makes Lea's asthma act up.

It takes only a minute to aim the water at his yard, a big stream so he doesn't need to seal the edges of the gate with mud—what runs on by won't matter. It is also simpler to walk back around the block, so he does that, his shovel balanced on his shoulder by his wrist crooked over its handle. He crosses the tracks he supposes they are on the wrong side of, though in Cedar the distinction hardly exists, and walks into the hard glare of mercury-vapor lamps along the highway that runs straight west to the interchange. He dislikes the lamps for the livid cast they give to skin, the tarry-looking shadows they throw around even pebbles, so he is glad to get past the big, blocky furniture store-warehouse, turn the corner, and walk in dark toward his house.

Out of the glare, he can look up at the stars, thick, clear, shining a steady, warm light. Living at home, he'd use his telescope on any night like this, could find his way from constellation to constellation, predict where, aimed carefully, the six-inch mirror would dazzle him with a nebula, a far galaxy like M31 in Andromeda, the jewelled globe of stars in Hercules toward which the whole solar system slowly spins. It felt good to know the sky, and he'd wonder what it was like to know it as God does, galaxies and even clusters of galaxies flung like seeds to the far fences of the universe. He'd read that a planet within the great Hercules cluster would be seared in the light of a thousand suns, and supposed that to be like the place where God dwells.

The sidewalk runs straight to the edge of his yard, stops for a foot-wide strip of bare red clay, then resumes as his own front walk angling up to the narrow concrete steps. In the back yard before the water, he has time to check his dams for watering the trees and flooding the small lawn. He really doesn't need all the water this second turn of the season—their garden is only half planted, peas, carrots, lettuce, thin grasslike spears of onion sets. He remembers last fall, when he came out from hanging several onion-stuffed nylons in the storage room and saw their cat leap three feet into the air to claw down the hummingbird that had darted at the hollyhocks all summer. He himself pounced on the cat to rescue the bird, got it in his hand, felt the shock of its unimaginably intense life, saw at its throat what he first thought was blood, then realized was the ruby, glowing in the dusk as if the bird bore the summer's whole harvest of light. Then, his hand stunned open, the bird flew away.

Kneeling in the grass to wedge a chunk of brick more firmly in the bank, he smells fresh mint growing along the ditch and bends closer to breathe it. He has seen Lea put a leaf to each nostril and inhale, an ecstasy of breath. They should learn to make mint tea.

Now the water arrives, a finger-size trickle swelling to fill the ditch and start spilling on the lawn. He stands, steps back near the house, and follows its spread by silver flickerings in the grass. The garden furrows were set right last time—he won't need to check them for an hour. He did not think he'd like gardening. His parents had a large garden and made him help weed it, a chore he escaped when he could. He still doesn't like weeding, but to have something grow by his own labor, something they can eat even if not at much less cost than buying, feels good. When the lawn is a still, blade-pricked sheet of dusky silver, he turns to go in.

He'll sleep on the couch near the bedroom door, and he steps into the bedroom to get a light blanket in case of cold. Coming back out he kneels by the bed to kiss Lea on her warm, pulsing temple, again half-wishing to wake her. The faint odor of the vinegar she rinsed her hair with last night reminds him how she came from the shower, blossoming from sharp spray. How she tangles sense and memory. There is no loneliness like the body, nor any delight. "Sleep," he whispers, content that she'll not know this riffle in the hidden stream of her ear. He will sleep without resetting the alarm, and see if his mind will wake him again in an hour.

But when he does wake again it is because one of his daughters has cried in her sleep. Guessing why, he takes a dry diaper with him, untwists her from her covers, changes her, for once without rousing her to open her eyes, and turns her warm, tumblesome body end for end so she lies as she should. When he stands and turns to check the older girl, he sees through the windows, taking both in at once, unbelievably, snow. The sight stuns him with delight and fear harmonized like a major fifth, and then he knows, barely trusting this, that it is some surprise of the light.

Stepping to the east window and bending to look out and up, he sees it is so: pale light pouring from a risen last-quarter moon and resting on bare clay, on weeds, on barely flowing water, on apple branches like silvery weightless snow. Looking at it, he is weightless, in free fall as if the earth has dropped from under him, or as if he is drawn up with the world's tidal bulge and loosed in the gravity of light, yearning farther out and from deeper within than in any prayer he has ever spoken. Undeserved, abounding, grace rings in his bones.

The Age-Old Problem of Who

Kevin Cassity

Peter could have walked but feeling the excitement and relishing the slight danger he ran, water pack and equipment jostling against each stride, the fire moving slowly after him through the dry grass. At the edge of the heavy brush he threw down his equipment and moved back to the field, pumping water through a fog nozzle. Dancing yellows turned to cold black. Seventeen year olds were not supposed to work fires but in Peter's case a mistake had been made, and he gladly let his age be forgotten. He thought of the work he was doing in rather unusual terms. It all came down to winning eternal life, which is what he wanted. It was Alaska, the summer of 1975.

He heard his name sung out from the mountainside where the main body of fire rolled upwards through thirty acres of tall pine and brush. He followed the sound. Through the haze two indistinct figures slowly took human form, each bowing and rising in rhythm with its swinging trench tool. Peter soon made a third, and the three passed the night moving slowly up the slope, cutting a line in the earth. Weariness came and then curiously passed away again as the sun rose.

Firefighting for a summer Peter would earn enough money to attend the church university. Then he would go on a mission, become a church leader, raise a family, become great in some field, die, and live in the celestial kingdom. This summer was his first time away from home.

During the morning he and Willis, the stocky, unshaven fellow, found a small stream, dammed it, set up a pump, and ran a hose up the mountain. Peter spent the day climbing up and down the slope, hosing the perimeter of the fire. It seemed to be under control. In the heat of the afternoon the wind carried a spark across the line, and it set fire to a thicket high up on the mountain. He saw himself on a movie screen, ragged clothes on his heroic frame. The city of Los Angeles was at stake; there was a stubble beard on his chin (here the scene had become, perhaps, implausible). A blonde haired girl he knew was involved. Although Grade B movies ran in his head— almost unremarked, as is common— the conscious, moral part of Peter had pretty much shunned television. Normal people watched T.V., but he believed that those who wanted to gain the celestial kingdom had to be more seriously minded. He realized, as he read church books and pondered quotebooks, that there were more important things to do with one's life than watch T.V. He had once given a talk to that effect in church. It had had a sobering influence on the ward. He was congratulated afterward for the hard-hitting wisdom of his talk. He gave the credit to the Lord and the Deseret Book Company.

As he climbed upwards, the weight of the preceding day, night, and day bore down, his movement becoming lethargic, dreamlike. By the time he reached the spot fire it was in thick brush, roaring and whirling before him. He stood and stared. A grey rabbit, confused by the thick, hanging smoke, loped up to him and then off again toward the center of the fire. Peter moved toward it, speaking a reflexive "no," but it jumped more quickly in the same direction. Sitting down he let his mind spin and his eyelids close. When he opened his eyes again it was to the sound of cries, like those of a human baby, downslope. It was the rabbit. He had heard the sound once before on a scout outing when his ward scoutmaster had shot a rabbit, missing its head but breaking its spine. The rabbit fell out of sight and cried until the scoutmaster found it and shot it through the head. There were a dozen tiny red teeth lying on the ground after the shot. The weeping now bored through Peter's stupor, and he stood up, rigid; it went on and on.

And then it stopped. When the relief crew arrived two hours later, he could not remember what he had actually done to stop the spot fire from setting a new portion of the mountain ablaze. He saw that it had burned up to a point where the organic land cover gave way to stone and offered no more fuel. The eastward wind had died down. So the fire stayed.

McKittrick, the magical one, called up to him, and Peter came slowly down the mountain. He fell once and lay there savoring his heaviness. Cold water leaked from the pack onto his shoulders and neck. He got up and moved on. McKittrick met him. "Fire Control just radioed and said they want all that dirt you're carrying around running through the sewers of Fairbanks tonight," he said. "We're walking out to the swamp where we landed." Willis handed Peter his gear bag, and the three set off.

Peter thought of McKittrick as magical because through McKittrick he saw common things as if for the first time. It was McKittrick who had told Peter one time, when they were talking about such things, that no one really knows what "matter" is other than a word for a purely mysterious, magical phenomenon. He said that by Einsteinian physics there was nothing solid about Peter's body—he was living in a state of crazy dance. It was not what McKittrick said so much that Peter liked but McKittrick's playful good will. McKittrick believed life was the greatest good, and he received it like a good gift. He did not live for anything hereafter. He said that you could see what was good or true in life itself without reference to rewards or punishments in the life to come. Peter didn't think it was right to proselyte him just now. At first he had intended to teach his co-workers the truth by example, but he came to realize that he had little to offer outside of words.

Willis was the leader of this three-man crew. He had spent considerable time teaching Peter fire tactics and the use of pumps and other fire equipment. McKittrick and others said he was the best crew boss in the district. He was also either a communist or socialist. Peter did not have the distinction down clear yet although he knew communists were supposed to be worse. Willis had given him literature to read on it. Willis said he was biding his time within the system until the moment for revolution came. He told Peter it was building quietly and exhorted him not to let the something something Mormons twist his head around. Peter could not remember what he had called the Mormons that particular time.

It took them an hour to reach the clearing where the helicopter waited. They strapped themselves in under the clear glass, and the whirling blades bore them off into the air. They never reached Fairbanks. Nor did they crash in the mountains and emerge ragged and starving a month later to the amazement and joy of those who thought they were dead—as Peter considered they might possibly have done. Halfway to Fairbanks new orders came by radio for them to stand by at Tignik, a small isolated village near the western ocean where it had been hot for two weeks. Lightning had been reported. After sleeping through two days of rain in Tignik they learned by radio that a four-seat light plane was on its way to take them back to Fairbanks. As they were boarding, a request came through to have a sick villager sent into town. It was okayed by radio, and the least important crewman—Peter—had to stay in Tignik until another plane came through.

It did not come soon. Peter sat in the plywood hotel for two more days of rain and tried to read the Book of Mormon he carried in his gear bag. He was distracted by the silence and emptiness. The villagers looked to him like walking cardboard. The hotel keeper, his wife, and her mother were the only whites in town besides the minister. Peter never actually saw the hotel keeper. The wife cooked Peter's meals, made his bed, filled out government forms, gossiped with her mother, and slept. That was her life.

The morning of the third day the sun shone. Peter walked through the run down, corrugated-tin town and to the river where some of the villagers were fishing. It took five minutes to peruse the mud banks and fish wheels. That left twelve hours in the day, two of which he could spend reading and two sleeping— leaving eight hours to stare at the river, the scrawny black spruce trees, or the plywood walls of his hotel room. He knew this would not have been hard on McKittrick, but he was not McKittrick.

He walked a ways down the river trail, rounding a bend where three dirty native children were playing in an old discolored washtub. As he was passing, there emerged from a wooden shack behind the tub a young, bearded man with a Roman nose, baggy trousers, and galoshes for shoes. The fellow ran up to the tub, rocked it wildly, and said something in the village tongue which sent the children into hysterical laughter. It was the village minister. As he parted from his playmates and walked toward the trail, he saw Peter and called out a greeting.

"Hi, I thought I'd just see where this river goes," said Peter, feeling he needed to explain himself. In one village he had been through earlier in the summer the local minister walked around in formal clerical garb. Willis said he fit in like a band of Nubi pygmies at Queen Elizabeth's coronation. Peter had laughed and then changed the subject because he did not want to hear any jokes about Mormon missionaries. Peter had met the minister who now stood before him on the day he had arrived in Tignik, but he didn't know exactly what he was minister of. He was not sure it mattered a lot, having himself been raised in the truth. He had marvelled over his good fortune many times. He felt moved to tell the minister about it. The two walked down the river path away from the village.

"It's interesting that you're out here," said Peter. "I'm a Mormon." He realized that this transition was a little awkward, and he would not generally have been so blunt but he was, after all, talking to a minister, and ministers knew their cues. The young man did indeed seem interested, and Peter plunged enthusiastically into an explanation of all the finer points of Mormonism—no Hell, eternal bodies and families, becoming gods, prophecy, stories of angelic visitations, archaeological evidence for the Book of Mormon. The village was far back in the distance when they came to a sudden halt. The trail was gone. In front of them the river swung tons of water round and round in a spinning, sucking vortex which ate at the land. His mind having been elsewhere, Peter was momentarily confused. The minister suggested they sit down and rest a bit. They sat in the spongy moss and watched the water. Realizing that he had been talking most of the time, and wishing to be polite, Peter asked, "What do you believe?"

"In Jesus," the man said. "I had an experience three years ago while I was living at a ski resort in Colorado. I don't know how to describe it. I love how John compares it to the wind—that spirit was like the wind—'the wind bloweth where it listeth and thou hearest the sound thereof but canst not tell whence it cometh or wither it goeth. So is everyone that is born of the spirit.'" Something in this caught Peter off guard. He thought about the minister's words and wanted to tell him that there was no contradiction there. His conversion to Jesus could just be the first step in his conversion to

Mormonism. But the minister spoke again. "This all came as quite a shock to me. At the university I thought I had this all worked out, but now I'm saying 'thank you, Jesus' along with the people I used to despise. The spirit told me to go see a man whose name I'd never heard before who was the head of a seminary in Carolina. I found the man's name, lived there and learned, and now Jesus has called me here."

The sound of the swirling river cut off the first words Peter spoke, which came out rather softly anyway. "Do you think you could have been deceived? I mean, you know, there is a devil, and sometimes he confuses people." The minister looked at him quizzically, then back to the river. Peter thought perhaps he had responded too quickly.

"Perhaps the devil is smarter than both of us," he said, "or maybe between the two of us you're the smarter and I'll go to one of your lower Mormon kingdoms." He said this simply and without sarcasm. "There has never been much in my life that meant anything until this call. I know the rightness of it like I've never known anything before. I've healed people too, by the power of Jesus, and felt full of the spirit to bursting. I've never done so much good or held anyone so dear as I hold the people here and Jesus." He said, "Hallelujah," quietly to himself.

The weight of this place seemed heavy, and Peter wanted to go back the way they had come. They did not say much as they walked back to the village. It was only four in the afternoon when they arrived. Peter went to his hotel room, took out his Book of Mormon, and read. A half hour later, when he found himself still reading at the spot where he had begun, he put it aside and dug around the hotel till he found an old *Time* magazine, which he read cover to cover. Night came and he was not sleepy. Early in the morning his mind drifted into the place between sleep and waking where dreams are. He dreamed of fire. It was an enormous fire. The radios would not work, and they could not come to a resolution as to what to do about the fire. Willis wanted to put it out. McKittrick said it was just a big campfire, sizeable enough for everyone to enjoy, and he wanted to sit by it and roast marshmallows. So in the day they fought it, and at night they slept by it for warmth. Peter's father appeared in the suit and tie he always wore and asked why Peter didn't put it out. Willis began to hose his father down, and somewhere in the commotion Peter found a pulpit. When he awoke he was explaining the situation to an empty room. He stayed in his room the next day, and when a message came over the radio that a plane had been dispatched to pick him up he got down on his knees and said a prayer of thanks.

He was ecstatic, upon reaching Fairbanks, to see McKittrick and Willis again. It was not long before they were out together on another fire—this time it was a tundra fire which required no work. They were just supposed to sit around with the mosquitos and see that the fire did not burn into the nearby forest before winter. The orders did not make a lot of sense. Winter was two months away. This was one of those things they did because the central fire control office, which issued the assignments, knew better than they. They were paid according to the work they did, not to think on things of which they could not see the whole scope. None of the three expected to be there more than a week.

The first day was warm. They lay out in the sun and swam in a shallow lake nearby while the insects were seeking shade. McKittrick dove to the bottom of the lake and brought up a seedy plant. He combined the seeds with fat from their C-rations and popped it like popcorn. They ate the few seeds with delight and smacking that any impartial appraisal by ordinary taste buds would have found unwarranted. Having slept during the day they sat up late into the night around the fire.

The conversation somehow got around to seeds, and Peter was reminded of a Thanksgiving story. "One Thanksgiving my folks put five kernels of hard dried corn on our plates and told us that's what the Pilgrims had as their daily ration during one hard winter. While we were all sitting there pondering the significance of that, one of my brothers flipped a seed at my big sister, and all hell broke loose. The folks were pretty pissed about the whole thing and made us spend the rest of the afternoon hunting down all forty-five seeds out of our tan shag rug before we could eat anything." They laughed.

Peter was conscious of having said "hell" for the first time in his life outside the context of the scriptures, and the "pissed" was absolutely inexcusable. He had only sworn once before in his life, and that had been an accident—"Oh God" had slipped off his tongue once from pure fright when he had gotten his head caught and almost crushed between speeding sled runners and the icy road beneath them. He did not think it had been an accident this time.

Swearing was so common among the people he worked with that it sounded natural to him until he said the words himself. But words did not mean the same to these people as to people in the ward back home. The day Peter had come in from Tignik, Willis had called him a name he could not repeat, but there was a smile on Willis' face and a tone in his voice that changed the meaning of the word. It was just Willis' way of saying that he was glad to see him. The fire swirled upwards and illuminated Peter's face. "We found the last kernel in my juice, and then Mom brought on the turkey."

Willis grew serious, and from his first few words Peter could tell what was coming. Willis had tried to explain the Revolution to him before. "Most of the world still eats like Pilgrims," he said. "They don't bow their heads in remembrance and then bring on the turkey. Most have never tasted meat—they live on gruel while their bodies waste away and their stomachs bloat and they die looking like something out of Dachau or Auschwitz, but it's an economic concentration camp. No one has the right to gluttonize himself while someone else is starving. Food is a basic human right in a world where there's enough to go around. That's what the Revolution will solve. The rich will sit on their fat asses until they start to feel pain, and then they will begin to care." He was speaking low, his eyes staring into the center of the fire and his own pain coming through. Willis reminded Peter, oddly, of an Old Testament prophet. All Peter knew of his background was that he had grown up in Chicago. Peter thought of telling Willis that he fasted once a month and gave the money to help needy Mormons. But finally he said nothing.

Everything was silent. The silence extended across the tundra desert and into the darkness that surrounded them. The fire popped occasionally and spun ashes upward into the night. The three huddled closer as it grew colder across the land.

"Peter, would you open one of those cans of twenty year old cake roll, toss me the cake, and throw the can at Willis?" McKittrick said. Willis lightened up a little, half smiling. "I used to worry about laughing," McKittrick went on, starting a little bit strangely into something that Willis had brought into his mind. "There were times when I was happy, and then I would think about it and realize that there were children starving in India and Appalachia, and that there was torture in Russia and in the upper-class suburbs of Detroit, and that at that very moment someone somewhere was dying and others were in pain, and I thought that perhaps I should be more sober. I visualized how I would disappear, myself, one day, and there would be nothing. I put a lot of effort into being sad because this world was such a bad place. But my sadness wasn't what anyone needed. They needed things done, in Appalachia, in Detroit, or wherever I was. And as much as that they needed happiness to balance out hard times. There are times when happiness is given like a gift and it's wrong to turn it down. To everything there's a season. Right, Pete?"

The words seemed to interest Willis. He was still silent, but he rocked back and forth in a squat, as if it required physical action to fully understand the words. The surging cry of a loon came from the lake, and two loons answered. He seemed soothed. A cool night wind had sprung up, the kind that came before storm clouds. It tousled Peter's hair. Looking up, Peter realized that McKittrick was gone. He heard a sound like the puff of a blowgun and felt a soft plunk against the yellow pocket of his fire shirt. He looked down and saw a dark red stain on the shirt. It was spreading. In his lap lay a mashed red cranberry.

"Defend yourselves!" came a cry from the darkness. Peter and Willis were up bounding across the tundra toward the forest where grew hollow, wild celery reeds and berries. As their eyes adjusted to the moonlight, they darted in among the trees to do battle. Ah, McKittrick had it. At last they could solve the age-old problem of who got who. Peter was laughing. The whirling began again—it was in the blustery wind, in his head, in the slowly shifting earth beneath his feet.

With Voice of Joy and Praise

Wayne Carver

Josiah bumped the car onto the shoulder near where the culvert used to feed the creek under the road, and for the first time in ten miles Louisa bobbed awake.

"Lord, Jos, why stop out in the middle of this God-forsaken place? Here I'd like a good cold Seven-Up, and you stop by some piddling creek I wouldn't water a horse in."

"This here's the place, Lou," he said, "where I was telling you Hal and me fished that summer before we were married. Late spring—actually."

She fanned down the front of her dress with the road map.

"Yes, sir. This is Bone Creek—or whatever."

He took the map from her, half unfolded it, and looked hard.

"Not even marked." He handed it back to her. "Yes, sir, we parked Hal's dad's new Winton right about here and we just fished and talked for about two days. By jolly, did we have some talk! One night we spent in a cabin, especially. When we came back the car was right where we left it. Doubt anybody had so much as passed along the road."

"Nobody in his right mind'd go along it now," she said, fanning.

He slipped out of the car and walked to the bridge. Looking upstream he smelled fish and grass, hot and heavy as if he could reach out and take the odor in his hands. He breathed deeply, held his breath for a long time, then the odor was gone.

"Does kind of help to stretch your legs," Louisa said behind him. Now she was looking down at the water. "It's funny, Jos, you never told me you'd been up here that I recall."

"Like you say, Lou, we've had more to do than worry about fishing. But do find it pleasant to recall that trip. Didn't see much of Hal after that, for one thing."

"Just as well you didn't."

He smoothed his hand across the two-by-four railing and saw the dark shale of the stream bed flutter beneath the current.

"Let's go," he said. They moved back to the car. "I ain't never been able to hold it against him. Could of been any one of us left the Church. Hal always was a little wild."

"It couldn't of been you, Jos," she said, heaving herself into the seat. She sighed. "But anyway, his folks had the temple work done for him and the work will go on and he can be with us yet."

"I know," he said, starting the engine.

"It's a great blessing, a great promise," she said, settling into the corner against the door. Jos pulled onto the road and the steady motion of the car lulled her back into her easy sleep.

II

The fat lady in men's Levis hooked the nozzle on the gas pump and came inside, wiping her hands on her denim apron.

"That's a good wet drink," Jos said, setting the Seven-Up on the showcase and taking out his wallet. "There was a time there this afternoon we didn't think we'd ever be cool again.

"It can get hot all right," the lady said. "But today was about ordinary. Nice cool wind most of the time."

"Nice cool wind!" Louisa said, deep in an unraveling wicker rocker beside the oil stove. "Lord! I thought I'd melt. Still think I might."

She put her bottle on the floor, took a postcard from the souvenirs on top of the stove, and fanned down the neck of her dress. "Don't see how you stand to live here."

The lady looked at her. "Nights get cool—mostly. And Birch Creek cools things some. We manage." She began to put Snicker bars in the freezer.

"Birch Creek?" Jos asked. "Hear that, Lou? That little stream I called Bone Creek is Birch Creek. Got thinking of bones from seeing all those steer bones in the borrow pit all afternoon, I suppose."

"More bones around than birches by a long shot," Louisa said. "Stunk like a carp slough to boot. Look, Jos." She held up a card with a copper arrowhead stapled to it. "Cute. Says 'Souvenir of Lemhi, Idaho.'"

"So this is Lemhi," Jos said.

"This here's called Gilmore," the lady said. "Lemhi's up the road a ways. But we sell Lemhi souvenirs. Or try. Whoever heard of Gilmore?"

Jos chuckled. "Well, now, whoever heard of Lemhi, for that matter. Now back in Utah we've got Lehi, Nephi, Manti, and Moroni. Never did hear of Lemhi, though."

"You study the map you'll see Lemhi's common enough hereabouts. We're in Lemhi County, this here's Lemhi post office, there's the Lemhi River, and them mountains off to the west, they're the Lemhi Mountains."

Louisa stopped fanning and went outside.

"Can't say we studied the map a good deal," Jos said. "Though, myself, I've been through here once—forty year ago."

The lady finished packing bars away and stood up.

"Where're you headed?"

"Nowhere particular. Me and the wife came up with the ward to see the temple at Idaho Falls. Never had occasion to see that one until the ward organized this excursion. Just had an idea this morning for a ride. Figure to spend the night in Salmon and hustle on back tomorrow."

"Better stay around and take some fish," the lady said.

Louisa came back carrying a set of black books.

"Well," Jos said. "Was never a great one to fish. Though did fish the creek out yonder once—forty year ago."

Louisa thumbed through one of the books. The fat lady began to dust around the oily room with a rag.

"You still can take a limit of rainbow out of that creek," she said. "I've got licenses and gear."

"Jos," Louisa said from behind the book she held close to her face. "I knew that was a familiar word to me. Listen: *Mosiah* twenty-two, verse twenty-five: *Now King Limhi*—only that postcard's got it wrong. Should be L*i*-m—not L-*e*-m—*had sent, previous to the coming of Ammon, a small number of men to search for the land of Zarahemla but they could not find it, and they were lost in the wilderness.* Twenty-six: *Nevertheless, they did find a land which had been destroyed; and they, having supposed it to be the land of Zarahemla, returned to the land of Nephi, having arrived in the borders of the land not many days before the coming of Ammon.* Twenty-seven: *And they brought a record with them, even a record of the people whose bones they had found; and it was engraven on plates of ore.* Twenty-eight: *And now Limhi—*"

"I incline to think you've made your point, Lou," Jos said. "Funny thing. Now how do you suppose I didn't recognize that name?"

"You pay more attention of a Sunday, the word of God might not appear so strange."

Jos turned to the fat lady and shook his head. "You just can't get the best of her."

The lady flicked the rag at the keys of the cash register. "I recall the Mormons did settle this valley till the Indians drove them out. There's an old fort up Salmon way. Myself?—I always figured Lemhi had something to do with Lewis and Clark— name of one of their squaws or the like."

"It's a great and faith-dealing story," Louisa said, closing the book. "How Ammon took Limhi—you'd think the Church'd make them spell that name right—and them sacred plates of ore from the land of bones and took them to King Mosiah and he translated them just like the Prophet Joseph and how Alma and Zeniff got delivered out of bondage. It's the promise we all have that all our pain and sorrow is overcome if we are righteous. It's a great promise, a great blessing."

"Well," the lady said, putting the rag away, "I wish some king or other would come by here with some sacred ore and buy some gas. I'd call that a blessing."

Jos laughed and turned to Louisa who was staring at the fat lady. "We'd better get on the road."

She turned to the souvenirs on the stove and riffled through them.

"If she wasn't so snotty," she said half under her breath, "I'd buy them moccasins for Ellen's girl. They're cute as can be."

"Suit yourself," Jos said.

"I can get all that stuff I want anyplace," she said loudly and started for the door.

"Much obliged, ma'm" Jos said.

The fat lady smiled. "Too bad you can't take some fish. It's a good year—specially over Challis way."

"Some other time, maybe," Jos said and went out to the car.

Louisa was settled comfortably in her corner and began to nod as he drove away.

III

Beyond Lemhi where a waitress talked fish to them over hamburgers, the valley narrowed to high mountains framing log houses and sheds and corrals and hay derricks and stacks of wild hay, smooth and brown like loaves of new bread. The breeze smelled of cut grass, and feeling the coolness of the evening air, Jos remembered the hot valley he and Hal had walked through, how it had filled with mist after the sun went down and how inside the cabin under their blankets the heat from their bodies had warmed them at last through their dank clothing.

The heat, the nose-crinkling smell of sagebrush on the wind, the creek, the fish, the mist, the dew, the cabin in the draw, he and Hal close and warm in the darkness—he looked at Louisa and felt as if it were all here inside the car to reach out and take again; and he moved his arm toward Louisa who was staring across the wheeling land and touched her lightly on the hair, stroked it once before she turned to him.

Jos, I've been worrying about us getting home on time. We've got to be back Sunday for sure."

"Figure on it myself," Jos said. "That shouldn't be much trouble."

"Ellen's boy's getting his Duty to God award at sacrament meeting. There's no prouder time in a mother's life than when her children get their Duty to God awards. I'm glad all our children kept their testimonies, Jos."

"They were pretty good kids," he said. All of them."

"We've knowed the joy of walking in the paths of righteousness, Jos." Her face softened. She sighed and settled back into the corner.

"Yes, sir," Jos said. "it's not more than ten miles from right here where Hall prophesied us two. There we were in that pitch-dark cabin—not even a chink for a window, though there was a full moon outside. Lou, I can't get over how clear all that is to me right now, and I've hardly so much as thought about it for twenty year. I remember it was a full moon because them rainbow shone like mirrors when they was lying in the grass before we went inside. I'd caught only three and we'd fished all day. Hal? He must of caught ten, but after I gutted mine and slipped a willow through their gills, I just laid them in the grass there and waited for Hal to finish with his. I remember you could look down the stream and see spirals of mist coming off the water. Well, them three fish of mine kind of lapped over each other so they fanned out there in the grass and the grass had dew on it and when the moonlight hit the fish and the grass and the drops of dew, it just shone out from that little nest all over the valley, so it seemed. I was mighty cold and dank before we got inside that night, I tell you; but I don't know when cold and wet ever felt so good against a man's skin."

Jos stopped for a moment. Then he chuckled. "That Hal did have a way with him, didn't he, Lou. Lou, old girl, did I ever tell you what old Hal said about Betty Errington when he was gutting them fish?"

She was asleep. Beyond her the mountains, fields, buildings, and tiny streams wheeled in the bright cooling sun. Jos shifted his weight to the top of his spine, let the wheel balance under the tips of his fingers, and watched the black stripe of the road reeling under him.

The fish packed between layers of grass and slung in a wet gunnysack high in a corner of the cabin, their heavy smell, he and Hal shivering under the blankets, gradually warming—he remembered it now with his whole body, could feel his arms and legs vibrate under its presence. A hardness formed at the back of his mouth that he could not swallow away. He heard Hal's voice as if it were beside him: "Put in simple terms, Son, you're saved and Old Dad here is damned and for good. Everything I do—or want to do—damns me. Just look at it: Betty Errington (godalmitey, Son, but you don't know how that can be!), cold beer out in the field under the cottonwood tree while the team nips redroots, a right powerful hankering to goose certain of the girls Wednesday nights after Conjoint. Then, hell, too, Jos. I ain't had the bringing up you've had. The folks go through the motions at church, but just to save trouble. It's my old man who brings me the beer and my old lady who makes it. Jos, did you ever drink any of my folks' home brew left in the trough overnight? No—you wouldn't have."

"No, I wouldn't've," Jos had said. "I'd of been skinned alive."

There had been a long silence.

"You take righteousness too lightly, Hal," Jos said.

"Well," Hal said, "righteousness didn't take me, Jos. I don't see no reason to pretend it did. Now a guy like you is set, Jos, and it'd take a damned fool not to see it. Course, I'm set, too, for that matter. I ain't proud of it, but there we are. Me and Betty Errington down in the cattails after ball practice going at it like it was on sale. And you and some Gleaner girl rutting for each other on the way home from Conjoint, pretending it's your testimonies speaking out loud and clear, talking about the Word of Wisdom and how long it will be before God's judgement overtakes the nations."

"I don't see it's got to be like that."

"Then they got to start holding Church down in the cattails."

"That aint't just too likely," Jos said.

They lay on their backs and looked up into the fish-smelling night.

After a while, Hal said quietly, "Jos, Son. Old Dad here is going to prophesy. You ain't going to suffer much. And it shall come to pass between you and that Poulson number. You'll be speaking your testimonies to each other any day now. I have spoken. And it shall come to pass. Even in these, the latter days. Verily I say unto you; even yea."

"Oh, shut up and go to sleep, Hal," Jos said. Then as he spoke and turned away to sleep, Louisa Poulson filled the empty spaces of the cabin. Her slim, straight, swaying figure trod the air, slowly stepping. Her dusky face floated down to him from out of the blackness, the straight, dark gash of her mouth glistening, parting, sighing a whisper: "Jos," she said. Then, "Jos, oh Jos." He reached up to take the face in his hands, to run his fingers lightly over the smooth lips, to touch the high hard cheeks beneath her eyes, to soothe away the tightness in her voice and soften the eyes stricken and crying with desire.

IV

Louisa slept while a large stream boiled white against rock canyon walls that cut out the sun and all but stopped the wind. Blue and cold the evening came as they passed the lake behind a large dam, the water ruffling darkly under the breeze, and came out on a bench overlooking a round valley. The traffic thickened around them as they approached the belt of motels fringing the city.

Some of the cars had fishing rods jutting out the back window or poking from under tarps of trailers. Others had them tied alongside under door handles or lashed to the top carriers. Bait cans swung from front and rear bumpers or were tied across the grillwork. And on the ledges of rear windows he could see yellow and orange creels and metallic grey tackle boxes; or sometimes they were rigged to bumpers or to corners of trailers or tied to the corners of top carriers.

"Does appear to be a general expectation of fish," Jos said.

Then in front of him a pickup, with bows and tarp arching above the bed, suddenly slowed. He braked quickly. Three girls about fifteen or so scrambled back to the tailgate, holding up a fish that must have been a yard long and forty pounds. Its deepcut gills were twisted and wrenched open by the girls' grip so that the head was like a hood above the body, and the body cut a white stripe down the middle of the truck opening. Jos had never seen such a fish, though he had heard of them being taken in the Salmon during the proper season and in sports pages had seen pictures of grinning fishermen in waders holding up such catches as this. He shook his head and sucked in a side of lip to show his disbelief; and the girls whooped and waved their free hands. Then the traffic jumped ahead. Jos waved to the screaming girls, then quickly slipped into a right turn that took him under a big flashing motel sign that said not everything was taken yet.

By the time they had checked in, unpacked, washed up, and eaten a bite at the coffee shop on the left tip of the horseshoe-shaped motel, the whole valley was jerking with neon color.

"Some town when it gets all lit up," Jos said as they walked back to the room. "Whole sky lights up."

"Pretty," Louisa said. "I wish I had an alka-seltzer. All this restaurant food gives me gas."

"We're living high tonight, Lou," Jos said. "Look."

In a glare of lights behind the motel office there were half a dozen deeply tanned people in white bathing suits. Jos could hear the thump of the diving board, the splash of water, and the cries of swimmers.

"Just some baking soda would do," she said. "Them greasy foods."

A brown body in white skin-tight trunks arched high and fell into the green water, disappearing quietly under a spreading cap of bubbles.

"There's a fellow dives like he don't want to get wet," Jos said. "Lou, I'm afraid we'd hardly cut a proper figure out there."

"Jos," Louisa said as he watched a girl pull herself onto the edge of the pool and flip the cap off her head, shaking out her hair. "Jos, I'm going in and lie down till this passes. Lord, that drive today, then this food you have to eat, it's a wonder anybody stays alive."

"A walk might do you some good. Wonderful air."

"Some soda would do me more good." She kneaded her stomach with both hands. "You go on ahead. If I feel better later maybe I'll look up one of them curio shops." She looked at him for a moment. "I sure would like a dose of soda."

"You go on in, Lou. I'll see what I can do."

He handed her the room key that was hooked into the mouth of a red plastic trout curved in a leap. Then he walked over to the office. The man recognized him.

"Comfortable?" he said.

"Fine, fine," Jos said.

"Well, then, what can I do you for? Fishing info you want? Over Challis way I recommend Bud's Bait Shop, Fifth and Lewis, for everything but the fish, hay? Bring your smaller catch to the cook in the coffee shop, he'll cook 'em up for a dollar. You gut 'em. One meal only."

"Was never a great one to fish," Jos said. "Though used to a little. Thanks anyway. The wife's got a stomach ache, and I wondered it you might have a little baking soda handy."

"Damn near everything's biting this week," the man said. "Hate to see a man come through here without wetting a line. We've had parties this week take the best fish I every seen. Everybody's filling. Course, you got to know how to take 'em. There's salmon over Challis way pick a man's meat from his bones, he don't know his business. You want soda? Don't carry it on me as a rule, you might say, hay? But what's your cabin? I'll call the wife—we live out back in a trailer, the two of us—and she'll take your missus something. Just passing through?"

"Wife's in 16. Much obliged," Jos said.

"Nothing to it. I'll just put it on your bill, hay?" The man laughed pretty hard and Jos went out.

He walked toward the swimming pool. A girl ran past him and threw herself headlong into the pool. Water slapped against his shirt and filled his eyes. He half fell into a beach chair, took out his handkerchief, and began to dry his face.

"That was a dumb trick," the girl called from the edge of the pool, lifting herself half out of the water. "Can I get you a towel?"

"No," he said. "Go ahead and swim." He waved the sopping handkerchief over his head. "Just push me in next time, though. It'll be warmer."

"I'm sure sorry," she said, then was gone.

Jos pulled the shirt away from his body, released it, and shivered as it settled against his skin. He unbuttoned his shirt as far as he could, pulled out the tail, then undid all the buttons. He leaned back on the chair and let the cold night air flow over his temple garments. He closed his eyes, and in the distance heard the sound of splashing water and thumping boards and calling swimmers. All around him was the night capped by the pink mist, and he smelled the gassy pool, heard the swish of traffic on the highway beyond the motel, heard, suddenly, music coming across the water, and sat upright, clutching the chrome tubing of his chair.

Around a picnic table in a corner across the pool, the swimmers in their white suits were gathered around the big bronzed diver, who with one foot up on the table seat was strumming a guitar. As Jos watched, the big man said something in a low voice, strummed a fanfare, and began to sing and play so softly that only a muffle of words and an occasional plink of the strings carried through the cold air to Jos. Then, as the tanned singer played and sang there in the light from a single hooded lamp above the fence, other people joined the group. Some were still in traveling clothes, some in swimming suits, others wearing robes and carrying beach chairs. Some sprawled on the wet blotched cement, curling their legs under them or grasping their knees with their arms. Some lay full length on towels, their hands under their heads, and others propped themselves up on their elbows. Some couples lay quietly in each other's arms, their bare legs softly locked together. The area gradually filled with people who simply strolled in and took their places, as if the music, the songs, the loving on the towels, the whole easy formation around the singer, were what they had sought in coming to the motel in the first place.

Darkened and cold, the wet shirt hanging loosely at his sides, Jos moved a hand under his garments and felt the hairy edges of his ribs. He buttoned the collar and the next couple of buttons, slid back on the chair, closed his eyes, and let the distant sound come to him; and he was whirling away with the cold wind whistling in his ears when he felt a hand shaking his shoulder and heard a voice saying, "Now don't pretend you're asleep."

He sat up. It was the girl who had splashed him. He quickly closed his shirt around his midsection.

"We want you with us. Come on." Laughing, she took his hand and pulled him to his feet. "It's better with us. Come on."

Every joint in his body aching, he stumbled along with her. At the edge of the group he tripped against a boy and a girl on a beach towel. He began to apologize.

"You can see how much they care," the girl said. "Come on."

Then she was shouting "Here he is," and the group burst into applause. Jos was pushed to the end of the board seat along the table just opposite the singer who was idly strumming his guitar. The rough dry terrycloth of a robe was folded around Jos's neck and he twitched his head away from the smooth flesh of her arm that rested for a moment against his jowls. He pulled the robe around him, looped the belt, mumbled that he didn't need it.

"After all," the girl said, squeezing in beside him, "who got you all wet and cold—after all?"

She thrust a beer can toward him. "To our getting wet together—oops! A beer! A beer! A can slid the length of the table and stopped in front of him, an ooze of bubbles growing above the triangular holes in the top.

"Well, now, no—no, thanks," Jos said, looking down. "Much obliged, but was never much of a one to drink beer."

But the girl was holding out the toast as if she hadn't heard him. Jos picked up his can, touched hers, and after watching her drink for a long moment, carefully bit off the cap of bubbles and sipped a little beer. The brassy taste turned bitter in his mouth, and he gulped the beer down, tasted the yeastiness that rose to the back of his tongue, then spread into his nose and throughout his mouth. The girl shouted, banged her can on the table, and the guitar player began to play and the noise of the crowd slowly died away.

Sometimes the tanned singer stopped after a chorus to give a few hard strokes and call out, "Now, everybody," and the group would join in. At first the girl, who sang with a clear voice and beat time on the table with her beer can, would turn without missing a syllable or a beat and raise a shoulder and an eyebrow at him. He would smile and move his can in wet half-circles around the table in front of him. Once in a while he would sip a little beer, letting his mouth fill, then drop the beer with a single swallow into his stomach. But after a few songs, the girl pushed at him, pinched him on the forearm, wrinkled her nose at him, and said, "Now sing, sing, sing. This one everybody has to sing." He found he was following after the words he picked out of the air:

"Oh, Shenandoah, I can't get near you—
Away—my rolling river.
Oh, Shenandoah, I can't get near you—
Wa-ay, I'm bound away
Across the wide Missouri—

The jagged words tore a raw passage through his throat. But the long, slow, wailing music moved into his body; and he felt his body drawing out and swaying toward the receding sounds that would suddenly return in waves only to subside in little pools at his feet. When the singer shouted "Again!" Jos sang loudly and painfully:

Oh, Shenandoah, I love your daughter,
A-way, my rolling river—

The song ended in a burst of applause from the group, and Jos lifted his can and drank as fast as he could to ease the dry scratching of his throat. The singer strummed a fanfare, then put the guitar on the table and waited for the crowd to be quiet.

"Now," he said, "a new song." He took his foot from the table seat so that he stood straight. He talked in the low voice he sang with. "A Sheepeater Indian chant—the Tukuarikas who used to have these high canyons and wild rivers and windy peaks, who used to fish with hooks of bone the river they called the River of No Return. They lived here where lava flowed from cracks in the earth, where the headwaters of the Salmon once heaved mightily ten feet into the air from the old riverbed, fell, and rose a second time even higher than before, and turned muddy and warm. Oh, I tell you, these mountains and rivers are shaken by the foundations of the world most of the time if we only knew it; and where we come to fish, to take the big ones on our slender lines at Challis, are strewn the bones of men who came into these changing places long before we came."

He stopped, keeping his eyes on the center of the group. Suddenly, he shifted his body by lifting his foot to the seatboard of the table. The immobile group broke into anxious movements and nervous smiles. Jos kept his gaze on the singer's face. The singer put an arm across the almost level thigh of his cocked leg, leaned forward, and clasped his hands. "Just north of here," he continued softly, "on 93 you may have passed a little trickle of a creek the Sheepeaters have named Weeping Child Creek. Now this next song tells how it got its name. The country out that way is stony, and white boulders poke through rows of the best apple trees in the world. Big white boulders rounded and pocked by the weather, but smaller white rocks, too, piled high in walls or in heaps or just strewn about the hillsides. They are the color of clean-picked, sun-and-wind-bleached bones. And that is what they are. For this chant says that a long time ago as a solitary traveler passed along that creek, he heard a sound of weeping coming from the foothills above. He followed the crying and came to a child sitting in a litter of bones. The fat, pretty child was crying for food now that the bones of her mother and father had failed to give her surcease from hunger, and the pitying traveler sat among those bones and took the child on his knee and placed in its mouth to soothe it his own soft, moist fingers. The child began furiously to nurse, and in only a few minutes had sucked the flesh from the fingers in her mouth, though the traveler felt no pain. Then she moved upward to the flesh of the palm, then the arm, and on and on, gradually, all the while inflicting no pain—until the entire tender covering of sweet pink flesh melted into the child's wet, sucking mouth, leaving only a glistening skeleton for the winds and rains and birds to cleanse and dismember. Then the child, its suckling over but its hunger ravening still, cried out over the drying bones, across the creek to the next traveler. And he too, filling with pity, would seek out the weeping child; and soon his firmly fleshed bones would be scattered bleak and dry among all the others on the hillside. Through the ages this went on—perhaps is still going on—and this song is the story of the little rocky creek and the succulent rocky orchards and how they were made by the weeping child."

The singer straightened up. A shuffling sound ran through the group and the people looked at each other.

The girl beside Jos gave a nervous little laugh. "Sweet kid," she said.

Jos walked the can across the table and said, "Course, a painless way to go, so it seems."

"Who's looking for a painless way to go?" the girl said and looked toward the singer plinking strings with an ivory pick.

He plinked three or four times, hummed briefly to himself, then began to chant the legend he had told.

The music was harsh and monotonous. Jos twirled his empty can across the table top. Suddenly, the singer threw back his head and cried:

"Eee-eye-ee-eye-eee-eee-yi-yi-yi—"

Jos smiled a little while everyone else broke into laughter and squeals. Then the song began again.

Surrounded by the smell of beer and the odd strains of music, Jos felt his body floating lightly about in the air. The chanting, the girl, the cans of beer, the presence of others around the table and at the edge of the circle of light came to him only faintly through the spaces that now opened on all sides of him. He stopped playing with the can, rubbed his tongue around his mouth, pulled his fingertips over the bones under his eyes and into the soft pockets of his cheeks and rubbed lightly. He pursed his lips. Warm juices flowed over the back of his tongue where the tightness in his throat hurt him. He swallowed. His adam's apple rose in his throat like a jagged stone and soft music came to him from far away. Tingling and floating, he untied the robe, slipped backwards off the bench, worked his arms out of the sleeves and handed it to the girl.

"Much obliged," Jos heard himself say from far away, and he moved out of the circle of light, beyond the chanting voice and he sat back down on his beach chair and closed his eyes as the

"eee-yi-yi-yi-eee-yi-yi-yi"

descended to him on a thin cold wind from remote canyons of rock.

Across a sagebrush plain strewn with bones a band of ancient warriors carried the sacred plates of ore to a sagging cabin in the draw. Turning the folds of wet gunnysack he saw the plates sparkle in the darkness. With his gift and sacred stones he reached down saying, "I'll read the promise and the blessing." Slowly he turned the large, slippery fish scales and stared perplexed at words he could not understand. "Hurry up, Son," a voice from a dark corner said, "or does Old Dad have to read it for you?" "No," he cried, "I have the sacred gift," and faster and faster he turned the slimy sheets, panic rising in him as the words faded faster and faster into the darkness of the cabin. "Hurry," the voice said, as the darkness fell once and for all and everything was lost in the fishy odor, until just above him a dusky face floated down to him from the depths of the eternal darkness, the dark glistening line of its lips opening to whisper, "Jos! oh Jos," and he reached up to take it with a cry of joy as a scalding ache trembled through his whole body and dissolved it.

He sat up in the darkness, gripping the piping of the beach chair, his teeth chattering. Over in the corner the picnic table was deserted, and in the pool—a light mist spiraling above it—the lights from the cabins glittered crookedly. The sound of traffic on the highway had died to an occasional roar. The stars were big and bright and seemed very near. Jos sat there for a long time while the world touched him all around. When he finally stood up, the lightheadedness was gone. He breathed in deeply, felt the pain cut into his throat, held the air in his lungs for a long, luxurious moment, then exhaled, and walked across the court to their room.

V

Louisa was sitting on the bed with her shoes and stockings off, moaning quietly as she rubbed her feet.

"Lord," she said, "where have you been? I walked all over this fool town trying to find something nice to take back. I'd like to have killed my feet."

"Sorry, Lou." Jos pulled up a chair, sat down, and leaned toward her. "But it does appear that soda helped you some."

"But where were you, Jos?" she said, rubbing. "You might of gone along to carry."

"Out there where those people were singing and drinking beer I—"

"I didn't hear no singing," she said. "No doubt, though, there's plenty of beer drinking in this town. You should of walked up town with me. What a place! Mobs of people, and what you don't see going on right on the sidewalk! And everything stinks of beer and fish, to boot. I'm dead, I tell you. Would think you'd be."

She stopped rubbing her feet and began to look through a paper sack on the bed beside her.

"Lou?" Jos stood up and walked to the window. He collapsed the venetian slats downward and stood there for a while with his hand on the cord.

"Just a second, Lou," he said.

He went outside and came back in unfolding the road map. The bed was littered from the sack so he spread the map on the floor and kneeled over it.

"I do suppose we know the way back," Lou said. "The quicker the better far as I'm concerned. Look, Jos. I got this for the table. Don't you think it's kind of cute?"

She handed him a small black ceramic terrier with a white bone between its teeth.

"Take the bone out," she said. "Go on. It's the cleverest thing."

Jos removed the bone and let it hang from the chain around the dog's neck. It clicked back into the dog's mouth. Louisa laughed.

"I got a half a dozen for the kids, too." She put them beside her on the bed.

"Lou," Jos said, "it just sort of seems like something in me today wants to reach out to this country here."

"Well," Louisa said, "it sort of seems like something in me wants to get to bed. Don't know, Jos, when I've heard you go on so much about something as over and done with as that fool trip you and Hal Peterson took. Don't myself see what's so all-fired great about this country up here. Suffocating wind and snotty gas-station keepers and drunks everywhere a person wants to walk." She held up a miniature cup and saucer with some plastic milk spilled under the saucer. "For Ellen's knickknack table."

Jos traced his finger over the map. "We could, Lou, if we had the mind to, go out of here along 93 south to Challis, right along the river where they get the big ones. Then from Challis we cut litter-skronchways to Arco and Idaho Falls. Wouldn't lose much time, and do hear that river country is mighty rough and wild and awfully pretty. That singer out there by the pool awhile back said they used to call the Salmon the River of No Return—that rough it was to navigate in the canoes—or whatever. Strikes me we might miss a good deal not going back in that country, seeing," he laughed, "as how it's likely to be somewhat changed about in another forty year when we get back up this way."

"I guess I got something for everybody," Lou said. "Not much, but shows I remember them. I got these for us to put in the china closet." She handed him a cardboard box. "I thought they was kind of nice," she said.

She picked up the terriers and bones and began to fold them into tissue paper spread across her lap.

"But Jos," she said. "Just don't you talk about gallivanting around on our way back. I just don't know what's got into you, anyway."

"Wouldn't be but maybe a few miles out of our way, Lou, old girl, going by way of Challis," Jos said.

"A temple excursion's one thing and it's our duty to do the work for the dead, but tramping through all God's green earth is another. And following some fool river called the River of No Return appears somewhat out of the way to me," Louisa said. "Take a gander at that stuff so's I can put it away."

She put the paper sack on her lap with the dogs and bones and waited for him. Jos lifted one end of the lid to the box she had handed him. In a nest of white tissue paper two ceramic trout speckled brown with pink and yellow stripes rested snugly, their heads and tails arched as if they fought a fly. He put the lid on the box and handed it back to Louisa.

"They got printed underneath 'Salmon City, Idaho, where fish are always in season.' They're salt and pepper shakers, did you notice? Seasoning?" She laughed.

"I did notice they were," Jos said.

He walked to the window and tilted open the slats. For a while he looked out at the street behind the motel sign, the oblong orange light dulling the trees at the side and blurring the cars that went by. Then, the world spinning away outside, he heard Louisa's voice behind him, "Jos? oh Jos."

Heavy and warm with sleep, he walked to the bed where Louisa rested among her gifts and sat down. Her face floated near.

"Jos?" she said. "Jos, I just don't know when I been so wore out."

"Well, Lou," he said, "I guess we better get to bed. If we don't want to fall asleep on the road tomorrow and kill ourselves."

He stood up, reached down for the road map, and began to fold it up as he walked over to flip off the light so they could undress in the dark.

Four Walls and An Empty Door

Linda Sillitoe

I was fifteen, almost sixteen, about to start my junior year, when I met Steven Wiscomb. I'd read about him in our Mormon ward news flyer and even in the *Deseret News*, the afternoon newspaper.

The news flyer came first. I always took turns reading it aloud with Patty, my best friend, as we walked home from church. Sister Jackson tended to print her family news first, then whatever else she heard second. But that time her family news was really news. She asked for our prayers for her grandson. He'd broken his neck diving into a creek to rescue a neighbor child. The kicker was that the child was found next door, playing with a kitten under the porch. Meanwhile, Sister Jackson's grandson was rushed an hour and a half by freeway from Spanish Fork to a Salt Lake hospital where, we read, he was in critical condition.

"Geez," I said to Patty, "that shows what being a hero will get you." We were in our ironic phase then, so the story really knocked us out.

A few weeks later, the *Deseret News* did a little story with a photo of the grandson in his hospital bed, with his parents and a doctor standing beside him. Steven was quoted as saying he knew he'd recover and that he didn't harbor a grudge against the neighbors.

Then about a month later, Sister Jackson asked me for a copy of my Sunday School talk so she could take it to her grandson in the hospital. He was such a good public speaker himself, she said, that she knew he'd like it.

My notes had scribbles and arrows all over, so I offered to type a fresh copy. It wasn't *that* great a talk, so I polished it a little as I typed. I'd been assigned the Beatitudes, and I worked out a rainbow metaphor with different kinds of people different colors. Not black, red, white, brown and yellow like people really are, but green, turquoise, pink and so on, according to their souls.

When anyone, especially one of the youth (meaning anyone under thirty who is unmarried) gave a talk in our Sunday School that neither offended nor put to sleep, it was considered a masterpiece. Half the youth stuck with the Golden Nugget booklets and church magazines in preparing talks. The other half tended to tie in the nuclear arms race or how our ward didn't support the campers as well as other wards supported *their* campers, especially in meeting the 5 a.m. bus. I'll leave it to you to decide which half I leaned toward.

A few weeks after I gave Sister Jackson the talk, a woman I didn't know stood during testimony meeting and thanked the ward for their faith and prayers. I soon figured out it was Steven's mother. After the meeting Sister Jackson introduced us, and Sister Wiscomb said how much Steven enjoyed reading my talk, and would I like to come to the hospital to meet him?

Of course I said yes. Already I admired him. I knew he was a few years older than I, a freshman at Brigham Young University. All the way to the hospital, his grandmother grieved over how bright he was, how he'd played the clarinet in the band, how he'd been on the debate team in high school (so was I), and now he couldn't even move. She added that he was much better than he had been at first. He was in satisfactory condition. I wondered how anyone could be paralyzed and still satisfactory, but I said nothing.

So it started out a little like a movie, with me walking into the hospital not really knowing what to expect, a little scared, wondering what I'd gotten myself into.

When they introduced me, Steven looked at me, looked away, then back without meeting my eyes, and said he'd liked my talk and understood I was a bishop's daughter. I said yes and waited patiently for the joke. The boys I knew on the debate teams around the city usually rolled their eyes and waggled their eyebrows if my status was mentioned. They'd say, "Oh, no, a bishop's daughter! Look out!" like I was sure to be wild and easy just to prove I wasn't a self-righteous prig.

Steven's room was full of relatives and friends from Spanish Fork, so I stood back and smiled and watched. At one point, I remember, his dad asked him to show everyone how he'd learned to move his right arm in physical therapy.

We stood in a respectful circle around the hospital bed while the face below the triangle of dark brown hair turned red, and the big gray eyes bulged slightly. I saw sweat break out on his forehead and across his bare shoulders above the sheet. Then his wrist shifted about an inch. Steven sagged in the bed, limp and soaking, while everyone exchanged looks, then praised him.

I couldn't believe it—so much effort for so little motion. But I smiled and nodded with everyone else, my throat aching.

The conversations about who had given him priesthood blessings, who'd come by to visit or had brought goodies all floated around me as I wondered whether he had anything on under the sheet. Not that it bothered me; I have brothers. But I thought it might bother him to be practically naked in a room full of people. And I wondered how he went to the bathroom if his whole body was paralyzed. I thought how awful it would be to have to be fed, washed and changed like an enormous 19-year-old baby. And be smart.

When Steven called me about ten days later, I was surprised. The male voice on the end of the line sounded familiar, but at first I couldn't place it. I was discouraged with boys generally. The ones I burned for always liked the platinum-haired girls who never wore the same outfit to school twice in a semester. True, those boys would flirt with me if their favorites weren't around. But after a few pleasant encounters that turned hollow, I decided that no matter how sweet boys could be when they wanted some kissing, they cared only for games and themselves. If Mormons had nuns, I might have applied at fifteen.

But Steven was older and he was nice. On the phone it was as if he were any young man calling me. Our voices met over the wires as we chatted, explored, flirted, retreated, then laughed together. Not until the receiver rolled away from his head did I really remember his condition.

"Nurse!" he called over and over and over and over again, while I gripped my telephone with a hand that finally shook from tension. We were both depressed by the time his voice returned, from the sheer frustration of being unable to reach out a hand and grab the receiver.

"Some days there are footprints all over the ceiling," he said.

"What?"

"Because I climb the walls all day."

"I can believe it," I told him.

"Do you think you might come to see me again?"

I found out the visiting hours, and that evening asked Dad for a ride to the hospital.

In the few weeks remaining before the start of school, I visited Steven fairly often. In between visits, he called. We talked for hours. He knew more than I did about debate, college, politics, and the Church. I didn't always agree with him, and he loved to argue, nailing down facts with twice the nails he needed, then returning to give them another smack after I'd lost interest and conceded. I began to realize, though, that even at three years his junior I was more confident socially. When school began, he loved hearing about my classes, teachers, and friends, and even my exclusion from drivers' training as one of the youngest in the class.

"I knew what those bus trips to debate meets are like," he said one evening, as I perched on the wall register in the yellow light of his room.

I smiled coyly. "Oh, come on. Nothing ever happens."

He whistled. "That's not the way it was on the Spanish Fork bus. I generally sat right behind the coach up in front so we could talk over the rounds. But my partner—he was all over the place." He shook his head in a way that looked as admiring as it did rueful. "We always left town in the dark and arrived home after dark, and old Frank thought that was great. He said he'd score on the bus if he didn't score in the rounds."

"And did he *really*?" I was going to ask cynically, wondering how Steven knew if he'd been talking to the debate coach all the time, but two men in suits and white shirts pushed open the door. We were both startled.

"Oh, hello," Steven said, as if he knew them, then introduced himself.

"I'm Elder Reed and this is Elder Martin. The nurse at the desk told us you might like a blessing."

"Yes," Steven said, his voice serious now.

"Have you been administered to before?"

"Yes. I'm not asking for administration, just a blessing."

This priesthood technicality meant little to me, but obviously mattered to them. The pair glanced at me inquiringly. I looked back at them, wondering what they wanted.

"Oh, she can stay," Steven said with a smile. "Her father's a bishop."

So I folded my hands in my lap and closed my eyes while the two of them repeated his name to be sure they had it right, then blessed him with health and strength. They didn't promise he'd walk, but they sounded optimistic.

Part way through, I began to wonder if I should have stepped outside after all. The thing is, I'd had experience with this kind of thing. Coming from a big Mormon family, I'd seen people recover after blessings, and I'd gotten well myself. But I also knew what Steven might not—that when a no-medical-explanation, genuine miracle was the single hope—well, it just didn't pan out. People did die. People stayed crippled or blind.

I couldn't bear it if Steven set his heart on white light, and sent a quiet counterprayer to that effect even as I said Amen.

Afterward the men looked at me sharply, picked up Steven's limp right hand one after the other, shook it, looked as if they wished they hadn't, and left.

It was a funny thing. Steven's parents and relatives— everyone— admired the way he wouldn't give up, his determination to recover. Yet I wasn't sure they believed it, even though they wouldn't say so. He may have suspected it, because he could out-faith anyone. He knew by heart the scripture in the Doctrine and Covenants that said if the sick are not appointed unto death and have sufficient faith they will be healed by the power of the priesthood. Period.

"And if I were appointed unto death," he would sum up, "I sure had plenty of opportunity to go. Some nights death was so close I could taste it."

That conviction, in fact, lay beneath a discussion between Steven and his favorite uncle the next Sunday. Uncle George congratulated him on becoming an elder, right there in his hospital bed. Steven had wanted to wait until he went on his mission. That was soon enough.

I could tell he felt that ordination now was a statement that he wouldn't go on a mission after all. Of course, I reasoned silently, he wasn't going to be doing any of the other things elders do, either. It was just that he'd turned nineteen since his accident, and they wanted him to keep up with the other young men of his age. As much as possible.

His uncle assured him he'd been right to have it done. It was good to have the priesthood as a comfort to him. Steven finally agreed. Everyone was always telling him how much his faith and courage helped people.

Later that evening, the nurse shooed us all out of his room so they could do something to him. They didn't say what, and I didn't want to know. Steven's parents and I walked down to the lobby by the elevators and sat down on the vinyl chairs. His uncle and aunt went to find the restrooms.

The hospital intercom was right above us. "Dr. Monson, Dr. Monson; please report to emergency," a voice said.

Steven's father sighed deeply, then said, "You know, we were sitting right here the night after Steven came to the hospital. The doctor came out and sat down by us and explained the damage to Steven's spinal cord. He showed us the X-rays up against the light. He told us Steven will never walk again, that he'll always be just about like he is now. If he lived, he said.

"And then the Lord's Prayer came on over the intercom, like it does at nine o'clock every night. We just sat here and listened to it." He shook his head and took Steven's mother's hand. "I'll never forget how I felt."

I made a sympathetic noise, then waited for the rest—for him or for Steven's mother to say, "But we know the doctor was wrong. We know he'll get well." But they were silent, looking out the windows to our right at the valley sparkling below us like a crowded firmament.

I felt uneasy, as if I'd been warned of a danger that wasn't supposed to exist. At last I said, "That isn't what Steven thinks, is it?"

They stood then, and we walked back to his room. "No," his father said. His mother smiled tightly and shook her head. I liked both of them. They looked older than they had the first day I met them only weeks earlier, as if they aged before my eyes. We all smiled as Steven's father placed a hand flat on the door, then we walked in together.

Uncle George and Steven were arguing about stockpiling nuclear weapons. Steven insisted that a balance of power was necessary. The Russians were overtaking us militarily and were not to be trusted, he said. His uncle called it a balance of terror, and talked about the insanity of overkill and the likelihood of accidental war. He clearly had Steven cornered, but Steven kept fighting. Inch by inch, his uncle began backing down, not because Steven's arguments were better, but because Steven was paralyzed.

It made me mad. I was tired of Steven's stubbornness and his repetitions, which weakened as he grew more desperate. Why didn't he throw in the towel?

"I tell you, there will be no peace at all without a massive array of weaponry," Steven exclaimed.

"Or war either," I put in quickly.

There was a pause. Uncle George opened his mouth, looked at me, then shut it again. Everyone looked at Steven nervously. He glared, then looked relieved. He laughed and tossed his head in a way that showed he was really flinging an arm in a wide gesture of generous defeat. "What did I tell you?" he asked rhetorically. "She's not only cute, she's smart, too."

Everyone laughed, and I blushed and sat down.

Later, after the others left for Spanish Fork, Steven and I watched an old movie on the television high on the wall opposite his bed. I was waiting for my dad to pick me up after his meeting with his counselors.

"I saw Jared," I told Steven when a commercial came on.

He grunted. Jared was another BYU student down the hall, who'd suffered a spinal injury in a car accident about a month after Steven was hurt. They'd met in the hospital, but had not become friends as everyone thought they would.

"So how is he?" he asked after a minute.

"He's okay." Jared wasn't hurt as badly as Steven. He was a quadriplegic, too, but he had more movement in his arms, and more feeling in his skin. I couldn't tell whether Steven could feel me smooth his long, curled fingers. Every time my fingers came to the end, his curled inward again.

"Jared's a quitter," Steven said.

"He told me he wants two things: to be home for Christmas, and to push his own wheelchair. He says he's pragmatic."

"Same thing," Steven said. "Okay, the show's back."

He couldn't jerk his hand out of mine, but I sensed that he wanted to, so I put it back on the bed. When I looked at him instead of the television, I saw a wet track from the corner of his eye to his ear. I turned quickly toward the movie.

Then I heard my dad's quick tap on the horn in the parking lot below the window and grabbed my sweater. Steven said my name just as I reached the door.

"What, Steven?" I turned back.

He lay looking at me, his dark hair and gray eyes shadowy against the television's bluish light on his white sheets. In the dark room, he looked like a picture on a black-and-white screen, himself.

"Nothing," he said. "Just—thanks for coming."

"See you," I said, and hurried down the hall.

I was never the type to line up outside a seminary teacher's door after school like some girls do, so I worked in the school library on my debate plan for half an hour, then dropped by the seminary. My timing was good. Brother Kane, who'd taught seminary only one year before, was showing Karlene Smith out of his office door. *She* would stand outside his door for hours, and cried when she talked about anything more serious than her pep club uniform.

"You're here late," he said to me in a surprised voice.

"Do you have just a minute?"

"Certainly," he said, standing back so I could come in . He shut the door. "So how are you this year?"

I told him about Steven. He listened intently. "He sounds like a very courageous young man."

"Well, he is. He sings when the pain is bad, did I tell you that? One of the nurses told me. He's so bright, too. I've learned a lot from him."

He nodded.

"And he's positive he'll get well."

"Maybe he will."

I just looked at him. He looked back, straight into my eyes. "Where's your faith?" he asked finally.

"Do *you* think he'll get well?" I asked pointblank.

He shrugged and shifted in his chair a little. "How can I tell?

Only the Lord knows. But I can tell you this. He won't get well without faith. If anything can heal him, that will."

"Yes, that's true," I said. "The thing is," I began, then stopped.

"Yes?"

"The thing is, I think he's getting serious."

"Serious? He's in a serious condition."

"I mean serious. You know . . . about me. About our friendship."

His eyebrows went up. I always wondered if he practiced that in front of the mirror, he looked so cute and teddy-bearish when he did it. He did it a lot. "So why is that a problem?" he asked.

I stared at him, exasperated. "I told you. He's paralyzed. According to the doctors, he won't get well. I've just turned sixteen. And he's getting serious. Isn't that a problem?"

Suddenly he leaped forward in his chair, his forearms on his knees as he leaned toward me. "Listen," he said. "He's in that room all day long, right?"

"Except for therapy."

"Okay, except for when he's killing himself in therapy. Reading is hard for him. Television is stupid. He needs people. He needs friends who care about him. He needs you. Go on—give him something to live for. Something to get well for."

"Oh," I said.

So that was kind of like the movies, too. Then our telephone conversations got longer. That made my sister mad since she had a new boyfriend. Her telephone conversations were long, too. In fact, she timed them. She'd heard he once talked to Jean Phelps, a cheerleader, for an hour and twenty minutes, and she wanted to break that record. To me, that seemed trivial. I didn't think her conversations were a lifeline the way mine with Steven were, after his day in a room with four walls and an empty door.

One night when I went to see him, I passed Jared in his wheelchair in the hall.

He looked up, panting a little.

I dropped to his level, perching on a nearby bench. "Hey, you're doing great."

"Home by Christmas," he said, and winked.

I winked back, then walked slowly to Steven's room. That night Steven was strapped into a wheelchair, too, but still had a tendency to tip. His trunk muscles wouldn't support him.

"You want to go for a walk?" I asked, "figuratively speaking?"

"Yeah," he said. "I want to go see the chapel. I'll bet it's a little strange. I've been watching all these priests and nuns all the time. You know how Brother McConkie said that the Catholic Church is the whore of the earth mentioned in the Book of Mormon."

"Wait," I said. "Is that fair? I think this is a pretty hospital, and they do take good care of you."

He ignored me. "Graven images," he said, glancing at the statue of Mary across the hall from his room. "Idols. I got into an argument with a priest today. I guess I won, because he finally said, 'I'm leaving, you Son of Satan, and I won't be back.' I just waited until he got to the door, and then said, very politely, 'Thank you, Father.'"

"Ha," I said, turning his wheelchair from behind. "I've heard versions of that joke at three of my cousins' missionary farewells."

I guess he was miffed, because he didn't say anything else except to give directions to the chapel. We got lost once. I didn't mind. I liked skimming the polished halls behind his wheelchair, the heels of my pumps clicking above the quiet hiss of the chair. I was thinking about a quiz in Advanced Placement English the next morning when Steven said, "This is it. To your left."

I stopped the chair. There were double closed doors down a ramp to my left. To the side of me stood a guest book and a stack of paper doilies.

"Don't sign us in," Steven said. "But you do have to wear one of those."

"Now, what?"

"You know. You have to put one on your head. Like a hat."

"Really?"

"When in Rome," he said, and chuckled.

I took a doily from the pile and set it on my hair. It slipped around. "It will never stay."

"Sure it will. Okay. Let's go in."

I turned his chair and started down the ramp, but I hadn't anticipated the weight of the chair, his limp body and the force of gravity opposite my slick-shoed, one hundred and twelve pounds. In an instant the chair dragged us both straight toward the closed doors. I tried to brace my heels, but they squealed on the polished floor. I turned the chair sideways, and took a deep breath as it stopped sliding. Steven was slumped toward the right.

"Geez, I'm sorry," I said. I could feel my heart thumping. The doily lay on the floor like a dishonored flag, but I didn't dare let go of the chair with even one hand to pick it up. I looked around wildly for help. We were mid-ramp, and I didn't see how we could proceed up or down.

"Okay," Steven said as calmly as I was pretending to feel. "Now turn me backwards, with you behind the chair. Slowly."

I did, bracing my weight. We rolled slowly against the doors and stopped. Unfortunately, they opened out, not in.

"Damn," I whispered under my breath. Again I looked up and down the hall for help. No one.

I turned the chair parallel to the doors and slid it past the center where they met, trapped a back wheel with one shoe, pulled the door past me, and somehow got him through. We settled for stopping in the back of the chapel.

It was dark, with a little red candle glowing up in front. No one else was there. My cold sweat slowly evaporated in the darkness. It had everything to do with that headlong plunge down the ramp, and nothing to do with being in a Catholic chapel. I didn't feel anything, good or evil, just my own thoughts quizzing me how I could get him back up the ramp without killing him or worse.

By the time we made it back to Steven's room, he was crumpled in the right corner of the chair. "Get a nurse," he said out of the corner of his mouth that wasn't jammed against his shoulder. I did.

It wasn't too long after that visit to the chapel that everyone started talking about Steven going home to Spanish Fork. I was surprised. True, he was stronger. He could sit up a little straighter, and he'd learned to use a brace to turn pages, change television channels by remote control, and even type. He held the brace in his mouth, and a long plastic finger extended from it. Steven's color was better, too, and he wasn't in so much pain.

But Steven didn't want to go home. "Why not?" I asked, thinking how I would miss him.

"Oh, there will be a big fuss."

"Well, maybe just for a day or two. Then everything will calm down. Your friends can come to see you."

"They've probably all forgotten me by now."

"Not Angie," I teased.

He wrinkled his nose. "Last thing I heard, she was chasing after a football player at the Y."

"What is it, really?"

There was a long pause. "Well," he said, gazing at a point above my head, "you weren't here the night this happened. Nobody was. That's too bad, because there should have been witnesses." He glanced at me sharply, but I didn't challenge him. "The elders came to give me a blessing."

I nodded. I'd been present several times for that.

"That particular time they blessed me that I would be serving a mission by the first of next year. I figure there's no way I can be on a mission by then unless I walk out of this place pretty soon. By November first, in fact."

I took a minute to absorb that. I made him repeat it while I thought it over, then I asked, "They set a time limit?"

He nodded slowly. "That's about it. So it's going to be soon, if I just have the faith. I figure that if I'm well by November first, I'll have time to get organized and receive my call and all the rest."

But—even if you went home, that wouldn't invalidate the blessing, would it?"

"I'm not going home like this. I promised myself I'd walk out of here and I have the faith to do it. Don't you?"

I talked to Brother Kane again in his office. I told him about the blessing, the mission, and about Steven going home soon.

"Did you hear the blessing?"

"No."

He dropped it. He seemed restless that day, skidding from one idea to the next as if they were patches of ice on a sidewalk. At one point, when he asked about Steven's condition, I described his hands, how thin and white they were now, with inward-curving fingers and long nails.

"Atrophy," he said. "That's what will happen to his muscles if they're not used. You know what the life expectancy of a quadriplegic is? An infection could just snuff him out."

"You mean—you're saying he could die?" It was the same man in the same room, but it sounded like a different tune.

He settled down, leaning toward me. "He could die," he said, looking into my face in his sincere way, getting a little excited. "You've got to be prepared for it, and you've got to help him prepare for it, too. That's how you can be of service."

"But. . . . " I said, remembering the night before when I stayed after visiting hours. I'd shut the door, and the nurses left us alone. The television was on, as usual, throwing its light onto his bed where I perched watching him, not the show. Moonlight poured through the window to my right, brighter than the television's aura. Sunday moonlight, as pure and drenching as they said God's love could be.

Steven and I couldn't look away from each other's face. My heart quickened, and I realized I was waiting for him to take my hand, touch my face, put his arm around me, waiting without knowing I waited. But of course he didn't do it.

"Wait a minute," Brother Kane said abruptly, his voice jerking me back to his office, his intent brown eyes. "Just how far has this thing gone? How involved are you?"

Did he know I was recalling how I'd leaned toward Steven, laid my hand along his face, and for the first time ever, initiated a kiss? A nice one. Not too long. And found in the last instant before our mouths touched that he was surprised.

"You said to get involved," I told Brother Kane. "You said to give him something to live for."

He sat back in his chair and stared at me, then sighed. "Well, you have to be smart about these things."

"I've got to go now," I told him. "It's too late already."

The dark fell faster than I could walk home, maybe because I was crying. Even through my tears I was grateful for the hard, fast sidewalk under my shoes, the late autumn air chilling my face as I hurried, the will in the muscles of my legs to run if I wanted to run. I knew I had no right to cry for me.

It was about ten o'clock before my sister hung up the telephone, but often the nurses had more time then to place a call for Steven. By the time he called, I was ready to talk to him. Our conversation was slow and quiet. I was exhausted. For once, I caught him with his faith down.

"You know," he said wistfully, "I've been thinking that if I don't get well, if I just have to accept this, I'm really going to miss things like playing soccer."

I took a slow breath, closing my eyes against the pain of seeing the real clock on the real paneled wall, my real legs, folded and trembling underneath me. "Do you think you might have to accept it?" I asked, my voice calm and casual.

But he didn't answer. Instead he recounted his favorite high school soccer game, his voice gathering its usual cheer and tempo. With my eyes still closed, I leaned into the rhythm of his voice. It almost took me back with him to his senior year, but not quite. There was a pause. When he spoke again, his voice was rougher.

"I knew this was going to happen, of course," he said. "Did I ever tell you that?"

"What do you mean?" I opened my eyes.

"I knew something was coming. Something like this. You know how I wrecked my car spring semester."

"Yes. But that was an accident."

"It was an accident. But it totalled the car, and I was a bit surprised to find I was still alive." He laughed. I didn't join him. I noticed that the trembling in my legs had spread. It was everywhere.

"And I still just had this feeling," he added. "That something would happen. Something was coming."

Impatience surged in me. "Steven, are you saying the devil pushed you into a creek? You jumped, remember? Because you thought there was a little kid in there."

"I dove. I didn't jump. If I'd jumped, I'd have just sprained an ankle, maybe not even that. I never dive into that creek. Never. It's stupid. Why did I dive that day?"

I let the silence stretch. "Shall I repeat my question? Are you saying that the devil. . . ."

"Not the devil," he interrupted. "No. Not the devil. You might ask the opposite, though."

There was another silence except that our breathing rushed through the telephones, back and forth. "I just—I just don't think the Lord pushes people into creeks, Steven."

"Not even for a purpose? Not even for His glory?"

"You mean so that when you get well, it will be for His glory?"

"It could be that. It could."

I was quiet.

"Or maybe something else. Maybe having to do with my mission. Let's not be so dreary. Tell me about your day. You don't have to believe me if you don't want to. I know it sounds crazy."

But I had nothing bright, nothing funny to tell, so we soon said good-by. Before I placed the receiver on the hook, I heard Steven's voice, smaller now, calling "Nurse!"

Steven lost his battle to walk out of the hospital and his

campaign to ride home in a hearse—he wanted to go home in a hearse if he had to go home still paralyzed. His parents were aghast. He thought it was funny. A coffin inside the hearse would be even better, he said. He was ninety percent dead, anyway. They could leave a foot hanging out to represent the portion that was still alive.

But, in the end, he went home in a chartered ambulance, feet tucked into a white blanket, and my head was strangely silent for a few days. Every time I thought of Steven, I pictured him riding home in a hearse. I saw the lid closing on him, on the future that had always been a many-peopled, multi-faceted diorama with "Happily Ever After" stenciled over it in gold. Now the future was all sealed up.

For a few days I felt bittersweet, as if a summer romance was dwindling and dying as the leaves rushed like yellow rivers through the gutters. On my way home from school, I walked through the leaves like a little kid, and their friction caught the rhythm of Steven's voice over the telephone.

Then he called me long distance to say how he missed me and to tell me a letter was on its way. "It took most of the day to type it," he said. I could picture him with the brace in his mouth for hours.

"Oh, Steven, that's such a lot of work. Why don't I just call you on Sundays when the rates are low?"

"No, typing fills my time, and I won't be back in school until next semester. Will you do something for me?"

I could still see him darting at the keyboard, the brace like a long tongue. "Anything."

That first letter told me how, upon arriving home, he'd found that his parents had sold the VW he bought after totalling his Ford. He knew they needed the cash, but still it upset him. I knew it was another sign that no one expected him to recover.

His letter also told how he hated the glassed-in family room his dad had remodeled the year before. The schoolchildren looked in and saw him sitting there, a freak in his chair, he said.

Also, in that first letter, Steven let me know he knew ways even a quadriplegic could choose to die, to escape an almost-dead body.

"It is so hard to endure this separation," he wrote. "But I must remember we are planning and preparing to be together through all eternity. Compared to that, this seems almost bearable."

So instead of our relationship dwindling in absence and silence, our devotion to words on paper made what had been before contained in a pause, a tone of voice, or a kiss in the noisy loneliness of the hospital as real and final as a loop of rope between Salt Lake City and Spanish Fork.

In his letter he made the same requests he had on the telephone. He asked me to write him every day. He asked me to come to Spanish Fork whenever I could. He said I should date and have fun, but to remember he loved me. I wrote back, my typewriter loud and furiously fast, that I would do all those things.

Only now, looking back, can I see that I also did three things I didn't tell Steven. I did them because, for the first time, I saw just how important it was to me that he get well.

First I lengthened my prayers to hours, pleading in the dark recreation room, begging the Lord to be fair and make him well. When my prayers met only darkness hanging like moss from the ceiling, darkness rustling like bats in the corners, I began fasting surreptitiously, skipping meals until my mother or Patty or a teacher noticed me shaking or hyperventilating and insisted I eat.

Second, I spent more and more of the school day with my forehead cradled on my curved arms on the desk, imagining a dozen, a hundred ways of learning that Steven was well again. He would knock at my door during Thanksgiving dinner. I would answer to find him standing casually on the porch with the fat, holiday newspaper under an arm, grinning as if he had just dropped by to deliver it.

He would pull up beside me as I walked home from school, tooting the horn on the VW he had somehow managed to buy back. He'd spin around a corner out of the honking traffic, as I fell into his lap, laughing at the impatient drivers who were ignorant of our great blessing.

Or I would bump into him while Christmas shopping downtown, astonished to see him healthy and on his feet. "Oh," he would say, "I'm just on my way to your house, but I wanted to pick out your present first," then hand me a gift-wrapped box, striped red and silver.

Hauled back into the classroom by the dismissal bell, the flat of one hand casually wiped the wetness off the top of the desk as I slid sideways to my feet. Soon every desk I sat at had a clean smudge a little to the left of center.

Third, I tussled a secret yearning for every male debater who sat down beside me on the slow bus home, every date to a school dance or party, even the occasional senior who gave me a ride home after play practice or a seminary service project, a guilty, desperate hope that he would reach out his magical, movable arms and fold me in.

Low Tide

Karen Rosenbaum

Crouched on the rocks, he tipped onto his toes over the little waterfilled crevice and stuck out his hand. "Cherry," he whispered, "the bucket!"

"Here. What is it?"

"Shh. That orange rock. Look." He lifted it up and touched its underside with a stick.

She shivered. It was alive. It rippled. Writhed maybe. "Hey," she said, "don't hurt it."

Twisting his mouth at her, he plopped the orange thing into the pail. He ladled water over it with one hand.

"Remember what pool you got him out of," she leaned over for a better look, "so he won't be disoriented when we put him back."

"C'mon," he snorted, "they spend every day and every night in a different puddle. Wherever the ocean deposits them."

"Really? She poked the crusty shell tentatively. "No family ties?"

"No family ties." He was feeling the crater where the creature had been.

"How conscious are they?"

"Conscious of pain probably. Hunger. Let's see what we can find for the old boy to eat."

She gagged aloud. "Maybe it's an old girl," she said. "Maybe she'd like crumpets and a laxative." She stood up and checked out Shasta who, her whitish fur browned with water, was sniffing at some kelp behind them. "All this supposition," Cherry said, "that lower forms have no feelings the way we do. Maybe they aren't even lower forms. Why do we assume they don't feel?" Her tennis shoes squished behind his on the wet rocks. "Just because we can't look them in the eye?"

He crouched at another indentation and dangled a hermit crab in front of her face. "Here. Let's see if Jumbo Jim wants lunch."

"Maybe," she said, "Jumbo Jim's a vegetarian."

"Not a chance."

"Just because we don't know how different creatures think." She leaned over his shoulders as he turned the orange shell and dropped the tiny crab onto the cold soft stomach flesh of the rock creature.

The rock creature was not a vegetarian.

She stood up. "Now dogs," she said to the grey ocean receding in front of her, "dogs have eyes we can look into. We know dogs have feelings. They care for their pups. Their owners. They're family-oriented." She noted that Shasta was not following them. "Familiar. We can communicate with dogs."

Keith bent his thin legs and crouch-walked, motioning her towards the next tidal pool. "And how do you like being Shasta's god?"

"I'm not Shasta's god."

"Shasta's mère and père may be responsible for her birth. But you," he turned and pointed a wet finger at her chest, "are responsible for her continued existence."

Cherry chewed on the inside of her cheek.

"You feed Shasta," he said, "and get her shots and let her sleep on your bed even when she smells bad. I," he said lightly, "need a god like you." He started to search out the water at his feet, but brought his chin up. "See that one?" He pointed. "That pool's yours. You can be its Juno or Hera or whoever. See what you have there."

She squatted, her wet tennis shoes overseeing the indentation.

Tiny limpet shells lined the sides. "Limpets don't go anywhere," she said. "They probably have family and community like us. Of course they don't seem to have much contact with each other. Probably some kind of telephone or radar."

"See if you can find the PTA president." She heard his hand dive for something behind her. She looked back. "Missed. Big crab."

"What would you have done with him if you'd caught him? He wouldn't have stayed in the bucket."

"It would have been an interesting encounter though."

She sniffed. "You cerebral sorts are so humane."

"Hey now. What's the purpose of life anyway, according to your religious tenets?"

"To learn things," she responded automatically, "to grow." She dabbled her hand in the icy water. "What do you mean, my religious tenets? Don't you believe that?"

"Yeah." He looked up. He'd pushed back the sleeves of his CSH sweatshirt, but the cuffs were still dark and wet. "That much I believe."

She fingered the cold hard limpets. "No more?"

"I don't know." He let out an abrupt breath and set to prying a mussel off the side of a stone.

Her fingers were losing sensation. She lifted them out of the water and shook them, spraying the rocks around.

"You'll never surprise anything that way," he said. "Be sneaky."

"I'm going to be a benevolent god," she said, "not a skulking, scientific one. My world's fine." She crawled next to him, pressed her cheek next to his leg. He was feeding the mussel to a large anemone. "Oh Keith. Why don't you serve up the whole thing now to Jumbo?" She was instantly sorry she'd said it. His eyes opened wide.

"For a benevolent god," he said, "you have some interesting ideas."

She waded off by herself over a smoother stretch of shore towards the cliffs that walled off this part of the beach. Seagulls stalked the water. She searched for a sand dollar but whenever she bent to pick one up, she found the part stuffed into the sand jagged and broken. The one round shell was marred by a gaping hole in the center where a hungry gull had pecked out its dinner and destroyed the pretty design. She slipped it into her pocket anyway. It would probably crack there. Shells were so brittle. She held up to the sky two broken angel wings.

"Shasta!" she called but Shasta apparently didn't think her voice sounded urgent enough. I am, she thought, too lenient a mistress. She took a big step to avoid walking on a quivering layer of violet—part of a jellyfish probably. Or maybe all of it. If Shasta came now, she'd nose it, destroy it maybe. Or did jellyfish secrete stuff to hurt their enemies? She stooped, scooped wet sand over it, walked on.

Her feet were rather numb, didn't even feel uncomfortable since they didn't feel at all. Her toe was wearing through the top of one of her treadless tennis shoes and she had to be careful now that she'd reached the slick rocks. These were the old-fashioned tennis shoes, the kind that weren't a status symbol, not a symbol of anything. She remembered buying them, hung by their shoelaces on a pole marked 8, in Woolworth's.

Stream of consciousness stop one. The first Friday afternoon with Keith. Bowling at that place up on College. He'd asked for size 7 shoes, and, embarrassed to ask for size 8, she'd asked for size 7 too. She joked uncomfortably about her feet being as large as his and bowled even more uncomfortably, her cramped toes curled under. That was eight months ago, she counted on her fingers, June to April, right after she'd stopped worrying about spring exams. Right before she'd stopped worrying about big feet.

Shasta didn't come again when she whistled but Cherry didn't feel like exercising her authority. Her levis were starting to unroll so she made new cuffs around her knees. She straightened and bent her spine the other way, threw her head and neck back. The sky was fog still. If there's a heaven, it's inside you, Keith had said last week. It's not up there. Jupiter's up there. And Io. She couldn't even see the sun though today. But she could still see Keith and his bucket.

Funny. All their lives human beings spent in conflicting modes. To be alone and stand straight and tall and shout I am. And to reach out and lean against someone and hold someone up and to whisper Are we?

She waded out to where the tide still was foaming against the rocks and sat on a tall stone. The water washed over her feet every few seconds. How long were the intervals? Keith might time them. Her watch was in the glove compartment though and it didn't have a second hand anyway. She looked over at Keith whose head was up, fixed towards her. She raised her arm high, waved. He waved back.

God, she whispered. The world was so complicated. She pulled out her emptied sand dollar. Even this, simple and round, had so many parts. And the rocks and the fogs and the rings of Saturn. Human beings, parts and passions. So many parts to their passions. And even the existence of all the questions. Could it all just have happened? Big Bang. Little Bang. Lord I believe said a Biblical voice out of her brain. Help thou my unbelief.

Shasta trotted up as though she were promptly obeying that last, five-minute-old whistle, a smooth piece of wood between her teeth. Cherry took it, patted Shasta's damp head, tossed the stick down the tide line. Turning so fast her fur sprayed, Shasta galloped down the beach. Shasta, now Shasta, was a true believer. Well. Belief depended on the object of belief being unseen. Shasta had an advantage.

Behind Shasta, a smooth stick between his teeth too, loped Keith. Cherry laughed, took both sticks, threw Shasta's back down the tide line, and dropped Keith's into his now empty bucket. "You put Jumbo back?"

"I fed him to an octopus." He sat on a neighboring rock, lower than hers. "No. I put him in the hole where I last saw the big crab."

"I don't want to hear about it."

"Okay," he said, pushing his heels into the wet sand. "Communicating with the Great Beyond?"

"Yeah."

"Make connections?"

"No."

Shasta, holding the stick between grinning teeth, jostled her. Keith took the stick this time, threw it even further and deeper.

"Not so far in."

"She can swim."

"What if she's sucked under by a current?"

"Nah." Back on his rock, he tipped the bucket upside down and put his feet on it. He'd taped one of his shoes with wide grey metallic stuff. It wasn't holding very well.

"What if Shasta were a child?" she said.

"We'd have fed her to Jumbo Jim."

"You just don't want to talk about children."

"I don't mind talking about two children. But I don't want to talk about ten."

"I don't want ten."

He played with the metallic tape. "You want five. That's as bad."

"It's not just a religious thing. I like being one of five children."

"If there were only two kids in your family," he said, "you'd like being one of two."

"No I wouldn't."

"Cherry." He got up as Shasta trotted back. "This is not one of the things I can give in on. I can handle an occasional church meeting. I don't intend to smoke tobacco or dope. I drink milk with every meal. My idea of a binge is club soda in a nonreturnable bottle." Shasta dropped the stick at his feet and rubbed her wet body against his bare legs. "I'm into the idea of marital fidelity and family home evenings. I can handle the whole thing on sex. Right?"

She looked at her levi cuffs. "Right."

"And the kids can go to Primary and Sunday School and be baptized and be in temple pageants and be Eagle Scouts—all two of them."

"It's not just that," she whispered. Shasta looked worriedly from Keith to her. "It's that it's hard for me to keep believing when you've stopped."

He crouched beside her, his hands on her sandy legs. "I'd believe for you, sunshine," he said, "if I could." He stood up. "Look. Maybe I'm wrong." He shrugged. "Probably we're all wrong. Probably we'll never know." He tried to smile but his mouth was wrinkled. "C'mon, Shasta," he said, throwing the stick in front of him. "I'll race you to the treasure." His sneakers slapped the wet sand. Dazed for half a second with joy, Shasta reared, then bounded off beside him. Shasta's faith was whole.

Cherry pulled the bucket over to her rock, upturned it. Sand streaked the sides and rimmed the bottom but all the little live things were gone. A grain of sand. A pismire is perfect and a grain of sand. It sounded like a psalm. And a mouse, Whitman had said, and if a mouse then why not a hermit crab? Why not a hermit crab is miracle enough to stagger sextillions of infidels?

They weren't infidels though. Exfidels she thought. And she did feel staggered. Shasta had beaten Keith to the stick and relinquished it and he was once more throwing it further down the beach. They both took off again.

Swinging the bucket, she waded back over to the smoother sand. The water washed out over her feet. She fell onto her knees and dug furiously. Sometimes if you fell on your knees and dug furiously you caught a little sand crab. She brought up a handful of heavy drenched sand, the sea leaking out her fingers down her arm. She opened her fist and the sand slid out too. No crab. Or if there had been one, it got away.

Another Angel

R. A. Christmas

And I saw another angel fly in the midst of heaven, having the everlasting gospel to preach unto them that dwell on the earth, and to every nation, and kindred, and tongue, and people. —Revelation XIV: 6.

I

Professor R. L. Robinson woke up on a jet from Los Angeles to Paris and discovered that his wife of one day was not in her seat. He had fallen asleep during the movie, and she, it was clear, had turned off his headset and the overhead lights, and left him to it. The champagne had done—no, was still doing—its work. It was close to midnight by his watch and the plane was quiet; the spaces—inside and out—mostly dark.

He turned himself on and began a survey of the channels. Comedy: it was that Vietnamese kid who did a take-off on Ted Kennedy. Rock: Bob Dylan's old "Popera." Next was Mozart, so he lingered. He packed his pipe and relit—but it wouldn't hold—so he put it back in his pocket. He closed his eyes again.

When he opened them there was light coming through the window, and the seat beside him, he noticed immediately, was still empty. It was certain now that his wife had collapsed in the restroom, and no one suspected what lay behind the locked door. She had been sucked out of a faulty hatch and had plummeted, silently, into the Atlantic—while he snored. For a few seconds, Robinson's mind rang drowsy changes. Then he was moving up the quiet aisle.

He found her, sitting in the empty forward lounge. She was hunched over—elbows planted on uplifted knees, chin wedged in her hands. A stubby paperback was open on the table in front of her, and her face was concentrated. As Robinson entered, one hand started down to turn a page.

"Good morning," he said.

"Well hello," Holly said, straightening up, smiling. She pushed a strand of brown hair from her eyes.

He sat down. She kissed his cheek.

"The film was a bore," she said. "I didn't want my light to bother you."

"It wouldn't have," Robinson said. "I was blind. In fact I still am, a little."

He glanced to see what her book was. "You'll never guess what I'm reading," she said.

She took the book by the open halves and turned it over. He saw hazy, vertical bands of bright and pale blue, and on the right side a golden figure, robed to the ankles, standing on a grey ball. The right hand held a long, single-stemmed, golden trumpet to the lips; the head of soft curls angled back—blowing a blast. On the other side was the title, The Book of Mormon, in white letters.

"Where on earth did you get this?" he said, taking it from her.

"At the used bookstore," she said. "Do you mind?"

Robinson closed the book and turned it over in his hands. It had a familiar weight and thickness, except that the ones he remembered had black covers and smaller angels.

"Charles told me you used to be a Mormon," she said. "I was just curious."

"He did, did he?" Robinson said, handing the book back. He took his pipe out while Holly lit a cigarette. When the stew came by they could get some coffee.

"Look at this," Holly said.

She turned to a page that had a dark ballpoint circle around a verse. Robinson leaned over and read:

> Now I, Nephi, did not work the timbers after the manner which was learned by men, neither did I build the ship after the manner of men; but I did build it after the manner which the Lord had shown unto me; wherefore, it was not after the manner of men.

"It's so repetitious," she said.

"Yes it is."

"It's all sort of like that," she said. "It isn't anything like the Bible."

Robinson struck a match. "Well," he said, between puffs, "it was all written by one man."

"That's not what they say."

"No," he said. "But the style is his, at any rate. That's what gives it that wordy tone."

He reread the passage.

"It sounds like he's buying time," he said. "Trying to think of what to say in the next verse. He just repeats himself until he's ready to move on."

"Could be." Holly took a pull on her cigarette, so Robinson read another verse. This raised two images in his mind, and he knew the connection between them perfectly well. The first was of a young man in farming clothes, sitting in a room that had been divided in half by stringing up a blanket. There was a wooden box on the floor near the man, and he was holding a black hat, upturned, in his hands. He was bent over, gazing at a stone in the bottom of the hat. On the other side of the blanket there was another man, dressed like a schoolteacher, sitting at a desk. Every now and then the man with the hat would say something, and the man at the desk would write it down.

The second image Robinson saw was simply himself as a young man, reading the Book of Mormon on a bus headed into Los Angeles.

"It's really strange," Holly was saying. "A bunch of Jews build a ship and go floating off to South America. It's sort of like what you'd get if you asked John Bunyan to rewrite the Aeneid or something. Maybe it's some kind of folk epic disguised as a bible. Is there anything in print on this?"

"Nothing respectable," Robinson said. "There might be by

now," he added, "but I wouldn't know about it."

"I bet I could track a lot of this down in English and early American sources. Folklore, sermons, things like that."

"A lot of people would be grateful if you did," he said. "But I wouldn't recommend it."

"Why? It's American lit. It's in my field. I'm surprised *you* haven't done it."

"I wouldn't touch it," Robinson said. "It wouldn't be worth your time."

"Why?"

"Because there's nothing there. There's nothing literary about it. It's simply propaganda."

He glanced out the window. They were over land now, a horizon of small farms, purple-grey in the dawn. The one place this does not look like, Robinson noted, is Utah. But that was a thought he had not expected to have on his honeymoon.

"Do you think those witnesses really saw the gold plates?" Holly was saying.

"Nope."

"Do you think they lied?"

"Who knows," he said. "I think they thought they saw something. I think they wanted very badly to see something, so they did."

"It does make you wonder," she said after a pause.

"The book is designed to make you wonder," Robinson said. "That's the best reason I know for not believing it."

"How did you come across it in the first place?" Holly said. "Your parents aren't Mormons."

"There was a girl," Robinson said, trying to find the right tone.

"Your first wife?"

"No. Before that," he said.

"Now we're getting somewhere."

"If you like."

II

Senior English, Inglewood High School, 1957. Robinson, Smith—we sat together on the back row. She was new—from Utah. A Mormon. Her parents owned a restaurant, and they were getting rich because they gave ten percent of everything they made to the Mormon Church and tried to keep all of God's commandments. I was a Methodist but I told her I had no morals and she threatened to "send the missionaries over." She couldn't keep religion out of her head—not for more than a few minutes. But she also worshipped Scarlet O'Hara, and she had read *King's Row* twice and *Forever Amber*. Some days she wore so many crinolines she had to fold herself into her desk. She had a nineteen inch waist but she wanted a waist that a man could circle with his two hands. Her mother had had nine kids and she was going to have twelve.

I was president of the Senior Class, but I didn't have a date to the graduation prom. I didn't even think to ask her until the last minute. She wasn't what I would have called pretty. She was a little too tall; her hair was too curly on top, and (this puzzled me) slightly darker in back. Her cheekbones where too high and rosy, her mouth was full of teeth, and her calves were skinny. She made up for these defects by trying to have what we called in those days "a great personality." She thought it was almost sinful to be shy. She also thought it was possible to be romantic without "committing adultery." She had been "sweet-sixteen-never-been-kissed." Unfortunately, her younger sister hadn't even made it to fifteen. It finally dawned on me that I was amused by the way she talked (partly because she shamelessly flattered and flirted). I figured that if we didn't "make out" after the prom, at least there would be no awkward silences.

"I'll bet it was a blow to your ego," Holly said.

"It surprised me," Robinson said. "I don't think I'd ever been turned down before."

"You mean you had to become a Mormon before you could take her out?"

"Not really. It was just a bluff. But I fell for it."

She was dying to go with me (I could tell), but when they came down from Salt Lake the girls had all taken a vow not to date non-Mormon boys. But she promised to plead my case at their next family council if I would just wait a few days and please not ask anybody else. After all, this was her once-in-a-lifetime high school graduation, so she deserved a teeny-weeny exception.

Did they open your mouth and examine your teeth?"

"Not quite. I remember they asked me a lot of questions about my family and my goals in life. They wanted to know what church I went to and whether I thought it was 'true' or not. I never thought much about my church one way or another. I was just a Protestant like everybody else."

"Deep down you probably felt like telling them to shove it."

"I should have."

"I can just see you, with that murderous little polite smile on your face. I'll bet you decided to seduce her then and there."

"Not hardly," Robinson said.

There were at least six bedrooms, two fireplaces, and a maid's apartment over the garage out back. The front door was eight foot of solid something with a big brass knocker in the middle, and just inside there was a stairway that would have made Rhett Butler pause. Carma slept in a four-poster bed with a pink canopy—I was allowed to see it on my short tour, accompanied by a chorus of giggling sisters.

But they hadn't lived this way for long—they let me know right off that this had all started with a small cafe in South Salt Lake (a family business that had grown—like the family), and a prayerful decision to "pioneer" the California Market. They were new money, full of enthusiasm and wonder at their success. We sat in the paneled study and her father played and sang a hymn on their new organ. A couple of the little girls recited poems and her mother gave me a copy of *Think and Grow Rich*. Carma's older brother was a missionary in Finland. They showed me his picture with the girl who was waiting for him to come home so they could get married. I was uneasy, but I liked them all right away and I think they liked me. I felt from the beginning that I was going to "pass," and that this was just a formality that would have to be endured. Her mother especially thanked me for helping Carma with her English papers. She said if it hadn't been for me Carma probably wouldn't have graduated. She said the rule about not dating non-Mormon boys was entirely the girls' idea, and the girls, she announced, had voted to make an exception in my case. All the little ones clapped and cheered at this, and I blushed—which made everybody laugh. After that, we had refreshments. Carma's mother wanted me to understand how important a temple marriage was to each of them, and I acted as if I did when really I didn't.

Graduation night Carma said that for every person living on earth there were at least a hundred evil spirits who wanted to inhabit their bodies because they couldn't have one. Her little cousin flew around the room until her father called the demon out by the power of the Priesthood. The Three Nephites and the Apostle John were still alive and might turn up anytime, anywhere; and there was a place called Kolob, which was a star or something where God lived where one day was equal to a thousand years. Somebody was doing genealogy work and found a hundred-year-old newspaper on their doorstep one morning. Utah looks just like the Holy Land turned upside down and there are pictures in the *National Geographic* to prove it. Joseph Smith saw God the Father, and His Son Jesus Christ, the Angel Moroni, Elijah, Moses, John the Baptist, Peter, James, and John—and if I had faith it could happen to me too. All I had to do, Carma said—again and again—was to read The Book of Mormon, and then "pray about it." She left me standing on her doorstep, early the next morning, while she ran inside and fetched me a copy.

I was sitting in the kitchen one night a few weeks later thinking about these things. I had finished Carma's Book of Mormon and I believed in a church I had never attended. My parents were away on vacation, and I was sure something terrible was about to happen; because people who had faith received visitations. And they were twice as tempted and tormented because they had found the truth. Two hundred evil spirits were probably assigned to them. I tried to read, but I couldn't shake off the sense of a presence. Whether it was good or bad I couldn't really tell, but I knew I was afraid of it. I wouldn't be up to it alone. I prayed a little and then I went to the telephone. I dialed every number but the last, waited too long and got the siren. Yes, it would look like I was doing it for a girl. I dialed the whole number. Worse yet, someday *I* might think I had done it for her.

Two hours later I was at a Mutual dance with my hands almost around Carma's waist, and she was beaming up at me. After that I figured I was in love, which justified everything until the day came when I decided I had figured wrong.

Suppose Sister Smith, in a silky fat nightgown, had suddenly turned on the lamp and said, "All right, when's the wedding? Don't move, I want Brother Smith to see this. The whole house asleep and here you two are having sexual intercourse at three o'clock in the morning. And we thought we could trust you. Get your hands off your faces and stop crying. Look at me, young man. It's a beautiful thing, but it's not free for nothing. Look at this, Lloyd. Sit up now and tell us what you think you owe one another. Rodney, I wonder what your parents are going to think when I invite them over for a little early breakfast?"

That was the only way it could have been. They lay upstairs on their bed and wondered and worried, but we were only mushing on the sofa, or grinding away in my car, or rolling around on the floor of the study until four a.m. for five straight nights, frenching until our tongues were raw. They wouldn't have admitted it for the world, but they wanted it. It might have been my salvation but I couldn't take the hint they never would have thought of giving. A thigh for a thigh.

Carma and I, at the piano in the living room. I'm trying to learn how to play "O My Father." Sister Smith strides in dressed in satiny black and a broadbrimmed black straw hat. Asks me would I like to take a little trip, to check out a restaurant she and Brother Smith are thinking about buying.

It's about ten and we head downtown. Sister Smith steers the big Buick and tells me a story. It's a sad story, and it reminds me of something in my own family. But I don't mention it.

"I thought you might like to see what happens to people who don't live the principles," she says.

A little tour of the plant. The man—husband—does most of the talking with a forced cheer plastered over fatigue. (When you've been caught in Vegas with one of your waitresses it takes it out of you.) The woman—his wife, his partner—offers a cutting comment now and then, when he forgets something, or when he doesn't.

Turning lights off and on, opening closets and cupboards, explaining machinery, showing us the parking out back. Sister Smith prevents silence with questions: the help, the daily figure, their banks, suppliers—prods a naugahyde stool, clacks a freezer door. I try to look like something besides eighteen-year-old boy. Everybody knows that everybody knows.

Finally, in a corner booth. Wife brings me a Coke from behind the counter, which I politely accept and dutifully sip. ("Every now and then you have to," Sister Smith says later.) They talk, about $20,000 apart. I nurse my poison, all ears. Suddenly, Sister Smith turns to me, smiling roundly, and says,

"Perhaps I should ask my future son-in-law if he thinks he can handle this."

She chuckles, and it's clear I don't have to answer. Just try to look modest and happy. The owners manage faint smiles, but I see they can't believe it. Their life's work in my hands. I smile back, but I can't believe it either.

They resume their haggle. Husband lights another cigarette, his hair in sandy tatters. Mrs. Fierce Menopause puts hers out. I sit there wondering if it wouldn't be better if I went away to college first, for a thousand years.

"You panicked," Holly said.

"Not right away," Robinson said. "I was always too polite to say what I really felt, so the whole thing dragged on for months. By then Carma had left college and moved back home—to wait for the wedding, I guess, or for me to officially propose or something. I didn't realize what was going on. I was just trying to survive Stanford. We wrote almost every day, but we couldn't keep it alive. So when Easter week finally came I went down and pulled the plug. I thought her mother was going to kill me."

"Did she make a scene?"

"Not exactly. I figured all hell was going to break loose, so I gave Carma the bad news the night before I went back. Late. Her dad I could have handled—he would have understood—but I was afraid to face her mother. So all I know is what Carma wrote me afterwards. She said her mother was thinking of suing me for breach of promise, and I guess she threatened to get me excommunicated too. Carma said she would never regret loving me because it had helped me join the Church, but she was afraid that someday my 'lust for power' was going to destroy me. She was always dramatic. I think she woke up her parents right after I left. All I know is her mom had her packed and half-way to Provo before breakfast."

"Was that the last you saw of her?"

"No. I saw her at church after that, when we were home on vacation."

"Did you ever try to get back together?"

"Not really. We went out a couple of times, but that was about it. I had my eye on a girl up at school by then. But nothing ever came of that either."

"What about her mother?"

"She finally cooled off a little. At least she never followed up on her threats. Needless to say, I avoided her as much as possible."

"You were quite a cad."

"Indeed," Robinson said. "Let's get some coffee."

III

From Orly, they went straight to the hotel and to bed— because of the time change. In the afternoon they wandered along the river poking in bookstalls, and that evening they rode up to the Place du Tertre and had dinner, under the Sacré Coeur.

Robinson's book was virtually finished, so the summer looked more like a reward than a chore. In Paris he might check a manuscript or two at the Archives Nationales, but aside from that, nothing. In ten days they would cross to England; there were a few things he had to do at the British Museum and the Bodleian, but this would take a week at most. Holly had her dissertation to think about, but so far she was just reading around. After London, a drive through Scotland, Ireland. They might take a cottage for a month, somewhere. Then back to the Continent.

They had both been in Paris before. This time, they decided, there was nothing they had to see, nothing to miss. They would start out late in the morning, let the Metro whirl them somewhere, and then walk back, shopping, people-watching, practicing French, holding hands. In the late afternoon find a restaurant, get a little drunk and return not long after dark. They did go to the theater twice, and once they ducked in and saw an American movie. At odd hours Holly kept at her Book of Mormon, and Robinson was reading *A Moveable Feast,* just for a lark.

"Guess what," Holly said, one morning when they were relaxing at the hotel. "I think I've discovered the secret of this book."

"Which is?" Robinson said, without looking up from his Hemingway.

"It's so outrageous," she said, "but at the same time so pious and preachy, that it creates an impression of truth. It forces it on you."

"It works on your fears," Robinson said, turning a page.

"I guess it's like the big lie. The bigger it is the more powerful it is. It's a strange feeling."

"It's the rhetoric," Robinson said. "Just as you say."

"It's probably the same feeling you had when you first read it."

"Could be."

"Jesus Christ visits the Western Hemisphere after his resurrection and preaches to the Indians. The *white* Indians. This has got to be the ultimate American fantasy."

"You may have something there."

"I still can't help wondering if by some weird chance all this actually happened."

"It didn't."

"I know. But there's something about it that makes you wonder, even when you can see right through it. Maybe it's just the style. It's so preposterous. So deadpan. It's such a flop, really. Why would somebody make all this up?"

"Why do people write books," Robinson sighed. "A profound question."

The next afternoon, as they were walking through the Luxembourg, Robinson said:

"This is where Hemingway first met Gertrude Stein. He says he can't remember whether she was walking her dog or not, or whether she had a dog then or not. But this is where he met her."

"I wonder where it was," Holly said. "I mean the exact spot."

"He doesn't say."

"I'll bet it was right here," she said. "That's why you thought of it."

"We'll never know," Robinson said. "Shall we stand everywhere just to make sure?"

They decided to walk to the rue Cardinal LeMoine, where both Hemingway and Joyce had lived, and then down the rue Mouffetard to the Place St.-Michel where Hemingway had done some writing. When they got there they found a cafe and feasted on a baguette and Préfontaines.

"I don't feel much like writing," Robinson said after a while. "I don't think this was Hemingway's table."

"Try not to think about it," Holly said. "Tell me," she added. "Are there Mormons in Paris?"

"Of course. There are Mormons everywhere."

"Is there a Mormon temple here?"

"Not that I know of. There's one in London. We can go see it if you like."

"I might like," she said. "Did I tell you I was in Salt Lake City once? We just drove through. My father wouldn't stop."

"I'll drink to that," Robinson said.

Dear dead town. Always grey, always sad. Crossroads of the West, once. Now only the crossroads of a psyche. Depressing, because you know what they wanted it to become, and at the same time you see what it has become. Just another city, tired mother of suburbs. 'And this is Mr. and Mrs. Young's bedroom,' your guide says, and it sounds so conventional, so singular. The sheepish tourists move down the hall. Postcards with bags of salt attached. Prostitutes on Second South joking about customers who won't take off their garments. A town not modern or holy or clean or dirty enough to exalt or debase the imagination. "I lost my sugar in Salt Lake City."

"Were you married to your first wife in the temple," Holly asked, "for eternity or whatever they call it?"

"Of course," Robinson said. "Who's been feeding you all this stuff? Charles?"

"I've asked some people a few questions," she said. "I'll stop if it bothers you."

"I just don't see the value of it," he said. "It happened a long time ago, and it's all over."

"You do mind," she said.

"Not really. Go ahead."

"Were you and Phyllis married in the temple?"

"No. Phyllis isn't even a Mormon."

"So in the eyes of the Church, you and your first wife are still married. As far as the next life is concerned."

Robinson had to laugh. "It's written on a piece of paper somewhere," he said. "But it doesn't mean anything. God isn't going to force people to stay married to each other, I don't think."

"What are the temples like inside? Is it just one big hall, or what?"

"Many rooms. Some big, some small."

"What's it like to be married there?"

"It's different. But one isn't supposed to talk about the details."

"You can't even tell your wife?"

"The last of my scruples," Robinson said. "Merely a courtesy."

"But why, if you don't believe in it?"

"I'll tell you all about if someday," he said. "I just like to add to my guilt one drop at a time."

"I can see you've really got a lot of it," Holly said.

"I was joking."

"But you have," she said. "I think you can still feel guilty about something you no longer believe in."

"I guess." Robinson lit his pipe and glanced out at the street. It was still there—Paris.

"It doesn't matter to me," Holly said, "as long as it doesn't bother you too much."

"It doesn't bother me at all," he said. "What put that idea in your head?"

"It's pretty clear."

"In what way?"

"In the way you say things."

"Like what for example?"

"Nothing in particular. Just everything."

"Oh for God's sake," he said. "That's ridiculous."

"I don't think so."

"But I don't take it seriously, for Christ's sake. That's why I joke about it. If I took it seriously I sure as hell wouldn't make fun of it."

"You could," she said. "It's not as simple as that."

"You're splitting hairs."

"Not really."

"Jesus Christ," Robinson said. "Can't we drop this subject?"

"If you didn't take it seriously," she said, "you wouldn't give a damn how I felt about it. But it's clear that you do give a damn. Because you don't want me to take it seriously."

He didn't answer that. He drank up, motioned to the waiter, and they got out of there, walking back to the hotel in silence.

It was a glorious afternoon—the streets filled with banners and honking. A light breeze and a rare blue sky. Shops freshly baited with things to eat and look at. Just like the song said.

Robinson strained after it, and failed. They might just as well be walking round and round Temple Square S. L. C. His honeymoon was coming apart. Turning into a goddamned cottage meeting. Christ!

He was afraid to let out his anger, for fear of losing her. But he would have to let it out, or he was sure to lose her. He touched her arm and they stopped.

"If you ever want to join the Mormon Church," he said, "believe me, I won't do a thing to stop you. You have my full approval to do whatever you want to do."

He bent to kiss her but she turned away.

"Why don't you stop being so damned polite," she snapped.

"Why don't you tell me what you really feel."

All right, he thought. I guess this is as good a place as any.

"I hate it," he began. "I hate it and I hate everything it stands for. And I'm damned mad at you for even bringing it up. I've spent most of my adult life trying to get away from it, so if you ever want it you can pack your bags at the same time."

"That's more like it," she said.

There was a bench nearby so they sat down.

"I don't have any intention of becoming a Mormon," she said after a moment. "But I'm going to study it, and I think I'll do my dissertation on the Book of Mormon. If you don't like it, tough."

"If it's all right with your committee, it's all right with me," Robinson said. "Just don't bother me about it."

"Don't worry, I won't."

"Fine."

"You creep," she added.

"You nut." He reached over and took her by the back of the neck. There was nothing like having your first fight in the heart of Paris.

"I know what," Holly said. "I'll prove it a fake and destroy the Church. Just for you."

"You don't have to go that far," Robinson said. "I don't believe it already."

They started walking again.

"Tell you what," he said, after a few blocks. "The next time we pass a pair of Mormon missionaries I'll point them out to you."

"You mean you've already seen some?"

"I think so. I can usually tell."

"Do they wear some kind of uniform?"

"No. Just dark suits, sometimes hats. Very clean-cut Americans."

"That doesn't sound like much to go on."

"It's enough," Robinson said. "Most of them look like people I used to know.

IV

Their second and last Sunday in Paris Holly got up and went to late mass at St.-Germain-des-Prés. Robinson slept in, met her outside the church, and they found lunch near the Place St.-Michel. From there, they took the Metro across the Seine and up to the Place de L'Etoile, wandered through the Arc de Triomphe and back down the avenue toward the Concorde, browsing idly through shops, with tickets to London marked for eight p.m. riding in Robinson's coat pocket.

"What ever happened to Carma?" Holly asked suddenly. I mean after you broke up, and she went back to college. What did she do after that?"

"She got married," Robinson said, "and had five kids in something like six years. It didn't do much for her figure."

"You saw her?"

"Now and then," he said. "I even had lunch with her a few times."

"After you were married?"

"Yes. When I was in grad school she called me one day, and one thing led to another. But not to another. I never slept with her, cross my heart. I wanted to, but I never did."

"Why not?"

"Well, for one thing she lost her nerve and told her husband. He made a big fuss. Accused her, threatened me. So we gave it up. They were divorced a few months later."

"And you were the cause."

"Not really. They had lots of other problems. She didn't cause my divorce either. By that time she was remarried and had even more kids."

"So you never did get together."

"We never would have," Robinson said. "I saw her a few times when she was divorced and I was still married, but there wasn't enough there."

"On your side or hers?"

"Mine. I was the one who cut it off."

"Do you know if her second marriage lasted?"

"Yes," Robinson said. "It didn't. She's divorced again, as far as I know."

"You've seen her?"

"No. She writes now and then, care of the department. About once a year."

"What does she say?"

"Repent. Go to church. Things like that. I guess I'm the only person she ever converted, so if I don't make it to Mormon heaven she says she's coming down to hell after me."

"And what do you write to her?"

"Nothing," he said. "I don't respond."

They walked on down the avenue, Robinson thinking that for a long time it wasn't going to matter where they were, that she was going to live only in these conversations until she found him all out. So why not volunteer a little information? After all, the girl had some catching up to do.

"What about her mother?" Holly was saying. "Is she still alive?"

I remember we had been rolling around on the grass down at the park. While I was holding her, I slipped my hand inside her blouse and unhooked her bra, and she got mad and made me hook her back up right away.

When we were inside the front door Carma's mother called to her immediately from the upstairs bedroom. I waited for a moment at the base of the stairs and then went into the study and picked up a copy of the *Improvement Era* lying on the "Postum table." Pretty soon I heard Carma calling, from the top of the stairs, for me.

When I came in Carma was standing flushed beside the bed with a couple of towels in hand and her mother was telling her to go downstairs and find the doctor's number in the desk directory. I could see two or three bloody towels on the tile just inside the open bathroom door.

Sister Smith was lying flat back on the bed without even a pillow. The blankets had been thrown aside to the floor and the sheet was drawn up over her slightly raised knees to her chest, her feet elevated, like two white spires, probably on the missing pillows. Carma set off without a word or a glance. Sister Smith had a grey smile on her face for me.

"Father's downtown," she said. "I can't reach him. I need a strong man."

"What do you want me to do?" I said.

"Go downstairs," she said, "and tell Gary to keep the little kids out back. Then I want you to go to the linen closet in the back hall and get me a large stack of towels. The big ones. I don't want to float out of this bed before the doctor comes."

I ran down, told Gary, and made two trips with the towels because the first stack was so large I dropped half of it on the stairs.

When I came back in Carma was in the bathroom—I heard the toilet flush—and Sister Smith was on the telephone explaining it all to a receptionist. The doctor was out. She said it was an emergency and then she put her hand over the mouthpiece while they tried to reach him.

"I want you to help Carma clean me up a little," she said.

Carma came out of the bathroom and I helped her raise Sister Smith so we could put fresh towels under her, and then we spread new towels all over the lower half of the bed. I turned away while Carma sponged her mother off with another wet towel and pulled the sheet back up.

"Anything?" Sister Smith said. Carma shook her head.

Sister Smith closed her eyes and put her head back, the telephone still at her ear, and Carma and I stared at each other across the bloody bed. Finally Sister Smith said "Thank you very much," and handed me the receiver.

"He's going to call an ambulance and meet me at the hospital," she said. "Carma, get a couple of my new nightgowns out of the drawer and my good robe and slippers out of the closet. And pack some things in my traincase. It's on the shelf in the closet."

We waited about twenty minutes, and during that time she passed some large clots and each time I helped her raise up so Carma could take them away and replace the towel. Once, while Carma was in the bathroom Sister Smith said, very quietly:

"My tithing baby."

I nodded, as if I understood.

"I'll bet you think I'm a foolish old woman," she added.

"No," was all I could say.

"Your mother would," she said.

I didn't know what to say to that, so I simply glanced out the window. My mother would have thought it foolish, I knew, but my mother didn't know about the millions of spirits in the pre-existence. She didn't know they needed bodies so they could come to earth and be tested. She didn't know how many Mormon women had given their lives for that principle.

I went down at the bell and let the attendants in. They hustled their litter up the stairs and put a dressing on Sister Smith while Carma and I pawed through the closet for the slippers. Then they eased her onto the stretcher, buckled the straps, and we followed them down. The ambulance was backed into the driveway and they opened the rear door and rolled her in. One of them opened the side door and let Carma in and I handed her the traincase.

"We'll be at Daniel Freeman," Sister Smith said. Carma looked away.

"If you hadn't come home when you did, she might have died," Holly said.

"I doubt it," Robinson said. "You couldn't kill that woman near a telephone."

"But she lost the baby."

"Of course. But that didn't stop her. A year or so later she had twins. A boy and a girl. She spent almost the whole nine months flat on her back and the doctor wouldn't let her leave the hospital without a hysterectomy. Beautiful kids."

"You've seen them?"

"Years ago," he said. "From a safe distance."

They continued down the avenue and Robinson turned the conversation to a small scandal they both knew of at the university. They passed two more blocks in this way and then stopped, when Holly turned abruptly to peer into a shop window. At almost the same instant Robinson saw the two young men, darkly dressed and looking like twins, who had come onto the avenue at the next block and were walking in the same direction, away. He fixed them for a second, then tugged at Holly's sleeve.

"There's your Mormon missionaries."

"What?" she said, without looking. She took a step closer to the window.

"Mormon missionaries," Robinson said. "I'm almost positive."

"Where?"

He started her up again, nodding his head to indicate the ones he meant. "Those two," he said, adjusting his stride to theirs and weaving from side to side to keep them in full view for his wife to study. They were both wearing American-style suits and ties, and one was carrying what looked like a triple combination—the Book of Mormon, Pearl of Great Price, and Doctrine and Covenants—all in one volume with a zipper cover. They were both very pale, and had unusually short haircuts; and they were walking almost in-step, talking and laughing. Robinson felt sure of it now, so he increased the pace.

He kept this up for about a block, not saying a word, as if his prey, the missionaries, might hear him, until he came to a difficult knot of strollers. As the knot broke, slowly and awkwardly, in front of them, he took Holly's arm and started to push and guide her, moving into a long stride.

"Let's catch up and meet them," he said, shifting her quickly in order to pass a couple who had stopped, right in the middle of the sidewalk, for a kiss. "Just for the hell of it."

He felt some resistance, but he kept up.

"Let's not be silly," Holly said. She seemed out of breath already.

"What's so silly about it?" he said without slowing. "It might be fun."

She pulled back very hard and stopped them.

"What are you doing?" Robinson said.

"I don't feel like it," she said.

"Why not? You've been talking about it all week. Why not meet the real thing?"

"I'd just rather not," she said.

"They won't mind."

"I don't want to," she said, "If you want to, go ahead. I'll wait right here." She turned and looked into a dark shop.

Robinson glanced up the street at the two figures. For a moment they disappeared in the crowd. Then he saw them cross the street and go into a building. He was surprised.It was a movie theater—or was it the place next door? There were some people in the way, so he didn't actually see them go in.

"They're gone," he said. "Forget it." He turned to his wife and saw that she was still staring at her shadowy reflection in the window, her back to him. He nudged her. "Hey." She didn't respond. She closed her eyes. She looked like she might be about to cry. But she didn't.

Counterpoint

Kent A. Farnsworth

The chapel was dimly lit and smelled of polished wood, with ranks of maple benches stretching from the scarlet-draped dais to heavy oak doors that opened out onto the high school compound. It seemed a world away from the city of mosques that sprawled in a labyrinth of narrow streets and high mud walls beyond the compound gates. An attempt had been made on the Shah's life two weeks before and he had taken a bullet through the jaw. The American community in Tehran was abuzz with rumors that his fragile government was on the brink of collapse and there might soon be an evacuation. Yet there were no signs of this turmoil here. Only a solemnity and reverence that made Brad equally uneasy. In the pew in front of Brad a white-turbaned Indian student bowed quietly as the chaplain's invocation echoed against the vaulted ceiling.

> Reveal thyself to us, Blessed Lord, and make us conscious of Thy greatness. We rejoice that while the teachings and theories of men have changed, Thy revelation of the fatherhood of God and the brotherhood of man changeth not.

Brad examined the long black neck hair of the Indian, pulled tightly up under his muslin wrap. He looked beyond to the black-robed figure of the chaplain who droned the liturgy, then down at the folded brown hands of the Iranian girl beside him. Nothing fit. He was part of a Schoenberg concerto—a composition of dissonance. He knew that he added to the dissonance and closed his eyes to shut it out, finding instead the tenor monotone of the chaplain.

> Help us to live Thy teachings, and to make them the rule and guide of our lives. May we give Thee the opportunity to lead us out of darkness into the light and liberty of the children of God.

"May we get Thee to leave us alone for a while so that we can just live our lives," Brad murmured under his breath. With head still bowed, he turned and glanced down the row to his left where Joe Brandon, head also bowed, was following the prayer in his book.

"If this were a piece of music," Brad thought, "even Joe would be out of harmony with me." Both were American and both were Mormons. But Joe was a gung-ho Mormon. The "no Pepsi" type. Plus he had no appreciation for Brad's passion for the cello. Instead Joe was a softball nut and could get more excited about "a well turned double play" than seemed possible for a thinking human being. In fact, the night that Brad's family had arrived in Iran, Joe had hauled him off to a softball game at the embassy; a game that Brad had endured only by finding it amusing. But it had given him a chance to learn a few things about Community.

"This high school is something else,"Joe had said as they watched the red uniformed team from the Atomic Energy Mission warm up. "It's just called 'Community,' but it's tougher than you can believe. Looks kind of prison-like—a big square brick building inside a walled compound."

"Oh, terrific," Brad answered. "But does it have a good music program?"

Joe shrugged. "Beats me. I'm not into music much myself."

"Too bad," Brad said. "I was first chair in the all-state youth symphony last year. I hope Community will have something challenging."

Joe turned and looked him over thoughtfully. "It'll be challenging—I guarantee it," he said. "Hey, watch this pitcher for the Atoms. He really throws smoke."

Brad watched the pitcher warm up without really seeing him. "What's so tough about it?" he asked.

"He's just super fast. And watch how this ball drops as it crosses the plate."

"No, not him. I mean Community. What's so tough about the school?"

Joe took a bite of hot dog, swallowed half of it and talked through the rest.

"Tons of homework. Real heavy stuff. The place is run by the Presbyterian Church and it's the only English speaking high school in Iran. Kids come from all over. Mainly foreign service kids like us—and some rich Iranians. There's no messing around."

"Church school, huh?" Brad said, opening his hot dog to examine the brown mustard.

"Yup. Chapel every morning first thing, and Bible class three times a week."

"Just what I need. More Seminary," Brad said, wishing that the game would get underway so that he could get home to practice the Boccherini that he had been working on.

Joe laughed and took another bite.

"Even worse. You march to Chapel in a line, sit and listen to them read prayers, sing old Protestant hymns, give sermons on the Trinity and that kind of stuff. It's really bad news. Great preparation for a mission, though."

Brad put the hot dog down on the bench beside him and watched the squad of red, overweight Atoms jog onto the field. Missions were time-buyers; delays for people who didn't know what they wanted from life. Brad knew what he wanted and wasn't going to let a mission mess it up. His brother had gone on one—left for England a terrific clarinetist and came home all thumbs and burdened down with scriptures. Now he was teaching junior high in Payson. Big deal.

The shuffle of students rising for one of Joe's "old Protestant hymns" drew Brad back into the wood-scented chapel of Community. He listened critically to the organist and sang the words from the book without thinking them.

> Once to every man and nation Comes the moment to decide, In
> the strife of truth with falsehood, For the good or evil side.

The hymn ended with the organist still missing one flat. Brad slumped back onto the bench as the sermon began, wondering how he would endure this every morning. Today's homily was not on the Trinity, but on the Fall, delivered by a man that Brad thought must be the personification of the theme—tall and gangly with a narrow, pitted face and a nervous tick that tightened his jaw and turned his lower lip outward when he paused.

Brad caught Joe's attention and rolled his eyes upward in mock disbelief. Joe nodded, ducking behind the row of students in the pew in front of him.

"Who do you have for Bible class?" he mouthed silently.

Brad fished the schedule from his shirt pocket.

"Cochran," he whispered back and stuck up three fingers to indicate the period.

Joe raised his eyebrows, mimed a whistle and pointed a concealed finger at the figure behind the pulpit.

"Likes to get Mormons," he said and drew the same finger quickly across his throat. "He'll murder you in class."

Brad's heart dropped into his stomach. The last thing he needed was to be hassled by someone else about church. He went now only because it was easier than listening to his mother whimper about how she must have failed him.

"You're a priest in the Aaronic Priesthood," she always reminded him when he announced that he wasn't going.

"I have whiskers, a voice that breaks and a driver's license," he would say. "It's part of being sixteen." His mother would cry and he would go to church and sit there with people like Joe—or "President Brandon" as their new priests advisor wished them to call him—who were "humbled by the experience." What a crock that was! And now some Ichabod of a teacher would be after him too.

On the dais the Ichabod leaned sternly forward and tapped the pulpit with his finger; the conductor demanding the attention of his mixed ensemble.

"'What is man that Thou art mindful of him?' said the Psalmist. 'For thou hast made him a little lower than the angels, and hast crowned him with glory and honor.'" Cochran paused, arms raised, then swept his hands forward, fingers pointed at his listeners in a dramatic downbeat.

"And why are you not all sitting here basking in that glory? Because you are limited by your own unbelief in God and in yourselves. *That* is the Fall, the sin that has benighted you. It is the sin of your own self-doubt. Your own inabilities to see what God has made of you."

"Self-doubt, baloney," Brad said, loudly enough that the Iranian girl slid an inch or two farther down the bench, and glared at him periodically throughout the remainder of the sermon.

He barely noticed as the litany began. Cochran, of course, wouldn't know that he was a Mormon—unless they all had to fill out a card or something. That was probably it. A card with religious information on it. He would put down "Protestant." No. "Christian" would be better. Why risk the fuss of true confession.

The Persian girl edged back toward him and slid an open hymnal onto his lap, pointing to the passage of the litany being read. She wasn't about to let him go to hell without a struggle.

> Our time is one of despair and expectation: despair because of
> our inability to save ourselves, of expectation because of our
> hope that you will make us a loyal and courageous people.

"Increase our hope, O Lord," read the girl in response, then pulled the book away, resigning herself to his fate.

The service ended and Brad marched in line out of the chapel and up the ramp that led to the main building. Cochran couldn't hurt him anyway, he decided. Suppose the teacher should find out. He couldn't malign what wasn't there.

In first period Literature the class read aloud Faulkner's "Barn Burning," moving from one student to the next as directed by a small Armenian woman with a polished British accent.

"Now," she said as the last line was read, "in the few minutes we have left, I would like you to take out a piece of paper and describe Mr. Snopes. We'll discuss his character tomorrow."

Brad scribbled a quick list on his note pad.

> Pitted face
> Twitching lip
> Probably a Presbyterian
> Hated string music

In orchestra next period he would play a dirge to Snopes. Instead he found himself in a four way struggle for first chair.

The music director, a stout balding man who puffed and wheezed as if just back from a jog around the compound, partially barred the door as Brad entered the room.

"What instrument?" he said, wiping his brow with a sweaty hand.

"Cello," Brad said. "I brought it in before chapel this morning."

The director thrust a small box containing folded pieces of paper under Brad's nose, forcing him to step backward to look into it.

"Pick a number and have a seat," the man puffed.

Brad unfolded the slip, glanced at the scribbled number 2, and moved into the room. It was a wide, semicircular chamber with a floor that rose away from a central open area around the door in tiered rows that held the student chairs. He stepped instinctively to the right where the cello section should be and found a seat.

"A round room in a square building," he thought. "I wonder how this fits in here without showing from the outside?"

The selection for the cello trials was new to him—a difficult piece by Hindemith with the cellos working in counterpoint to the dominant melody line. A plain, shapeless girl preceded him; playing plainly and shapelessly. She was stiff and mechanical, he thought, and stumbled on several measures that he knew he could handle. He tilted his chair back, tightened the hair on his bow and waited his turn, wondering if this was all there was to music at Community. When his turn came he took the chair in the center of the open area and showed the plain girl how it should be done, working his way carefully but effortlessly through the piece.

As he finished the director handed him a folded sheet of paper and called for the third performer. Brad loosened his bow, returned the cello to its case and opened the paper as a thin, fair-skinned girl with dark flowing hair took the trial chair.

"Technically correct, but lacking feeling or expression," the critique said. "You need to work on interpretation."

Brad surpressed a smile. Typical comments. The old fellow couldn't say too much the first time. He leaned back again as the dark haired girl began to play, but found himself drawn forward again into her music by rich, resonant strokes as she blended with the instrument, her graceful fingers caressing its smooth, polished neck. Lovingly she slipped Brad into second chair, then listened appreciatively as a smiling oriental musician moved him into third. Brad struggled through the rest of the hour, unsettled by the waves of fear and excitement that their music created within him, and realizing that he had not created the same in them.

The slender girl approached him at the bell and extended her hand.

"Leah," she said. "I'm Lebanese. And you?"

"American," he said. "Brad McDaniel."

"You play well, Brad McDaniel," she said.

"You also," he said, and left the room.

Cochran was standing in front of his desk when Brad walked into Bible class. The seat behind the turbaned Indian was empty and Brad plopped into it, then opened his notebook to review his Snopes list. Cochran sat awkwardly on the desktop that seemed much too small for his tall frame, carefully surveying the class.

"We have our usual mix again this year I see," he said, attempting what smile his twitch would allow. "It's helpful to me for discussion purposes to know something about your religious preferences. Let's start here at the right and have each of you introduce yourself and state your religion."

Brad felt his face begin to moisten. What about the card? At least that would be, well—private. More one-on-one. But now . . . ? In front of him the Indian straightened in his chair and looked around the room.

"My name is Kuldip Singh and I am Sihk," he said proudly. Cochran nodded and shifted his attention to Brad who stirred nervously in his chair. He was beginning to hate Community and Cochran. He drew a deep breath.

"I'm Brad McDaniel and I'm a Christian."

"Christian?" Cochran was on him almost before the word was out—as if he'd been expecting it. "What do you mean, Christian? Baptist? Methodist? Catholic?"

"Mormon," Brad said before he could catch himself. The room fell silent. Through the open window the sounds of the city beyond the walls began to intrude. He steeled for the attack.

"Why?" Cochran asked. Brad's mind was racing too fast for the simplicity of the question. He shrugged.

"Why not?"

"Why not is not a reason. Surely you have a better one than that."

"Do I need one for this class?" Brad knew that he was being impudent.

"Yes," Cochran said.

"Sorry to disappoint you; but that's it." Brad tried to hold his eyes steady.

Cochran's face relaxed and he leaned back onto his hands.

"Disappoint me? You aren't here to please me," he said. "But I should think that you would want a better reason than that for yourself."

In the quiet of the room Brad could hear the light breathing of Leah, the Lebanese cellist, who had taken the seat behind him.

"I have more important things to worry about," he said.

Cochran pushed away from the desk and stood looking thoughtfully at Brad, his hands thrust deep in his pockets.

"That's a pretty big load," he said.

When Brad left the classroom, Joe was waiting in the hall. He grinned and slapped Brad sympathetically on the back.

"He nailed you, didn't he," he said.

Brad brushed past him and headed down the stairs toward the outside and lunch. Joe laughed.

"Don't take it so hard. It happens every year."

"Not to me," Brad said, slamming the door against the stop as he pushed out into the compound.

"No. But to one of the Mormon kids. He finds out who you are —somehow—and asks to have you in his section. He was really a bear in my New Testament class last year."

They reached the poured concrete bleachers that rose in six uneven steps above an outdoor basketball court and opened their lunches, sitting in silence as Joe sorted through a wrinkled paper sack and Brad gazed absently at a soccer game that was beginning on the dirt field beyond the court.

"Did he work you over like this?" Brad asked, unscrewing the lid of his thermos.

Joe didn't look up from his sack.

"Nope. There was a member girl in my class," he said, stripping the peel away from a browning banana. "Seems like we spent half of each period listening to Cochran interrogate her about why she was a Mormon. She held up pretty well."

"Why does he pick on us?" Brad said, still following the soccer game. "Why not one of those strange religions like Kuldip What's-his-name?"

"Likes us, I guess," Joe said. "Why don't you ask him?"

Brad cast him a wry glance as he filled his cup with orange juice.

"How did you escape," he said. "No guts?"

Joe tucked the banana peel back into his sack.

"I wasn't a member then," he said.

Brad's cup stopped in mid-air, sending a stream of juice down his chin and onto his shirt. Again Joe laughed.

"In fact," he said, "I wasn't much of anything. You can learn a lot from Cochran."

The Gift

Levi S. Peterson

Gerard de Valois lived on Quai Marcellis overlooking the river Meuse in the Belgian city of Liège. On a snowy evening, as he returned to his apartment building, he found two young men at the door. "We are missionaries," one of them said, introducing himself as Frère Beckwith and his companion,who spoke no French, as Frère Haglund. They were Mormons from Utah.

"*Mon Dieu!* Who has ever heard of Utah?" Gerard said because he liked whimsy. "So you have created a new religion there? Is it anything like Islam?"

When the missionary had finished laughing, he explained that the Mormons were the inheritors of the authentic Christianity. They also called themselves Latter-day Saints.

"You call yourselves saints!" Gerard said incredulously. He stood back to scrutinize the missionary in a better light. "I would like to see this place called Utah. The seven deadly sins do not exist there!" He paused to join the missionary in laughter, then went on.

"But you are too late. I have already been a Christian. My parents were devout Catholics when they were alive. Now I am an existentialist."

"You are exactly the person we want to talk to!"

"You are very amiable and I am tempted to hear what you have to say just to know you better. But, no, when I think of it, I would be wasting your time."

The missionary pulled money from his pocket. "Let's gamble. This bill is worth two hundred fifty francs. I'll flip this coin. If it comes down tails, you get the two hundred fifty francs and we'll go away peacefully. But if it comes down heads, I keep the money and you listen to our message."

"Will you risk two hundred fifty francs on a chance to convert me?" Gerard said, laughing loudly. The missionary beamed. Gerard saw that he was perhaps twenty-one; his build was sturdy, and his hair, peeking from beneath his beret, was blond. He had a wry, affectionate smile and eyes that were simultaneously fine-humored and wistful. Already Gerard liked the young man immensely.

"Well, come along and I will introduce you to Katrine," he said, starting up the stairs. As he let them into his apartment, he was startled to see his sister Marie, who had not visited him for two or three years.

Having stared a moment from the threshold, he said elaborately, "I am honored, astounded, overwhelmed."

"Please withhold your effusions," Marie said in a bored voice. She sat with her pretty dark eyes half closed, her face impassive, her hands thrust into the pockets of the raincoat which she had not taken the trouble to remove.

"I invited Marie for supper," Katrine explained. "It was to surprise you for your birthday."

"My birthday!" Gerard exclaimed with exasperation. He turned to the missionaries. "I have turned thirty today. I had entirely forgotten the painful fact. Please forgive me. It will be very awkward to have your message tonight. You will have to return some other time."

Marie stood up, stretched languorously, and took off her coat. "Why chase them away so unceremoniously?" she said. She pulled chairs from the table. "Please take off your coats and have a seat. Really, Gerard, you are brutal. Have you forgotten your manners entirely? The least you can do is to introduce us."

He had no problem making his sister known to the missionaries. Marie smiled warmly and murmured her recognition. But it was not so easy in the case of Katrine. Unthinkingly he had been ready to tell the simple truth; he would not have used the word *mistress*, but certainly he would not have lied, as he finally did, by calling her his wife. Katrine was Flemish: a little taller than Gerard, well shaped, blond, generally placid, though not entirely predictable. She spoke French as Gerard spoke Flemish, with a heavy accent. She could not understand Walloon and was likely to be irritated if he broke into the patois of his region. Gerard had time to reflect that by calling Katrine his wife, he had given her an advantage; she sometimes said that it was time to settle down, that one should not wait forever to have children. The little lie had to be. Having known Frère Beckwith scarcely more than five minutes, Gerard was already hesitant to disappoint him.

"Wouldn't it be fun to share our supper with these gentlemen?" Marie said as she lighted a cigarette.

Katrine wrung her hands. "I am so sorry; I am truly desolated. I would love very much at any other time to show our hospitality, but the plain truth is I have not prepared enough."

"Forgive us," Gerard said. "We will make amends by having you back. How would it be if we think of the same night next week?"

"Don't be so niggardly," Marie said scornfully. "I will be happy to share my chop with one of them. A modest portion of food won't hurt any of us. Gerard regularly overeats."

Though at first Gerard shared Katrine's anxiety, he saw as the meal progressed that there was plenty for everyone—a braised chop apiece, a nice portion of salad, a serving of baked chicory sprouts aswim in bubbling gouda cheese, and a crusty roll. Frère Beckwith inquired a little into the lives of the three Belgians, but he was obviously pleased to respond to their questions about Utah and the Mormons. Utah was a land of high timbered mountains, arid sagebrush-filled valleys, and deeply eroded canyons. Frère Haglund came from Salt Lake City, while Frère Beckwith came from an isolated desert village called Hurricane. Frère Beckwith's eyes misted as he spoke of his valiant mother, a widow who supported her son on his mission with a tiny grocery store and a vegetable garden. She did not regard it as a sacrifice to keep her son on a mission; she shared his urgency to make known the wonderful fact that an authentic Christianity had been restored to the earth.

Gerard realized that the missionary had slipped without fanfare into a religious discussion. Katrine's dull, abstracted eyes showed that she had lost interest. To Gerard's surprise, however, Marie was attentive and alert.

"A living prophet on the earth today, even now!" she murmured.

The missionary was gratified. "That's exactly how it is—a prophet whose counsel it is our privilege to obey."

A little later she asked, "How does one know these things? How can I know that what you are telling me is true?"

The missionary exchanged a significant glance with his companion. "If you think about what we tell you, if you make sure your life is righteous and in order, and if you pray sincerely, then the Holy Spirit will touch your heart; your bosom will burn and you will know."

Gerard regarded Marie's radiant, sympathetic face with disbelief. He couldn't imagine a less likely candidate for conversion. He had never known her to be interested in art or history or any other serious subject, including the Catholic religion which she had abandoned instantly upon the death of their mother ten years earlier. Marie was outspoken and uncharitable. She spent beyond her means and failed to pay back money borrowed from friends. Above all she was concupiscent. At twenty Marie had been involved in an impossible affair with a volatile Dutchman who had a wife and children in Maastricht; Gerard believed that his counsel had helped her break out of that corrosive entanglement. He had attempted to intervene again when she first moved into her present apartment in Rue Lesoinne, for which her secretary's salary could not begin to pay. The man involved at the moment was M. Turpin, an entrepreneur in real estate from Verviers. Marie pointed out the fact that Gerard had a mistress. He admitted to the hypocrisy of his behavior; nonetheless, he insisted that there was something particularly malodorous when a woman from a recognized family misbehaved. Marie became livid. Gerard did not know that she had a capacity for such fury, and he went away chastened.

The missionary had pushed back his plate and opened a tiny appointment book. "This has been just a start," he said. "There's much more to tell. May we come back in a few days?"

"What about me?" Marie interrupted. "I do not live here, as you know. Is your offer for my brother only, or would you also come to teach me in my apartment?"

With an affable smile, Frère Beckwith turned to Marie, and in a moment they had negotiated a meeting at her apartment. The missionary returned his gaze to Gerard, who could not make up his mind. He stroked his palms together as he glanced at Katrine, whose eyes rolled upward in an expression of indifference. To Gerard's surprise, Frère Beckwith closed his appointment book and let it lie on the table. He said something in English to his companion. The two missionaries rose and rolled up their shirt sleeves. "We will wash the dishes," Frère Beckwith announced as he began to stack plates and collect silverware.

"No, you mustn't," Katrine protested. "I will not allow it. A guest cannot wash dishes."

"You can't deprive us of it," he said. "We are specialists in washing dishes. We love to wash dishes. We would walk ten kilometers anytime just for the chance to wash some dishes. You can show us where to put things when we are through."

"What will you think of my messy kitchen?" Katrine cried as the missionary pushed through the kitchen door with a stack of plates.

In a stentorian voice the missionary said, "In the beginning God created heaven and earth. And the earth was without form and was void, and the kitchens of the earth were without order, being filled with clutter, mess, and mayhem. And God said, Let us send Beckwith and Haglund to clean up these kitchens, that order may reign again. And so it was."

Katrine, who had followed him into the kitchen, watched with a gaping mouth. Gerard saw her astonishment. "You have to understand that this fellow cannot resist a jest."

As he scrubbed dishes in a pan of soapy water, Frère Beckwith told stories which he claimed were true. One was about an old woman in Hurricane who owned a dozen prize geese. One day a neighbor dumped a barrel of wet, soured mash into a feeding trough to dry. The geese crossed through the fence, gorged themselves on the fermented mash, and became drunk. When the woman came from her house, she found her geese wobbling and reeling; to her horror, they toppled over one by one, apparently dead. To soften the blow to her meagre economy, she plucked the geese and put their down aside for making quilts. By evening the naked geese had revived and milled in the woman's barnyard, honking angrily. That night she suffered the guilt of the damned, thinking of her poor denuded geese and the approaching winter. In the morning she rose with resolution.

She set to work with knitting needles and made a formfittng suit for each goose. During the entire winter her geese were to be seen wandering in her barnyard solemnly dressed in union suits of knitted wool.

Leaning against the kitchen counter, Gerard laughed until tears rolled down his cheeks. "Would it be so bad?" he said to Katrine. "We could have these young men to supper again. They could tell us whatever it is they have to say about their gospel, and then we could talk about America and perhaps learn a little English."

Very quickly the weekly visit of the missionaries became a routine, and Gerard came to cherish Frère Beckwith, though he was not entirely sure why. The doctrine which the missionary preached struck him as primitive and grotesque, something like a discourse from the theatre of the absurd. Oddly, its very absurdity appealed to Gerard. The proposition of his accepting the instruction of foreign heretics was an ultimate irony, an unprecedented joke. He knew that he did not strike other people as perverse. His enviable job as senior buyer in textiles at the Grand Bazaar depended upon the air of solidity and regularity he had. He was civilized, polite, tolerant, good-humored. Yet inwardly he was in a state of angry resistance; it could not be otherwise for any reasonable person, who of necessity must know the horror of the times, the purposelessness of human affairs, the ultimacy of the void. Underlying existence, as the existential philosopher Sartre had emphasized, was precisely nothing. Yet, being perverse, Gerard was free for just such a whimsical adventure as becoming a catechumen to these eccentric Mormons.

One Sunday afternoon Gerard decided to attend a sacrament meeting in the Mormon chapel on Rue de Campine. Arriving early, he saw Marie sitting alone at the back of the hall. As he took a seat beside her, she murmured a greeting in Walloon. He turned to her, wishing to say something light and friendly, then found himself swallowing an impulse to accuse her of perfidy. She was conspicuously out of place here. People filed into the barren hall, some of them taking seats, others clustering in the aisles; they greeted one another warmly and took up animated conversations. Obviously they were the kind of people who labored or kept shops. At best their clothes were merely decent; for many, a respectable shabbiness had to do. In a sense, Gerard too was out of place here. He wore fine Italian shoes with pointed toes and elevated heels and an expensive suit with tapered trousers and a coat having narrow lapels. Still he would not have imputed a sexual cast to his way of dressing. Marie's black hair brushed her shoulders in luxuriant abundance; her lipstick and eyebrow pencil were scrupulously etched; the neckline of her dress showed the barest hint of cleavage, above which hung a fine necklace with a gold chain and an enameled pendant. She was elegant and in a subtle way provocative.

A portly woman seated herself next to Gerard. Her aging cheeks sagged and her white hair was strewn wispily about her head. She introduced herself as Mme Jardins, though, as she told Gerard, people here called one another brother and sister rather than monsieur or madame.

"I am surprised," Gerard said. "This is not a large meeting place. Where have they gone—all the Belgians the Mormons have converted?"

Mme Jardins lowered her voice. "To tell the truth, there have never been many; people are unbelieving nowadays. Of those who believe, some go to America. That is what lurks in the hearts of those girls there." She pointed to a cluster of girls, the oldest of whom might have been seventeen. "They hope for a missionary; they will go to America, marry him, never come back. Or failing to find a missionary, they fall away."

An aroma of mildew and fried liver arose from the woman's soiled coat. Gerard said, "I am curious about this name you Latter-day Saints have taken. I am told you are like the primitive church; the members live lives of perfection. Are you truly saints?"

Mme Jardins broke into a grunting chuckle and poked her elbow into his ribs. "What a notion! Who is perfect? I will be happy for the merest corner of heaven if the good Lord will take me in."

"You are a true believer?"

"Oh, I am a believer. It is not the gospel that lets you down; it is people." She drew her tongue across the scattered whiskers of her upper lip. Gerard had surely known, she said, how things were during the war. The missionaries left; local brothers took charge; she had difficulty getting to meetings from her farmhouse near Flemalle-Haut. After the liberation, while things were still disorganized, her son had died. An unmarried man of twenty-five, he was irreplaceable; her husband had died long before and she had no other children. She went to Liège and asked the local brothers to come to the cemetery and consecrate the grave. But no one came. There had been only she herself, the sexton, and the driver of the hearse.

"There, it is the man you see," she said, gesturing toward a baldheaded man who conferred with Frère Beckwith at the front of the chapel. "He would not come because he considered my son an apostate. So I ask you: would you call him a saint? He preaches a pretty sermon; he loves to preside. But God will judge him for abandoning a poor woman when she had to put her only child into the earth."

By now the benches had filled. The baldheaded man stationed himself at the pulpit, and a woman began to play solemn music upon a small pump organ. Mme Jardins leaned toward Gerard and whispered, "That missionary, Frère Beckwith, he is the saint. I will not hide it from you: until he came to me, hardly six months ago, I was one who had fallen away. He came to my miserable room; he found me down, dying of despair; he gave me new courage. He has conviction; he touches people. It is like a fire in the wintertime to be near him. He has converted twelve or fifteen; that may not seem so many, but you should see how few the others convert."

Then her eyes blazed with disgust. She leaned forward and gazed askance at Marie. "The pretty young things flock to the branch to see Frère Beckwith. Unluckily for them, he has only three months until his mission ends and he will return to Utah. There will be a falling away, you will see!"

Marie, who seemed to pay no attention to the conversation, suddenly looked the old woman in the eyes. "There are also others who flock to this branch. It seems they have an abundance of aging addlepates."

To Gerard's immense relief, the service began immediately. Mme Jardins, furious for a while, stirred, snorted, and coughed, but gradually she became quiet and slumped into sleep. At the end of the service, many of the people remained to mingle in friendly, buzzing confusion. Children, who seemed to have miraculously multiplied, ran here and there in exuberant release.

Standing in the aisle with Marie, Gerard said, "They worship God in a strange way."

"Not so strange," she said pointedly. "Give them the benefit of the doubt; let them do it in their own way."

"Certainly, I have no objections, whatever their whim," Gerard replied. "Nonetheless, what do you make of this hubbub, this noisy conversation among friends in the chapel, and really, the sparse, mechanical procedure of their Mass?"

Marie shrugged. "As I say, it is their own way."

"I find it strange," he said in a softening voice, "that we who are the remnants of our family meet here in this place."

"Don't come if it bothers you," Marie said. "As for me, I like it here. For the most part these people please me; they are not complicated."

"That is true. Their minds are not burdened with ideas."

"They are decent people," she said with a rising irritation. "Why do you pick at them? You are free to go away."

"I didn't think I was picking at them," he said. Then suddenly, speaking compulsively in Walloon, he came to the question burning in his curiosity. "Why are you here? Do you believe?"

She also spoke in Walloon. "I will tell you so you are not surprised when you learn it from others. I intend to be baptized. I am thoroughly determined. There is nothing you can do about it even if you do not like it."

Gerard released his tension in a long expiration of breath. "You have even stopped smoking?"

"Even," she said.

"*Mon Dieu!* Well, fine, excellent, I congratulate you! Why not be baptized if it pleases you?"

Gerard took a tram to Place St. Lambert, where he transferred to another which passed by Quai Marcellis. Swaying in harmony with the jolting, twisting tram, Gerard gazed abstractedly out the window into the premature twilight of the rainy afternoon. He could not bring himself to believe in Marie's conversion. Knowing that the universe neither reasoned nor valued, he should have been prepared for such an absurdity. Christian conversion had always implied a certain irrationality; *credo quia absurdum,* Tertullian had said—I believe because it is absurd, the things of God being folly to the mind of man. But the prospect of Marie as a Mormon far surpassed Gerard's tolerance for the improbable. It was mindboggling. He could imagine nothing that the Mormons could do for her or, for that matter, that she could do for them.

Trudging along Quai Marcellis in the misting rain, Gerard recognized how severely he had been disillusioned by his visit to the chapel on Rue de Campine. The building was drab, the worship service barren, the worshippers impoverished and ignorant. It was a poor showing for a religion claiming to be a restored, authentic Christianity. The missionaries were apparently unequal to their task. Certainly Frère Beckwith had immense personal qualities; as the old woman had said, he radiated warmth wherever he went. But as Gerard now recognized, he was a cultural illiterate. He knew nothing about logic, art, history, and philosophy. He scarcely knew anything about theology. He had never heard of the Nicean Creed; he did not know that St. Augustine and St. Thomas Aquinas had ever existed. After living in Liège for more than a year, he knew little about the city—a fact which piqued Gerard's civic pride. For example, he had passed the church of St. Jacques many times without recognizing its distinctive architecture, which was widely considered to be the finest example of flamboyant Renaissance style in Belgium. By the time he was climbing the stairway to his apartment, Gerard had made up his mind to propose to the missionaries a tour of the cultural and historical sites of Liège. In fact, he would propose several tours. Ostensibly, the outings would be for relaxation and pleasure; in reality, they would be for the serious education of the missionaries. If they had nothing to give Gerard, at least he would give something to them.

On a cloudy Saturday afternoon, Gerard met the missionaries at the Place de la République Française. Although Frère Haglund had something on his mind, Frère Beckwith responded enthusiastically to the notable features of the city, and Gerard decided that his ignorance was nothing more than lack of exposure—a matter of youth and of isolation in that fantastic wilderness called Utah. During the rainy afternoon, they saw the gospel book, a thousand years old and jewel encrusted, which had belonged to Notger, bishop of Liège. They viewed the Perron, the columnar statue which symbolized the liberty of Liège. They discussed the statue of Grétry standing before the opera house, which the missionaries had often passed without learning anything about the illustrious composer. At last Gerard led them into the church of St. Jean to see a statue of the Virgin and Child entitled *Sedes Sapientiae—The Seat of Wisdom*. On the lap of the seated Virgin the Child sat upright; in the palm of his outstretched hand rested a jeweled sphere overtopped by a cross.

"What beauty the sculptor has achieved!" Gerard said, wiping his eyes with his handkerchief. "The Lord sits in calm dominion over all the world, as you see by the globe in his hand. And behind him, the Virgin—majestic, perfect, yet so human. I cannot see her without thinking of my own mother."

From the high dark caverns of the vaulted ceiling a concentrated light fell upon the statue. The thin, delicate face of the Virgin was caught in a mood of slight abstraction; an affectionate smile rested on her lips. The Child looked steadfastly outward, his face composed by simple, unquestioned authority.

Gerard waited expectantly, but the missionaries seemed reluctant and diffident. Perhaps they had been distracted by the odor of incense or by the scraping of shoes and the coughing of an old man who, across the expanse of the nave, placed a penitential candle before a small altar. Suddenly Frère Haglund, with an angry wave of his hand, said something harsh and contemptuous in English. Frère Beckwith replied in an embarrassed, coaxing voice. The younger missionary turned on his heel and strode noisily along the nave and disappeared through the doors of the church.

"He is offended. I am sorry for that," Gerard said.

"Please forgive him," Frère Beckwith said. "He has bad news from home. His brother is getting a divorce—he has not been married long—and my companion is angry about it."

"But something here also bothers him," Gerard persisted.

"He has never been in a Catholic church until now. Some of the missionaries are afraid of these old churches. They think Satan is in them."

"He thinks of Satan here!"

Frère Beckwith spoke reluctantly. "That really isn't what was bothering him. It was the statue. We aren't accustomed to thinking about Mary in this way. She seems to displace her son."

Gerard returned his gaze to the statue. He felt stung and vicariously insulted, a fact he noted with surprise. For the first time in years he acknowledged the hunger he felt for these venerable churches in which he had worshipped as a child. He had loved their soft darkness, the rose and amber splendor of their stained glass windows, the muted echoes of the high vaulted ceilings, the varied perspectives of columns, arches, and aisles. He yearned for the clarity of a Gregorian chant, for the pageantry of red, white, and gold vestments, for the murmuring recitative between priest and congregation, for the elevation of the Host—that moment of daring hope for the transmutation of wafer and wine into the substance of heaven. Against the Eucharist of his childhood Gerard posed the scanty, impoverished ritual he had seen at the Mormon chapel. Two missionaries had uttered brief prayers over plates of broken bread and trays filled with tiny cups of water, which boys had distributed to the members of the church. The Mormons did not call it the Mass, but simply the Sacrament, as if they did not consider their other rituals to be sacraments.

"I am for you, not against you," Gerard said to Frère Beckwith. "I see the remarkable things you are doing. You have dug up this old corpse, Christianity; you have drawn the embalmer's fluid from its veins; you are attempting to pump fresh, living blood into them. But, good brother, you are not doing it correctly. It is still a corpse."

The astonished missionary shook his head in denial.

"Do you have to start at zero—knowing nothing about Jerome or Boethius or Aquinas? Or this lady?" Gerard said, looking again at the serene face of the Virgin.

"You are still a Catholic."

"No, I am not a believer. Yet if I consider the matter without reference to myself, I still say you are empty. I am sorry to put it so bluntly. There is nothing in your bottle, neither old wine nor new."

The missionary turned toward the statue and said, "Your lady is not real. She is a fiction."

"A fiction? Yes, indisputably. That is why she is beautiful. The human heart has created her."

As Frère Beckwith prepared to reply, Gerard put his finger to his lips and silenced the missionary. From somewhere in the immense cavernous building came a light, melodic tapping. "That tapping—do you hear it? In my childhood home a clock from Zurich ticked with the same regularity. I am reminded again of my mother. She sat knitting by the hour; in the net of her lap, beneath the coils of yarn, were a prayer book and rosary. Wherever she was, there was order, undeviating regularity. She draped the dining table with lace from Bruges; she decorated the mantel with crystal from Val St. Lambert. She combed her hair into a discreet bun; she hid her face behind the severity of large, round spectacles. Yet she loved me and wanted me to have eternal life."

Gerard's eyes sparkled with tears. "What I do not see," he went on when he had wiped his eyes, "is how you span the abyss. Haven't you ever felt the need for a mother beyond this world? Doesn't it mean something that God had a mother, that a mortal bore God in her womb? This lady is a bridge between his infinity and your insignificance."

"There is no abyss."

"No abyss! So for you God is close, convenient, congenial. You will call at his house this evening; he will serve you cookies and Pero; you will converse on the affairs of the day or on the weather!"

"Tonight I will pray to him exactly like that," the missionary said. "You do not understand the Holy Spirit. Through the Spirit, God is always close—if you are worthy to have him."

Like Gerard, the missionary had stood these several minutes at the ambient edge of light falling from the ceiling. His hair, nose, and ears, his gesturing hands burned with chiaroscuro brightness against the shadows around him. "I have the testimony of the Spirit. I am telling you so that you can have it too," he said in a voice strangely elevated.

"I have read about the day of Pentecost. You cannot ask me to believe in the Spirit. It violates every rule of reason and logic," Gerard said urgently, feeling suddenly compelled to parry and forestall.

"How can you say that?" Frère Beckwith said with an impatient gesture. "I know what I know. I have the Spirit. Do you feel it?" He stared intensely into Gerard's eyes.

"Feel it! How could I feel it? Look, here is my hand!" Gerard grasped one hand with the other. "It is solid, real. But the Spirit! No, I feel nothing."

"It is with us," the missionary said in a voice close to terror. "Do you feel it?"

"Nothing!"

"This is your chance!" the missionary cried.

"There is nothing here!"

"It will leap to you now!"

Gerard was aware of the horripilation of his hair along the back of his neck. An ominous electricity seemed hung in the air; an inscrutable potency seemed to have just brushed by. Though neither of them had moved, Gerard suffered the illusion that he had been pressed to a wall. And then, looking again at the *Sedes Sapientiae*, noting again the tranquil marble smile of the Virgin, he said simply, "I do not accept it."

Already the energy of the missionary seemed to diminish, like the dying down of a spinning shaft when its power has been cut off. "I wanted it for you," he said. Tears glistened on his cheeks.

"I am sorry to have denied you," Gerard said. "I am not a Christian."

Afterward Gerard and the missionaries ate a little supper in an open pastry shop off Place St. Lambert. Gerard bought a slice of cheese and a basket of fine grapes in a grocery shop; he found crusty rolls in an adjacent bakery; and here, in the little shop where they sat on stools before a narrow counter, he bought them sweet waffles and apple juice. A Saturday crowd still filled the square and its surrounding streets. The rain had stopped; the clouds promised to break. Frère Beckwith had recovered his composure and talked cheerfully about a letter he had received from his mother in Hurricane.

Gerard poured another round of apple juice into their glasses. A trifle remained in the bottle; he gave it to Frère Beckwith. He was reassured to see that the missionary had not cast him off. Oddly, Gerard cherished him more than ever. An awe and a reconciliation had settled upon him. He would attend Marie's baptism. Having felt the intensity of the missionary, he no longer doubted the miracle of her conversion. He would make no further judgments against the worship of the Mormons. He knew that Frère Beckwith was the timeless Christian. He had no need for reason, for culture, for tradition; he had the Spirit.

On another Saturday Gerard went to the baptism. A hushed crowd had gathered in the basement of the chapel; afterward, because of the excellent spring weather, there was to be an excursion to the citadel at the head of Rue de Campine. Dressed in white, Marie sat at the edge of the font, in which clear water sparkled and splashed. Her black hair spread across her shoulders; she sat quietly, her hands in her lap, her lips slightly tremulous. Frère Beckwith, dressed in white pants and shirt, took her by the hand and led her down the steps of the font. He paused while she forced the floating hem of her robe to sink around her legs. He took her wrist in one hand, raised his other arm, uttered a brief prayer, and laid her back into the water. She arose drenched and spluttering. They clambered from the font and passed by Gerard on their way to the dressing rooms, leaving behind a trail of water. Gerard had not realized how muscular and well proportioned the missionary was. He seemed a perfect match for Marie, who despite her twenty-eight years had a splendid body; her drenched, clinging robe revealed the undercup of her breasts, her flat belly, her sinuous thighs. Yet Gerard could detect nothing concupiscent about the way she leaned against the missionary's shoulder, subdued, dependent, strangely unlike herself. Like

Adam and Eve before their fall, they seemed oblivious to the sensual perfection of their bodies.

Gerard had supposed that he would find the making of a Christian in this manner unseemly and indecent. On the contrary, the cleansing rush of water over his sister's body left him touched and elevated; for a moment, he felt renewed and purified. Then a sense of deprivation came over him. He could not remember a time when he had been free from guilt. His inadequacies and failures were innumerable; among them were his abandonment of his parents' faith, his refusal to marry, his recurrent doubt that mankind excelled in anything other than theft, butchery, and oppression. He could only envy Marie for having found a means of absolution. In his mind, he defended her before their father and mother, who would not have approved of her becoming a Mormon. If they could know how dead the old forms had become, how the old truths had lost their potency and conviction, they would understand. It was far better that Marie take on the eccentricities of this revivified Christianity than that she go on as she had been—angry, cynical, and promiscuous.

Afterward some thirty persons crowded into a tram in front of the chapel and rode to the top of Rue de Campine, where they got off and strolled along a tree-lined promenade to the citadel overlooking Liège. Seeing that no one waited to walk with Mme Jardins, Gerard fell in beside the old white-haired woman and kept her pace, although she was so piqued by the neglect of the others that she could scarcely be polite to him.

In time the two overtook the others in a courtyard of the citadel. Gerard knew already which object the quiet group examined. It was a wooden post, splintered and chipped until it was scarcely more than a stub. To this post the Germans had bound the best citizens of Liège and had shot them in retaliation for acts of the Resistance. Nausea crept over Gerard as he viewed the post. Each splinter and shard had been torn away by a bullet which had first passed through the body of a patriot. Dozens had died: lawyers, physicians, aldermen, men of commerce and finance—the most respectable, honorable citizens of the city, who now lay in the cemetery behind the citadel. He could remember clearly one of the executed men, M. Besier, a pharmacist who with his wife and family had frequently visited Gerard's father and mother. He pushed away from the crowding circle. It was an outrage too terrible, too irremediable to think about.

The group, broken into chatting clusters, strolled on, coming in time to an overlook of the city. A bank of clouds burned in the setting sun. Steeples, façades, and domes glimmered above the haze of the city's exhaust and smoke. The wide Meuse threaded a silver path through the city center. An aromatic breeze stirred greening plants.

Mme Jardins had come again to Gerard's side. He murmured a recognition of the beautiful evening, which she ignored. Peering beyond him, she grumbled, "Things would be better without your sister. She will be a troublemaker."

Gerard was startled, but he said with an increased politeness, "I trust you will find otherwise. She has already made many changes in her life."

"You have been a neglectful brother. She is only twenty-one and from all appearances you have let her live alone and do as she pleases for many years now."

"Only twenty-one!" Gerard whistled.

"It isn't true? She is younger?"

"Yes, of course, certainly, there's no question about it," he replied hastily. "Somehow I had imagined she had already turned twenty-two, but her birthday is several months away. How did you know her age? Doubtless she told you."

"*Par bleu*! She wouldn't speak to me in any circumstance. It is marked on her papers of baptism. I saw them in Frère Haglund's lap as we sat in the service."

Laughing and chatting, the people had turned back now. Mme Jardins motioned with her hand. "Notice that your sister has captured Frère Beckwith." Gerard saw that the missionary and Marie walked in a straggling cluster of young people, though they were not precisely side by side. The old woman went on. "He stays too close. You watch: she is always nearby; she will not leave him alone. She is in love with him."

"*Ça m'assied*!" the stunned Gerard said, wishing fervently to believe that the old woman was mistaken. "Well, what of it? Such things happen. A handsome young man, a pretty young woman—no harm can come from it, I suppose."

"No harm? You don't understand things in this Mormon church. Now as for me, no, there is no harm to this missionary, whom I respect enormously. We have an understanding, he and I," she said proudly. "But the others! It is unbelievable how closely they watch the missionaries. And when tongues wag, the mission president hears; then off goes the good missionary to another city—instantly."

"He has only a month or two before he goes home to Utah."

"That doesn't matter. If word gets to the president, off goes the missionary to another city. Such a pity that one so fine should go home with a cloud over him. And when he is gone, your sister will fall away. That is how deep her conversion is."

After returning to his apartment, Gerard fell into a lassitude from which he did not recover even after the pleasant supper of ham, oiled salad, buttered rolls, and wine which Katrine set on the table. He browsed in the evening paper and pretended to get into a novel but finally resigned himself to querulous thoughts. He could scarcely bear to remember his cheerful feelings at the baptism. He was swept by embarrassment for his romantic ideas about Marie's conversion. What a shameful exercise she had put herself through! Like a schoolgirl she had assumed this theatrical posture, giving up smoking, accommodating herself to a congregation of stolid shopkeepers and thickfingered streetworkers, performing the charade of baptism—her body clothed in white, her face painted with innocence. Passionate love! *Mon Dieu,* what people wouldn't do for it!

Two weeks later, on a Monday morning, Mme Jardins came by Gerard's office on the top floor of the Grand Bazaar and asked him to consult with her on a serious matter. At 5:15 Gerard joined the wispy-haired, soiled old woman on a bench in Place St. Lambert. The square roared and clanked and rushed with arriving and departing trams and crowds of people making their way toward home. Near Gerard and the old woman a multitude of pigeons bobbed, pecked, and pushed around the feet of a man who scattered grain to them; a pigeon balanced itself with fluttering wings upon the man's beret.

With decided firmness Mme Jardins said, "I have come to ask that you control your sister."

"Control my sister! What on earth has she done?"

"The missionary is on the edge of disaster. If your sister were not present, it would all end well."

"Those wagging tongues, I suppose," Gerard said with a sigh. "The mission president will send him to another city for his last weeks."

"It is not as simple as that. Things have happened between them."

"But of course!" Gerard exclaimed. "What else would you expect? Things have happened between them!" He shook his head.

"It is not so bad as it might be. But to prevent things getting worse—that is why I am here. It would be simple: you speak to your sister; she takes a vacation; or perhaps she makes herself scarce in the city."

"You do not understand things anymore," he said. "One does not control his sister these days."

The old woman, reeking of onions, leaned toward him and wagged a finger in his face. "There are things you also do not understand. I will say nothing about your sister; as for the young man, it will not only ruin his mission, it will ruin his life. You do not know how the Mormons are. They count adultery next to murder."

Gerard laughed. "Really, the missionaries are always together. Are you telling me that the three of them are having a love affair?"

"Your sister is a contriver," Mme Jardins protested. "I will tell you how I know. I thought I would give Frère Beckwith a tiny warning from a friend. I stopped him on the streetside before the chapel, and I told him how visible this attachment between them had become. I did not expect more than that. Suddenly he wept, he made a confession, he spoke of private moments between them that would astound you—on the stairwell between the basement and the chapel, behind the stage curtains while practice for the branch drama was in progress, in the kitchen of her apartment while the unsuspecting Frère Haglund snored in the living room, thinking that his companion and your sister were busy washing dishes."

"He would tell you this?" Gerard said incredulously.

"There is a loyalty between us," she said. "He saved me from despair, and he knows that I do not judge him, that I would not abandon him even if he fell. But if you know him, you know that he must go home honorable. That is the kind he is."

Gerard was filled with loathing for the intimate discourse of the unkempt, mildewed woman. Again he wished to believe that her gossip-honed mind had created the situation she pretended to see. He set himself to doubt, he willed disbelief—and could not achieve it. The only surprise he felt was that Marie had not contrived sooner and more completely, that she had not long ago brought the vulnerable missionary to the thing she desired.

"Will you influence your sister? If something is not done, Frère Beckwith's life is ruined; he will be excommunicated; he will live as a pariah. You do not understand how much chastity means with these Mormons."

"I prefer to have nothing to do with this matter," Gerard said. He was angry with the old woman for bearing this news. He was angry with Marie for being always in heat, always looking for an affair. Most of all, he was affronted by Frère Beckwith's defection. There was no such thing as a saint. Wasn't it true that the very word *saint* had a terrifying sound? To claim such a word, to bind it seriously to one's identity was like playing ignorantly with a dangerous object. Gerard was filled with disgust for himself. His own behavior regarding these Mormons was scarcely less shameful than Marie's. He must shake himself savagely awake; he must eradicate entirely his foolish intrigue with Frère Beckwith; he must deny once and for all his longing for an impossible innocence.

"Please influence your sister," Mme Jardins repeated.

"It will seem irrelevant to our discussion," Gerard said, "that my father was killed during the second week of the war. This post brings it to mind." He waved toward one of the green corrugated lamp posts which circled Place St. Lambert. "I fancy sometimes that the Germans tied my father to the post we saw at the citadel and shot him, but that isn't how he died. He was second in command at Fort de Malines on the heights between Namur and Charleroi. The defense of the fort was neither intelligent nor heroic. The blitzkrieg bypassed the fort; a week later a mop-up force arrived and burned out the defenders with flamethrowers."

"Everyone suffered in the war."

"Yes, and I have no right to complain more than any other. Why should I blame the Germans? Why should I blame them even for the brutal retaliations against the innocent citizens of Liège? They practiced a standard counter-insurgency, in which they were nothing more than the agents of reality. As Sartre and Camus correctly point out, life is absolutely senseless, absolutely nauseous."

"I know nothing about Sartre and Camus," the old woman murmured.

"So why shall I be concerned if this missionary compromises himself?" Gerard went on. "It is apparent that he is spineless, to say nothing of the fact that my sister would do something drastic if I spoke to her."

"Then I must do it myself. It would be better coming from you, but I will do what has to be done."

"*Zut alors*! What do you intend to do? If you think you can persuade Frère Beckwith to change his ways, good luck to you. But I warn you not to approach my sister. She is volatile; she is worse than gasoline or dynamite!"

"I am not afraid of your sister," Mme Jardins said. She grasped his coat sleeve and tugged his arm toward her. "I will also tell a story about the war. I myself was in the Resistance. My stable loft was one of the stations for downed aviators on their way toward the Channel. I once stood at the gate of my farmyard near Flemalle-Haut, knowing that six British flyers were in my loft, and I stared into the eyes of a German patrol leader, who stood on the road with his men. I gave him a fierce look which silently said, Come in if you dare. Luckily for him and his men, he chose to go on."

Looking into the old woman's resolute eyes, Gerard did not doubt her story. Who could explain why a poor country woman should have the nerve for such heroic action? "I am impressed by those who resisted. I honor and respect you. But, honestly, I do not think you can succeed with my sister."

"I will try. A person must not become weary of good causes. I know what is is not to have a good cause; one can die simply from despair. Frère Beckwith is worth saving. I have an interest in his innocence."

Gerard found himself agreeing. Innocence being a rare thing, the missionary ought to be retrieved. He had a vague notion that if he spoke to Marie with an immense tact she might also be persuaded. On the next afternoon, not knowing what he should say, he took a tram to the Guillemins station, then walked along Rue Varin, which offered a movie house featuring pornographic films and a dozen or more houses of prostitution. Even at this early hour, a few women were on display behind plate glass windows; they sat in padded chairs, their hair impeccably coifed, their evening dresses well-fitted and suggestive. It was a remarkable transition to turn into Rue Lesoinne, where recently renovated apartment buildings spoke of prosperity and social elevation. Their brick was new, their woodwork freshly painted, their façades perforated here and there by broad garage doors behind which automobiles were likely to be parked.

Marie asked Gerard whether he would take supper with her. He did not believe her to be sincere; in any event, as he told her, Katrine expected him. He could not keep his legs still; he crossed them first in one way, then in another. He admired the decoration of her apartment. It was painted in the merest tint of peach pastel; satin curtains hung at the windows; an excellent rug covered much of the waxed parquet floor. Gerard particularly admired one of the lamp shades, an import from Denmark whose quality he had the ability to judge because of his work at the Grand Bazaar. Marie shrugged off his compliments; it was an apartment like any other and not so badly priced.

'Well," she said, "you have come to see me, which is very nice, but there must be a reason."

Gerard came to his point, though not in a heroic way. "I think the missionary—Frère Beckwith, I mean—has only four weeks. Then he will go home to Utah."

She put out her hands with palms up and fingers spread, as if she wished to hear no more. "Yes, of course; sooner or later all of them go home."

"Perhaps we should let him go without complicating his life," he went on. "He impresses me as a fragile person. Really, it would be easy to crush him."

"By all means, let him go. I am not aware of anything holding him here," she said impatiently.

"He is naive. He does not know how to take care of himself."

"I find this discussion absolutely strange!" Marie cried. "You have come to preach to me about something. Well, for God's sake, tell me what it is."

"I have come to make an appeal."

"An appeal is always in order; I have never been known to refuse an appeal," she said mockingly.

"These Mormon missionaries are like our priests. They marry later on, but for the time that they are missionaries, they are persons apart, they are celibates."

"I don't need lectures on facts which I gathered for myself a long time ago," she said, rising and going to the kitchen. "Excuse me; I will get on with my supper." She picked up a knife and sliced a cauliflower into a pan.

Gerard stood in the doorway. "My point is that we can scarcely comprehend how difficult it would be for one of them if he should sin. It would destroy him."

She turned on him and spoke with an exaggerated calmness. "You have two choices: you can leave my apartment now, which is what I would prefer, or you can speak out clearly what it is you think I have done."

He sighed; his task might have been easier if he had known more precisely what he wanted to say. "Do you think to marry Frère Beckwith?"

Marie opened her mouth several times but finally, puckering her lips into a scornful pout, refused to speak.

"Do you think to go to America with him, because that is what it means, isn't it?"

"Why should I go to America?" she said defiantly. "What if he were to stay in Belgium?"

"It would be like holding a rabbit under water; he would die here."

She stared intently upon the last bit of cauliflower in her hands. Tears gathered in her eyes, but she spoke indignantly. "How is it that you have your pleasure with women but come relentlessly to me with suggestions of chastity?"

Gerard felt tears forming in his own eyes. "You are in love with him. You must do something paradoxical: you must let him go. Make pretexts; give reasons for missing church services; fail to be at home when the missionaries call. It is only for four weeks."

Her tears flooded. She seemed to have sagged, to have diminished in stature. He held out his arms and took her in. She spoke in Walloon. "Since Papa was killed, since Mama died, I am always lonely; I have no one."

He stroked her shoulders and pressed his cheek against hers. He said, also in Walloon, "We must see each other often; we must not abandon one another."

He was filled with strange, cutting emotions. He had been braced for tirades and explosions; he had no strength for her tears. They posed an irrefutable argument. If one or the other in this abominable love affair was doomed to suffer, why should it be Marie? What interest did Gerard have in the innocence of the missionary—or in the innocence of anyone, for that matter? He could not understand the passion the human animal had for penitence, self-denial, renunciation. Was the human conscience any less a genetic accident than the trunk of the elephant or the plumage of a male peacock? The missionary would have to look out for himself. If he fell and suffered, it would be no more than happened to anyone else.

Gerard left Marie apologetically and without any attempt to extract promises from her. He believed himself resolved to withdraw from the affair and let things unravel as they must. Yet before he had entered his own apartment, he was afflicted again with feelings that the missionary should be saved. He spent the evening in a confused paralysis. He did the usual things with an air of calmness while his mind looped and rotated like a wheel broken free from a speeding railway car. He ate his supper, chatted with Katrine, read the newspaper for an hour, lay on his bed, and tried to sleep. Tentative solutions coalesced and evaporated in his mind. The missionaries would come for supper on the following evening. If Gerard wished to speak privately with Frère Beckwith, he could arrange it as easily as Marie had apparently done.

Katrine had come into the bedroom. She sat on the side of the bed and undressed. She dangled her bra in Gerard's face and asked whether he was awake. She stood on the rug at the foot of the bed and did the steps of a little dance while she put on her nightgown. She turned out the light and got into bed. She snuggled close to Gerard, rubbed her hand along his chest, and nibbled at his shoulder.

"I have no spirit tonight," Gerard remonstrated.

"No spirit! Let me give you spirit," she crooned, running her hand along his thigh.

Marie was absolutely correct in accusing him of hypocrisy, he was thinking; he was always wanting her to make sacrifices which he was not prepared to make.

"I have given it up," he mumbled.

"But we haven't made love for five days," Katrine protested.

"It is time we were getting married," he said. "Really, this has been an indecent thing we have been up to all this time."

She took up an accusing voice. "You have been with someone else. That is why you were late tonight."

"*Mon Dieu,* no! I am thirty. I think it is time for children. And a little respectability."

Katrine withdrew to her side of the bed. It seemed to Gerard that she turned and sighed and threw off the covers and pulled them up again for a long time before she went to sleep.

The next evening after supper, Gerard and Frère Beckwith went onto the balcony overlooking Quai Marcellis and the river. Through the open door Gerard heard the faint murmur of voices from the kitchen where Katrine and Frère Haglund washed dishes. The ballooning canopies of the trees on the quay caught the yellow light of the late sun. The image of puffed clouds refracted across the wake of a deep-laden boat making its way up the river. The captain of the shovel-prowed boat, standing at the steering wheel, puffed calmly on a pipe; his wife took in clothes from a line stretched between the cabin and a mast; a little dog darted back and forth across the deck, barking at the city first from one side of the boat and then from the other. The missionary leaned over the balcony. He spoke of leaving Liège. He said it would be hard to go, though he had awakened in the night during these recent weeks thinking of the deserts and mountains of Utah. Gerard caught himself shrinking from his purpose; he would have to move with predatory abruptness.

"You are in love with my sister," he said.

The missionary scrutinized Gerard's face as if he doubted what he had heard. Blood rose slowly along his neck and colored his jaws and ears. "She has the Spirit, and I am not worthy of her," he said at last. "I have shamed myself because a missionary should not fall in love though I do not know how to keep from it. She is beautiful."

"But I think you are in trouble."

Frère Beckwith did not seem to understand.

"I mean that things have happened between you," Gerard insisted.

The missionary was silent for so long that Gerard thought his words had been lost in the high, melodious call of a rag merchant who pushed his two-wheeled cart far down the quay: "Rags bought here and old iron too; brass, glass, nails, pails, anything at all; rags bought here and old iron too."

When the call had died away, the missionary said, "I am glad she was brave enough to tell you. Don't be angry with her. I take full responsibility. I am horribly ashamed. I did not intend to take liberties. I never dreamed about any such thing; I am astonished at myself; I did not know I could feel so strongly."

"Please, I am not a judge; I would rather not know about it."

The missionary gestured impatiently. "Telling you is a relief. I didn't mean to deceive anyone. I should have confessed to the mission president, but I couldn't bear to do it. However, it is a matter of the past now. I do not think the Spirit has deserted me."

"The problem remains."

The missionary looked shamefully downward. "Yes, because I have compromised my mission. Now you will never believe."

"You are relentless; you think always of conversions," Gerard said. "I am not thinking about me. I am thinking about what will become of you."

"I will make it good to her; I will marry her if she will have me," the missionary said, his voice sinking more deeply into apology. "When I get home, I will write to her. I can't speak to her about it now; that would be breaking the rules again. Maybe she will come to Utah; my uncle would sponsor her immigration."

"In the meantime, you are still in jeopardy. What if things continue to happen?"

"I am resolved. It will not happen again. Your sister is safe."

"It is not my sister I am thinking of. What if she herself should contrive to give the two of you an hour, or even a half hour of unquestioned privacy? What if she let you know unmistakably that you could do with her as you wished? What if, in fact, she approached you so closely, so intimately, that the man in you had no choice?"

For an instant the missionary's face carried signs of collapse; he seemed to weave uncertainly, like a boxer whose senses have been shaken. Then his determination returned, and he spoke with a rapid belligerence, as if he meant to stave off a full recognition of what he had heard. "No, that is not the kind of person she is, no, not at all!"

A great pity welled up in Gerard. "I am trying to tell you that you are in danger."

"You are wrong," the missionary fervently insisted.

Gerard went recklessly forward. "She is not twenty-one; she is twenty-eight. And there is more to be told."

The two men stared at each other through a long, entropic silence. The missionary appeared to be on the verge of surrender; helplessness, defeat, pleading emerged upon his face. Then again, in time, resistance and defiance. "That isn't true. I know her better than that!"

Anger kindled in Gerard. Strangely, it was detached from the missionary. He was thinking of the old white-haired woman. He cursed her for having set him upon this haggling, hopeless business. He should have known by common sense that there could be no intervention in an affair such as this. He shrugged his shoulders and in a cool voice murmured, "I apologize for what I have said. There is nothing of importance in it. Let us go inside and see whether the dishes are done."

They sat at the table with Katrine and Frère Haglund. Gerard tried not to watch the face of the suffering missionary as he delivered the scheduled lesson. The others saw nothing unusual. Katrine yawned; Frère Haglund perused a notebook. Frère Beckwith stuttered, made false starts, paused, searched for words, broke off sentences. Within fifteen minutes he had concluded and with his companion went out the door.

Turning back after closing the door, Gerard bumped into Katrine, who had followed him closely. She smiled, searched his eyes, put her arms around his neck. "Sweetheart, I am so sorry about last night," she said affectionately. "I didn't listen to what you were really saying, did I? Please forgive me for pouting. If you want this little whimsy, if you think we should be chaste until we are married, well, I am willing." She kissed him again and smiled happily into his eyes. "It would be nice to be married. And little ones would be nice, too, wouldn't they?"

He resented her clinging to his neck. He had an impulse to scold her or at the very least to denounce his proposal of the previous evening as a mad irrelevancy. Before he could speak, the doorbell rang. Frère Beckwith stood alone in the hall. He beckoned Garard out and motioned for him to close the door. Terrible recognition was in the eyes of the missionary.

"What do you have against me?" he said. "Are you afraid of losing your sister?"

"I am truly sorry I said anything about it," Gerard said.

"I will not believe it. She would not lie to me."

"It is all right, whatever you do. My sister knows how to take care of herself, and you will have to learn how to take care of yourself too. I am not angry with you. If you want her, she is waiting for you."

The missionary tried to speak, found his words stifled, buried his face in his hands.

"You did not come back to tell me I am wrong," Gerard said.

"She doesn't believe," the missionary said.

"No, she doesn't believe."

The missionary wept with retching breath and heaving shoulders. Standing silently by, enduring the long minutes as best he could, his own face streaming with tears, Gerard struggled to maintain perspective on this episode between Marie and the missionary. The incident was not tragic; it was wrong to grieve. Yet

Gerard was shaken, even stunned.

"She is not a Jezebel or a Delilah," he said at last. "She has loved you, and she has honored you by the unusual exertions she has taken to be near you. I am sorry that for her love is an explosion. A few weeks, several months—you cannot guess how quickly she would have had enough of you."

They heard the opening of the street door down the stairwell. The missionary looked about in a panic. "It will be my companion. I told him I would not be long."

"This is good-bye then," Gerard said, stretching his hand to the missionary. "I have admired you and I will always remember you."

The missionary took his hand and seemed ready to say more, but the sound of mounting steps pulled him away. The image of the retreating, vanquished face burned in Gerard's mind. His gift hung in the air, and Gerard lingered in the hall, unwilling to relinquish this moment of seizing it. *This little whimsy,* Katrine had called Gerard's refusal to make love to her—a parody upon true renunciation; yet Gerard was determined to marry Katrine, to give children to the world, to forgive God for not existing.

Everncere

Eileen Gibbons Kump

Callie looked down at the folded paper grumbling in her lap and wondered if Laman and Lemuel had first exasperated Sariah by scribbling sour notes in church. Her own son Ted had decided at the age of ten that enduring to the end meant sacrament meeting and that he couldn't. Within fifteen minutes of the opening prayer he was manufacturing audible sighs, stares at the clock, and notes.

"I'm bored!" The letters looked like angry exclamation points. Ted's usually illegible hand was clear enough. "What is there to do? There's nothing to do," he wrote.

"Unscramble *rophetp*," she wrote back.

"Prophet. I'm hungry."

"Try to listen."

"I do, but it's **BORING!**"

"Unscramble *everncere*."

"Reverence. When is it over?"

Callie looked around her at children, hers and others. All of them except Ted were being sort of reverent. She saw no contortions.

She heard no growls. Other children seemed able to keep their restlessness average. But as she looked at Ted, he slid himself lower and lower on the bench, his knees up, his head frantically forward. Like an inverted insect kicking air, he suffered.

"Dear Ted. Daddy is looking at you. Make him proud. Sit up straight and try to pay attention and on the way home we will have a quiz about the meeting. Maybe you'll win." She laid the note beside him.

Ted read it while he took his shoes off. Struggling to a halfsit, he glanced toward the stand. His father gave him The Look, an ingenious combination of sympathy and stern expectation. Whenever George looked at the children that way, they repented. It was a temporary transformation, but better than nothing. Ted's face became a study in attentiveness.

As Callie took the sacrament, she tried to settle her thoughts on the great sacrifice and agony. Beside it, her son's discomfort seemed shallow and self-centered. But there it was nevertheless, and she watched him begin a game of tick tack toe with himself. Despite his advantage, he lost, and when the meeting ended an hour later, he leaped and was gone. No jack-in-the-box ever wore a broader smile, and no mother ever felt greater foreboding.

That night when she couldn't sleep, George would remind her again that Ted was just a boy at a tough age trying to make it through a meeting that, "let's face it, is not usually programmed for ten-year olds."

"Maybe I wouldn't worry if he were just bored," said Callie, "but he's miserable! Whenever he has to hold still, pain sets in."

"What you need is one of those stories about the ward terror growing up to be stake president."

"Stake presidents have *sensible* allergies, like chocolate or tomatoes! Ted can't tolerate a speech anytime from anybody. Why is he like that?"

"Well, Callie, he's young, and restless. He reminds me of your brother Andy."

"Oh dear!"

"As for acting bored in church, he's probably somewhere between Tracy and Jeff."

"Do they hate meetings too?"

"Chances are that whether they do or not, their mothers are worrying about what will become of them. And their fathers are trying to comfort their mothers so that their fathers can get to sleep. Let's count our blessings and say ten times to ourselves: He's a good boy."

Ted is a good boy. Ted is a good boy. Callie made it to ten. It was easier than she expected. In fact, lying there in the dark she realized that Ted prayed with greater eloquence than any of his sisters. Even after balking at having to kneel down, he could remember and voice sincerely every blessing and every need. He could conduct family home evening with a professionalism that made Callie wish it were a public affair: individual hand-written programs, elaborate introductions, exhortations, all delivered over a homemade pulpit that gave the whole meeting the kind of importance Callie knew it ought to have.

Of course George was right. At least Ted was not a bad boy. Callie convinced herself that she had never actually worried about any of their children, not really, not hard, except now, just a little, about Ted. The experience at church had already taken its place beside other memories crowded into the worry department of her mind. As she went off to sleep she felt it lying there restlessly beside Ted's tithing envelope full of IOUs. Next to the IOUs cowered the family prayers when Ted acted as if his dad had asked him not to kneel down but to break his leg in two places. Even if Ted was just a boy, and a good boy at that, he was worth some hard thought. Thank goodness next Sunday was a whole week away.

A typical Monday morning would have sent all thought reeling, but this morning was not typical. The children found their shoes without hysteria. They even finished their eggs. Hurrying to breakfast, Ted had whacked his head on the door and since hitting the door back meant getting hurt twice, he tripped his sister instead. But when George called on him to say family prayers anyway, Ted remembered everyone and everything. Then he went off to school without combing his hair or brushing his teeth. Seeing him like that, the teacher surely would not give him the benefit of any doubts, but Callie decided against calling him back. She could forgo that today. There was quiet for regrouping, disorder to vanquish before lunchtime. There was time for Ted. Work encourages healthful circulation, the books say, and thought . . .

Ted is a good boy. Ted is a good . . . young . . . typical . . . . Upstairs, Callie found his rumpled Sunday trousers under the bed and a missing sock in the chandelier. The sun burned in, like hope, as she shut a drawer on the broken slingshot with its year's supply of spitwads. What she needed for thought was a windowless house with no child prints, no sun burning in. What she needed was less love and concern burning pathways through her concentration. Walking those paths she would end up with straight rooms and not a single idea.

Finally, the windows were to blame because leaning toward the light Callie caught a blur of movement as Junior, the neighborhood dog, leaped into her dooryard, wrestling a shoe with his teeth. Growling with superiority, he fought his prey while Callie rushed downstairs and outside to recover the shoe. It would be Ted's for sure. He never took care of anything!

But it wasn't Ted's. She had never seen it before. Looking at it, standing there with somebody's old, ragged, unfamiliar shoe hanging from her fingertips, a present, upstairs worry fading but clinging, Callie saw other shoes. Still tender to the touch of memory, a long-ago day came back. Her brother Andy had had a dog, a chewing dog like Junior who fought shoes and mitts, and, these lacking, legs. Finally the dog had hurt someone, and Andy, all by himself, had called the sheriff and told him to come and take the dog. Andy had never seemed to love the dog, or feed it either (except maybe shoes). Like Ted, Andy the little boy hadn't done much right except finally grow up and turn out fine in spite of everything. The single act about the dog seemed to Callie, remembering, the only really correct thing her little brother had done, but it had given them all hope, and Andy the man had not been a disappointment after all.

Surely Ted wouldn't either. Surely there were noble acts in his young life. All Callie had to do was notice. Her hope would be verified, and all those boyish things would become insignificant. How old had Andy been? Callie couldn't remember. But young, very very young. She would watch and wait and by next Sunday she would have a noble act to cling to.

The following week was not the best Ted had ever had. He painted his name on the garage with the last of a can of blue spray paint. He hid his bedspread in the attic because it complicated bedmaking. Wednesday when it was his turn to do the dishes, he hired his sister to do them with money borrowed from the lady next door. Thursday he cut up the new *National Geographic*, looking for animal pictures.

Callie kept watching. After all, the act she was looking for needn't be dramatic. She must not give up, no matter what.

Saturday morning she began to practice her speech about Sunday and seriousness. If she had to use it, she would. After all, there would be other weeks.

Sunday morning came more abruptly than usual. Suddenly, there was Ted in the bathroom combing his hair. He always looked larger out of motion. His hair was thick. Combed or uncombed, it mounded like an old-fashioned haystack. The hair Ted couldn't see crossed crookedly, but Callie resisted helping. Actually, he was doing pretty well considering his lack of experience.

Callie hadn't intended to use her speech just then but Ted seemed so calm, so quietly in charge of himself, that she changed her mind. She took a deep breath.

"Ted?"

He stopped combing and looked at her.

"Ted, life isn't all fun. It's serious business. Our comfort isn't really as important as it seems to us when we're young."

"I know," he said, "I think about life and what's important all the time at school. I think, who am I? How did I get in this family? What about everything? Then I decide just to do the best I can."

As Ted himself would say, bull's-eye. Through the hoop, clean. Hole in one. Callie braced herself against the door frame. He had looked right at her, as sincere and earnest as Callie had ever seen him. Yet it was a casual, hair combing moment, and she wondered if Abraham Lincoln on the way to Gettysburg had combed unruly hair with one hand while he wrote with the other. Had Nathan Hale, comb in hand, regretted having as little as life to give for his country?

"Do you really do that?"

Ted didn't answer. It's hard to comb a haystack. Callie walked into the kitchen to sit down, but Ted called her right back.

"Mom, can you compete in the Olympics while you're on your mission?"

This time it was Callie who didn't answer, although she thought she had heard.

"Well, can you?"

She needed to say something. "What in?"

"The marathon and track events."

"Well, it hasn't been done yet."

"That's what I'm going to do." He ducked around her under his combed haystack and was gone.

Callie sat down by the kitchen table. Overdosed with joy, she had a hard time keeping her feet on the floor. Ted had combed his hair! He had assumed he would go on a mission! He had talked to her seriously, out loud, mind-to-mind! Not noble acts exactly, like giving up a dog, but enough. And then she began to know that she had put Ted into a box with words all over the outside: *Problem. Rebel. Worry. Doesn't love what I love.* Just now, for an instant, Ted had stood before her upright and right-side-up. Realizing that he was indeed beyond her, but that she could grow, Callie sprang to the task of getting everyone to church

A Mormon missionary in the Olympics? Of course it hadn't been done. Yet.

Lavender Blue

Donald R. Marshall

She bit into the back of her hand until it started to bleed, and then she began to cry. Why was everything so crazy, so crazy, so crazy? She squeezed her eyes tight to shut off the tears, then took a deep breath and threw her head back, staring at the blurred wallpaper across the room. "Well," she said sniffily, trying to breathe in to keep the tears back. "I know one thing anyway." And she did. If she really couldn't put her finger on the exact day the world had started turning ugly, Ginger was at least sure of something: she would never—*never*—tell anyone, including Mary Louise, what had happened Saturday night in the old wrecked car behind the cafe at Four Corners.

Stretched out diagonally across the bed with her feet hanging off one side, she kicked off one of her oxfords and let her cheek rub against the plaid bedspread. When was it all going to stop? Or did it just keep getting worse? No matter what anybody said, she hadn't minded being tall all that much. Even when she had been the tallest person in the whole seventh grade and for most of the eighth, it hadn't bothered her nearly as much as her grandmother had seemed to think it should. *Well, there'll be plenty of tall boys that'll just be looking for a tall girl like you when the right time comes.* What a ghastly thought. She couldn't remember whether she had drowned out her grandmother's voice by turning up the radio or if she had just gone into her bedroom and shut the door, but she hadn't been able to get rid of the terrible picture: a conglomeration of gangly, drooling, pimply-faced boys breaking loose at the sound of a gun or the word "Go!" to come stumbling up to where she had been made to stand in line, waiting to be chosen, with a freakish group of stoop-shouldered, stringy-haired teen-aged Amazons. *When it comes time for you to start dating*—how she had hated hearing that. But she had hated just as much overhearing things like "Well, Ginger'd rather be out climbing with the boys than in here playing with dolls," or "She sure takes after her Dad" or "regular little Tomboy." Why couldn't they leave her alone? Why did they always have to be putting labels on her? She squeezed her eyes shut. What kind of label would they find to put on her now? When she breathed, the mattress seemed to press up against her chest reminding her of the two little mounds—how she hated the word *breasts*!—that were becoming more and more a part of her. When her grandmother had first commented on them the year before, she had felt like finding a knife and cutting them off. For a long time she had hoped they would just go away—and sometimes she felt as if she had almost gotten her wish.

Why did it all have to be so awful? Everything seemed to make it so complicated and crazy—like the books. Where RaeLynn had got them, she really didn't know, but she wished she had never seen them. And what was more she wished she had never even heard of Mary Louise's cousin or even Mary Louise herself for that matter. She wanted to erase every word or drawing she had ever seen scrawled on the sidewalk or on the lavatory walls or traced by someone's finger on the side of a dirty car. Sometimes she wished that she had been born blind and deaf. Helen Keller's afflictions had always been more than her own mind could even cope with, yet she was beginning to feel that there was something wonderful about not having to see everything that people tried to thrust upon you. But she knew that it would be just her luck that somebody would come along and draw dirty pictures on the palm of her hand.

The thing that was hard for her to figure out was how long it had been going on. In some ways it seemed as if it all happened more or less within the week of her fifteenth birthday, as if she had just looked one day and there it was like some big ugly undulating blob breathing suddenly in the bottom of the aquarium tank that you passed every day. But sometimes it was more as if it wasn't really just the big slithery blob alone but was even all the little fish darting through the seaweed, first showing one side and then the other, flashing here then flashing there, disappearing totally then darting out from a piece of coral only to hide and disappear again—fish that had been there all along, that she had seen out of the corner of her eye yet never really examined. It was a little bit like finding out about Santa Claus: when the realization finally stunned you and didn't go away, you remembered all the little things you had been hearing from kids at school but neatly rejecting and forgetting, year after year, because they didn't fit in with what you wanted to believe. Once, long ago, when she had had her tonsils taken out and had been given gas, she had thought she heard people laughing, witch-like, just before she was sucked, whirling, down into some endless black funnel. She felt like that now: tricked, betrayed, being pulled down into some spiraling darkness while people shrieked and mocked her from all sides.

She wished there were a way of going back. *His body . . rippled with shuddering as an electric current.* She wished she had never seen the words and thought about the pictures. *It's a D.H. Lawrence novel,* RaeLynn had whispered, signalling with her eyes as though the information should mean something. *He always writes about that.* But even the words on the page had not meant much to Ginger at first, and RaeLynn had laughed at her and explained what the vague description only suggested. There had been passages passed back and forth in school before—sometimes even a long graphic verse copied in pencil in the back of someone's notebook, and once a dog-eared photograph that Freddie Beckstrom had held up in front of her before he had run off laughing. She had heard RaeLynn and Mary Louise and all the others blurt out, "You creep!" or giggle and slap some boy on the back for something he had said, and she had heard them snicker off by themselves at things they'd read together. But something different had been happening ever since last spring. When RaeLynn read *The Virgin and the Gypsy* and told her about it, there had been no giggling. RaeLynn had cut her hair that same month and started using eyeshadow.

Why, your eyes are downright pretty. Ginger turned her face toward the wall and bit down on her curled fist. There could be no going back, but going forward seemed impossible too—not only uncomfortable, but impossible—at least for now. *If you'll just keep your hair fixed pretty and wear a nice dress—* She cringed. What did Grandma know about what was pretty and not pretty any more? She had believed her about the eyes, though, but mainly because she had wanted to believe it—even though she had felt compelled to make a little grunt and slouch out of the room with her hands in the pockets of her Levis. But when she closed the door to her room, she had stood in front of the mirror for a long time studying her gray-green eyes and their thick dark brows. She thought of the class picture she had brought home last March and dumped on her grandmother's lap by the parlor window. *Well, there you are,* Grandma had said, holding the wallet-sized photograph at arm's length end straining her head back to study it. *Well, there you are.* What was that supposed to mean? The comment about the eyes had probably been thrown in because Grandma realized how empty her first remark had been. But Ginger wanted to believe it anyway. There had never been a class picture she hadn't despised, and this one—with her hair growing out and her eyes betraying how awkward she felt in the dress she had talked herself into wearing—this one she had dreaded most.

It would all be so easy if she could just fit back into the clothes she had worn three years ago—even two years ago—and not only into the clothes but into the person she had been. She still was that person, she felt—at least almost; it was just that things had been happening—crazy things—and they were still happening and no matter how she tried to go back in her mind there was always a clutter of things—words and pictures that she didn't like to think about—that wouldn't let her get through. *All drunk and throw his big hairy sweaty body on me*—It made her cringe to think of her father like that; something just seemed to shrivel up inside her, leaving her skin all cold and prickly. But she supposed it was true. *They just want what they can get; that's all they care about.* Maybe she should feel bad that it was her grandmother and not her mother who took care of her, but she didn't, and it was *this,* she realized, that made her feel bad. *I know it's none of my business*—no, it isn't, it isn't any of your business and I don't want to hear anything about it—*and I know your grandma means well and tries to do her best, but every girl really needs a mother, and I want you to know that I'd like to help you and if you ever feel like you want to talk*—please, no, no talking, no nothing, just let me be me, let me be how I am and how I want to be. Please, please, please. She pushed her face into the mattress, closing her eyes as tight as she could and grinding down on her back teeth. Why did everyone suddenly feel as if they had to help her? Ladies she hardly even knew were offering counsel and advice. What was wrong with letting her be what she wanted to be? She had been comfortable, safe even, in the old clothes—the Levis, washed until they felt right, the cut-offs, the T-shirts and sweatshirts, the shoes with the thick soles. Everyone had just accepted it; that's how she was. Why did they want to upset that? She raised her head and tried breathing deeply into her fist, staring blurrily across the room at the *Butch Cassidy and the Sundance Kid* posters. *Robert Redford and Paul Newman!* Big deal. She hadn't even thought of it like that, but trust RaeLynn. *So drunk he couldn't stand up and with his big hairy sweaty body—* She recoiled. Okay, so her father was like that, but Paul Newman too? *They're all alike; that's all any of them think about.* She thought of the barns and the dusty smell of hay and the hours spent climbing the rafters and shooting at each other from behind the bales. Rick and Louis and Arnie's big brother—is that all they ever think about? Did they think about it then? Last spring she had mentioned to Mary Louise something about the summer she and Rickie had practically lived in his uncle's barn and Mary Louise had raised her eyebrows and poked her, snickering, "Well, Ginger, *tell* us all about it!" That's what was wrong with everything: you couldn't say anything any more because everything meant something else. Why couldn't she have just gone on her own way, the way it used to be before it got so complicated? She laid her cheek back against the bedspread, knowing the answer even as she asked the question. *Hey, you'd look really neat if you'd let your hair grow real long and—* Last year it was true that she really didn't want to go with a boy or go to a dance or anything like that. She really didn't. And the way she felt right now she wasn't sure if she would ever want to. The changing was just too hard. *Hey, you guys, look who's got on a dress—and lipstick!* It was just too hard, too humiliating, and not worth it at all. Twice last year she had tried, in her way, but both times had been horrible and she had nearly died before three-thirty came. It was just too hard to try to do. That's what had been nice—at first—about Mary Louise's cousin from Modesto, California. *There'll be plenty of tall boys that'll just be looking for a tall girl like you.* Maybe it was because he was not only tall but seventeen and from somewhere else and didn't know anything about her or anybody at all in the whole town of Tremonton except for Mary Louise and her family—maybe it was because of this that he treated her like anybody else, like a person. *Hey, you're all right, Gingerbread.* A soft sock on the upper arm. No one had called her Gingerbread since grade school and she had hated it then. She wasn't sure why she didn't hate it now but it was probably because she had grown to despise all her other names. For some reason she hadn't called him anything—not Bernard certainly, and not even Bernie or Buff—nothing except simply Mary Louise's cousin, and that was only when he wasn't around. *You're easy to talk to, d'ya know that?* Another soft sock. There had never been anything like it. Not that there hadn't been other boys besides Rick and Arnie and his brother who treated her just like another one of the guys in the gang or the boys in her class who looked on her as some kind of freak: the Whitney boys who came up from Albuquerque nearly every summer to visit their grandparents, *they* had been okay, and one of them even sent her a Christmas card when she was in the seventh grade; and her own cousin Leon from Duchesne was a pretty close buddy whenever *they* were in town. But now with Buff it had been something different. He was a pal, yes—but even during the first part of the two weeks he had been here, she had known that he was something more.

She thought of his name—Buff—and wished again that it wouldn't always have to be that way. "They were swimming in the buff—not a stitch on either one of them," she had heard a lady say once about Carolee Jeppson and some truck driver from Tooele that she'd been caught with out at The Willows; and now, no matter how she tried, she couldn't help the pictures that kept coming to her mind whenever she heard the word *buff*. She didn't like it whenever he talked about Modesto, California, either, because the name always made her picture the big pink boxes of Modess next to the Tampax and Kotex in the back of the drugstore and the humiliation of having anyone see you even near those counters. But it was her own names that made her the most uncomfortable of all. She had been Ginny until the first grade, then mostly Virginia except for Uncle Harold and Aunt Galia who had always called her Ginger. But everything had begun to change during the seventh grade; and by the fall of the eighth grade she was signing everything Ginger and praying that everyone would forget her real name and how it sounded like *virgin*. And why, she had asked herself a hundred times, couldn't her last name have been anything but Peterson? Well, not *anything*. She had heard her mother mention once or twice a friend that had been stuck with the horrible name of Arvila Sexsmith, and more than once Ginger had experienced a little tug of pain in thinking about this person she had never known, wondering how her childhood had been and how she had ever endured growing up. She hoped that, if the lady was still alive and had not committed suicide before she was fifteen, that she had long been married to someone with a completely harmless last name like Jones or something like that. In fact, she had long ago decided that this was marriage's only redeeming feature: it gave a girl a chance to legally bury her last name if she simply hated it to death.

The names were bad enough, but there was something terribly unjust, something close to treason, about what had happened to the little songs she had sung as a child. Couldn't they leave anything alone? She had heard one rock group singing about Winnie the Pooh and Christopher Robin and several times on the radio she had heard Carly Simon and James Taylor belting out disrespectfully the words she had once loved to hear—"And if that mocking bird don't sing, Daddy's gonna buy me a diamond ring." But what bothered her most of all was that the words to perfectly innocent songs now had uncomfortable feelings attached to them in a way they never had before. Sometimes at night, even when her mother was living with them, her grandmother had often put her to bed and sung to her, "I gave my love a cherry." Now whenever she thought of the line, "I gave my love a baby," it always spoiled the song for her and she wondered if her grandmother had in any way been aware of what she was singing all those years. RaeLynn had an album by Melanie and one of the songs went "You can put your bread in my oven, any old time you want." Every time she heard a song any more, she found herself listening to the words and trying to figure out what dirty joke was probably behind it all. It spoiled everything. Mary Louise had found an old 45 record of her mother's—"Lavender Blue," sung by a black—and although neither one of them had been able to find anything really dirty in it, something about the man's voice and what he did to the words made her feel that if she thought hard enough she'd probably find something there.

If there were a way of going back, she would take it so fast it would make your head spin. She laid the side of her face against the bed again, realizing that her head was spinning already. It was just too much to take all at once—too much, in fact, to take at all, ever. She longed to go back to the days when she had walked down the street in her sweatshirt and cut-offs and not looked at people and wondered what they did with each other. Wondering about her mother and father was always the hardest—*He'd come in the bedroom all drunk and think he could just throw his big hairy repulsive body on me*—and her grandparents were out of the question. No matter how she thought about it, she was just sure *they* had never done *that*. But she didn't like to think about it. And yet it seemed as if RaeLynn couldn't think of anything else. How they had ever become friends in the ninth grade was beyond her imagination now—RaeLynn hating every day because she wasn't sixteen, and she hating every day herself because she couldn't stay twelve. Maybe RaeLynn liked her because Rick and Louis weren't afraid to hang around her and because RaeLynn thought Rick was the greatest thing in the world now that he had grown almost a foot in a year and had started combing his hair that new way. And maybe, she decided, it was also because RaeLynn felt that hanging around with tall, lanky, unshapely Ginger made her look all the more gorgeous and petite. She didn't like to think about it, but she was afraid it was true. And thinking about it made her want, more than anything, to let RaeLynn know at least part of what had happened with Mary Louise's cousin behind Four Corners on Saturday night, yet she knew that she could never tell anyone—not even Mary Louise.

It's called The Virgin and the Gypsy. *We seen the movie at a drive-in up in Idaho and I just loved it. That's why I'm reading it.*

What's it about?

Wouldn't YOU like to know? Giggle. *It's all about this girl in England who's got all these problems and her life is really dumb and then there's a big flood and she ends up spending the night with this real neat guy who's a gypsy and it changes her whole life and everything. The ending of the movie is real neat because it shows her getting out of bed the next morning and walking outside and finding everything really changed and all of her problems. . . .*

It seemed impossible. *He'd come home in the middle of the night and think he could just force his big sweaty repulsive body—* Impossible, impossible, impossible. *You couldn't pay me to get married again,* she had overheard her mother say. *They're all alike; that's all any of them ever think about.*

Little pitchers have big ears, Marva.

Well, that's the way I feel anyway, And don't worry about her—she'll learn soon enough what it's like. In some ways, she felt as if she had always known; in other ways, it was as if all the years of playing cops and robbers and climbing in the rafters of the barn had been done inside some gigantic silver-green bubble, and then one day, almost without warning, there had been a loud crash, a jolt, and when she had opened her eyes, everything around her was shriveling and turning dark, the color of a bad bruise.

A soft sock on the arm. *Hey, what do you guys do around here for excitement?*

Anything. Everything. What do you want to do?

Everything? Do you really mean that? I bet I know something you don't do.

Like what?

Do you want to find out?

Depends on what it is.

Like—A soft sock on the brain. No, not soft, not very soft at all, but hard, like a jolt. She couldn't remember what he had said or how he had said it, but she remembered the jolt and how the world had tipped and she had suddenly understood what he had said. She hadn't seen him for three days, had even gone out of her way to avoid him, to turn a corner when she saw him come, or slip out the back door when he whistled for her out by the front gate.

It's not as good as the movie, but read the part about the electric shock or whatever it is. It's probably like kissing a boy only about a billion times neater. Ginger, I bet you haven't ever even kissed a boy—have you? Kissed a boy, haven't even kissed a boy. *C'mon now, Gingerbread, you can do better than that. Just relax and open your mouth a little.* Haven't even kissed a boy—*smelling like beer and pushing his big rough whiskery face down into my neck and trying to*—A billion times neater and changed her whole life at least a billion times neater and everything was changed and a billion times—*forcing his hot breath and his big repulsive body*—if only there way a way of going back—*his body . . . rippled shuddering as an electric current*—if only there were a way, some way, any way, back, back, back, beyond the rising flesh, the undulating arms and legs that appeared and reappeared no matter how you tried to shut them out.

You're shaking.

I can't help it.

Are you backing out?

Back out, back out. *N-no.* Back out. *Just cold, I guess.*

It's not that cold. Are you afraid somebody'll see us?

The flashing neon lights from the cafe had kept sending slivers of blue-colored light in zig-zags across the shattered back window of the car, and the steady clinking of dishes from the back of the cafe had fallen into the summer-night shadows like crushed ice.

You won't back out, will you?

A billion times neater. *No. I'll be there.*

Darn it, I wish we had us a car. But I think this'll work. Just trust me—okay?

You can't ever trust them a billion times and everything was changed a billion times and that's all they want anyway a billion times.*Okay. But how come Four Corners?*

I don't know. Got any better ideas? You know this town better than I do. Do you want me to come by for you?

No. I'll just meet you there, I guess.

Okay. But by the old car, remember? It's out behind, you'll see it.

The upholstery had been cracked and where the stuffing was coming out it had smelled musty, reminding her of the mattress with the big yellow stains on it that Whitneys kept by the fruit shelves in their garage.

You're shaking.

She had not been able to stop the trembling, and when she felt his hand slide up under her striped pull-over shirt, it had grown worse. Above the far-away sound of the juke box and the clattering of dishes she had become aware of the fan's constant whirring in the kitchen window, and the whirring had gradually transferred itself to a place inside her head.

Are you afraid somebody'll see us?

She had been afraid of more that that. The seeing, yes, but more. Afraid that when RaeLynn saw her she would immediately know. Mary Louise, her grandmother, Rick and Louis, the lady who worked in the school lunch room, even total strangers she might pass on the street—wouldn't they all be able to see, wouldn't they *know* that everything had changed, that she was no longer the same person who climbed in barns and shot at birds with flippers, that she was not even the girl who had suffered wearing dresses in the ninth grade, not even the same girl who had sat on the big bronze bear in front of the high school with Mary Louise's cousin not more than a week before? Would they think of her name and look at her in some funny way, knowing that now it was no longer anything but a name?

Let's take this off, he had whispered, his lips brushing her earlobe and slipping down onto her neck.

A billion times, a billion times. *Repulsive. So drunk he couldn't stand up and trying to force his big hairy sweaty body on me*—She had shut her eyes tight and clenched her fists, hearing the far-away whirring of the fan from the cafe and the terrifying whirring in her head, yet telling herself that, no matter what happened, she had to know.

What's the matter? Are you chickening out?

She hadn't looked back. The handle of the door had come off in her hand and she had bumped the top of her head trying to get out, but she had not looked back once even though she imagined him climbing out after her and sprinting along behind her past the cafe and the parked cars and the man who yelled "Where the hell *you* off to, girl?" But he hadn't followed her. She could imagine him standing outside the car, looking puzzled, as she crossed the road and ran off into the dark toward the lights of town, but she wasn't sure, for she had never looked back. And the next day had been Sunday, the last day of summer vacation, and Buff Collins had gone home to Modesto.

She could feel the tears coming back and she pressed her tight fists against her eyelids, then bit down on one of her knuckles. One summer she had scraped her stomach badly on a bale of hay and had acted very brave about it until Arnie's mother put merthiolate on it and it had made her cry out and caused her eyes to get all watery right in front of Louis and Arnie and Arnie's big brother. Everything was crazy now. Nothing was certain, except that she would never tell Mary Louise or RaeLynn or anyone else about what had happened Saturday night. If she had been quite sure all day Sunday that she didn't want them to know, she was even more sure now, because the truth of the matter was, *nothing* had happened.

She dried her eyes for what she hoped was the last time and scooted herself toward the edge of the bed. There was no going back, that was another thing she felt quite sure of—that and the fact that the world was probably going to go on being as mixed up and crazy as ever. It was true that she hadn't found out what she had felt she had to know, but at least she hadn't proven that it was all a hoax, that nothing really changed at all, that it was all nothing more than a big, ugly, repulsive, dirty joke. And, for the time being, she would hang onto that.

Yellow Dust

Joseph Peterson

He knew it was Tuesday because he could see that the butcher's cart had a sow tied to the end of it, and behind the cart walked the peasant women in single file, like some kind of funeral procession, each waiting for her cut of meat. From where Elder Heaton sat on the roof of *Pit Prebol*, he could see the butcher stopping in front of his three-sided meat shop. He was wearing a pair of grey labor-pants and a greasy blue work shirt that was spattered with dark brown stains. The donkey jerked when the butcher pulled on the reins and the knives and cleavers, hung from hooks on the side of the cart, clattered and glistened in the morning sun.

Dismounting the cart, the butcher tethered the sow to the leg of his work bench and placed the sign, *Carniceria Abierta* on a peg. The women stood around watching him, each with her arms folded over her pot belly. After he had sharpened his tools and hung blistered slabs of black-smoked bacon and strings of goat-milk cheese around the opening of his shop, he centered his attention on the sow. The women immediately came to life, lining up behind his work bench, stretching to see him work.

The butcher took the sow by the front leg and rear flank and threw her over on her side. She squealed horrendously. The butcher then placed a sandaled foot in the middle of her chest and held her, letting her squeal to notify the women in the *barrio* that it was Tuesday—pork-day. After a few moments, he reached to the bench with one hand and grabbed the boning knife. With a quick motion, he sliced the sow's throat. Soon the gargled squealing stopped. The women, lined at the bench, looked on in a sort of stoic fatigue.

Elder Heaton turned away as the butcher started cutting the warm meat. Some of the women were squabbling like vultures, pointing crooked fingers at the fleshy flanks, while others were picking through the entrails.

The butcher shop irritated Elder Heaton. He hated the odor; it bothered him in the hot Venezuela afternoons. Despite the president's request that they read the Book of Mormon during the siesta, the elders slept. The heat was too much.

Heaton knew that reading the Book of Mormon was important. Once when Elder Heaton was a boy he had seen his father cry when he spoke of the Book of Mormon. His father had been a mechanic with a state road crew, and as far as Elder Heaton remembered, he had never seen him cry; but there he had stood in testimony meeting, crying in front of them all, holding his blue, paper-back Book of Mormon, saying, "I know that this book is true, and I know that reading this book you can find out 'bout anything you need to know."

He knew that the president wanted him to read it, he knew that it was important, but up until this time of his mission he had never felt the need to read it—he had read it already, once years before, and he knew most of what was in it.

While thinking of his father, he remembered that he was especially busy that morning; he had to prepare the funeral service for Sister Gallegos' illegitimate girl that had died of dysentery the day before. He had gotten up late because a movie had kept him and Elder Jensen out late the preceding night.

Shuffling from the roof to his room, he marked a discussion *C* on the *informe* since he had talked about Joseph Smith with a young couple that were waiting in the movie line.

Elder Jensen lay in his hammock with his Book of Mormon,

reading intensely. Slapping Jensen's foot, Elder Heaton, said "I thought that you'd have breakfast by now, flipper."

"I'll get it already—leave me read," said Elder Jensen.

Ducking under Jensen's hammock, Heaton walked into the bathroom and locked the door. He liked it there: it was cooler than the rest of the house because the toilet leaked and ran over the floor and green moss grew at the perimeters of every tile; and he was secluded there—he could be alone for a minute. At home, when his older brother Johnny moved away, he had his own bedroom with a lock, and before he had come on his mission, he had spent long moments stripped to his skibby shorts in front of the full-length mirror admiring his sun-tanned skin, his bleached-blond hair, and most of all his rounded and toned muscles. He was proud of his body: at dances when Susan put her hand on his chest he would flex, hoping she would feel; and at work he would stack eight two-by-four studs, more than any one of the crew had ever lifted, and carry them proudly to where he would use them, hoping someone would see. Before his mission he had been at the height of physical condition—his body was almost perfect and he sometimes felt omnipotent.

As he stood in the bathroom and stripped to shower he looked into the small, cracked mirror. Because of his diet of rice, beans, and corn flour *arepas,* he was developing a bulge above his belt-line, and he was getting flabby now. The tropical heat made him sweat profusely and great pimples and blackheads dotted his shoulders and neck, and his blond hair looked greasy after ten or eleven in the morning.

He quickly turned from the mirror and got ready to shower. The shower was a ten-foot length of rubber hose that connected to a faucet and the water was cool. Since the water came from a great tank on the roof of the apartment building it was better to shower in the mornings because the afternoon sun made the water warm, almost hot, and besides in the afternoon the mosquito larvae left the surface and swam down by the drain of the tank and sometimes they ran out with the water.

In the shower Heaton was careful to scrub his armpits and groin thoroughly but tenderly. He had a rash; the Latins called it "Mushrooms." When he first got it he had tried everything to get rid of it. Other missionaries had told him to use footpowder, to stand naked in front of the fan for thirty minutes a day, and to use petroleum jelly, but nothing worked. He first noticed the rash when he was in

Caracas on his first assignment—he was standing in front of the mirror making a muscle, and he saw it, a small red dot under his armpit. It grew from there and it terrified him; he felt as though his body were somehow rotting or dying, and he felt he could do nothing about it.

After Elder Heaton dried himself and dressed he walked into the front room. Sitting at the table, Elder Heaton pulled out his Bible, Book of Mormon, and D & C and looked until he found a scripture, and read: "And what if I will that he should raise the dead, let him not withhold his voice." No, No, he thought, it wasn't what he wanted. What does she need? he asked himself. He pictured himself standing there in the cemetery above the open grave. He would open his scriptures and raise a finger to expound; then he would bear fervent testimony of life after death. No, he thought, he couldn't do it—couldn't feel right. From dust thou art, and to dust thou must—; crud no, he couldn't say it. It wouldn't sound right.

Even though he had been in the mission field for over eight months, he had never gotten to the point where he was comfortable enough with the plan of salvation to teach it. As a junior companion, he had simply refused to participate in the discussion. Now that he was a senior comp, in a two-missionary town, he had just never given it, never confronted himself with having to teach concepts that he understood, but not really. The whole idea of life after death disturbed him.

As a child of ten he had been swimming in the St. George pool. As he had walked around to the other side, to where Michael was splashing some girls and needed some help, he saw a form in the corner of the deep end. Thinking that it was one of the older girls swimming along the bottom, holding her breath, he thought nothing of it, and jumped into the pool alongside Michael, kicking valiantly and splashing the girls as he went.

Behind him, he could hear a girl yelling at the life guard, "Hey lady, look down there—what's that girl doing?"

The young life guard stood on her pedestal, squinting at the water, but the sun was too bright; she couldn't see anything. As she descended the ladder, all of the children got out of the water and stood at the edge of the pool surrounding the deep end. Elder Heaton remembered how he had crowded to the edge of the pool, and how he had heard the children whisper, "What's she doin'? Hey, there it is, down there—no, over there in the corner; yes there."

After leaning over the pool and squinting, the life guard fell back, her face blank. In a hoarse voice, she softly cried, "Oh God, she's drowning." Then turning towards the office, she ran frantically yelling, "Oh God, help! Help, someone, for God's sake!"

Elder Heaton remembered how he had turned towards Michael shrugging his shoulders.

He and Michael waited and watched as a man dove into the water and pulled the girl to the surface. Then the ambulance had come and had taken the girl away, lips and fingernails blue.

And he and Michael had walked home slowly from the pool, kicking the Coca-Cola cans as they went. He thought of the girl a lot, and for weeks he saw her in his mind's eye when he lay in the bottom bunk bed, with his brother Johnny up above. When he closed his eyes he saw her, he saw her as he lay in the dark, and that's all he saw. Therela Romney was her name, and he saw her lying there at the side of the pool, her cheeks pale, almost green, her limbs strewn about her in disorder. He saw the water that ran from her nostrils and formed a dark circle around her head as it spread on the dry concrete. And then he saw her unmoving figure under the grey blanket they laid over her. For weeks he was afraid to close his eyes and he had watched the street light out his bedroom window until he could hold his eyes open no longer. For weeks he had awakened at night crying, "I don't want to die; I don't want to die!" Once his mother came into his room and sat on his bed in the dark.

"Mommy," he had asked, "what happens to you when you die?"

His mother had smiled and said, "You go to the spirit world."

"No, Mom," he continued, "I mean what happens to your body?"

"First they take it and they do things to it, and then they put it in the ground."

"I mean but what happens to it?" he had pressed.

"Well, it decomposes, Paul, I suppose."

"You mean like the rabbits on the highway; like the pollywogs that dried in the ditch? It goes all smelly and that?"

"Yes, I suppose so, Paul."

Elder Heaton remembered that he had felt a sort of emptiness, or a coldness, as if that's all there was to it—you just died, rotted, and that was it.

Elder Jensen started moving about the apartment, clanking

pans and cooking breakfast. Elder Heaton left his books, thinking that he would come up with something during the day.

Elder Heaton and Elder Jensen left *Pit Prebol* about nine, walking down the dirt alley past the butcher shop and corregated-tin huts till they arrived at *Avenida Bolivar,* the only paved road in the village. A beggar child with bulging joints and watering eyes approached Elder Heaton and raised a thin arm, extending his cupped hand towards Heaton's face. The beggar bowed his head and hid one eye behind his raised arm as he asked for a *pulla* to buy bread with. Elder Heaton pulled a handful of coins from his pocket and selected a copper piece. He plopped it into the child's hand and turned his back. He could hear the padding of the boy's feet as he ran excitedly through the yellow dust towards his shanty in the *barrio.*

God, he thought, thank you for bringing me to earth in the bounty of Zion—in the promised land, where the fear of death stands aloof, instead of hanging ominously over the heads of Thy children.

The government had errected a metal bench there at the bus stop but it was too dirty to sit on, so Elder Heaton waited in the sun. It was already hot and Heaton was starting to sweat and his rashes were irritating him like they always did when he started sweating. He turned to look at the fellow behind the *Chicharron* stand, and then, sure that the fellow wasn't watching, Heaton scratched at his crotch.

There were flies in the glass cases of fried hog hide at the *Chicharron* stand and the smell reminded Heaton of rancid cooking oil. The glass cases were spattered with oil and fat from the inside, but Elder Heaton could still see the umber chunks of hide, crisp, salted, and wrinkled, and here and there on the hide were patches of yellow hair.

Looking at the stands, Heaton remembered the long summer evenings when he had sat in the dining room looking out the picture window at the horses in the corral, and the steer grazing farther off in the pasture, and the rows of corn in the garden; and he remembered eating buttered rolls made of cracked wheat, dipping them into bowls of bottled applesauce, seasoned with cinnamon. Oh God, he thought, thank you.

He turned from the stand when he heard the bus and fished another *pulla* from his pocket for the fare to Los Obscuros, the government housing tract where Sister Gallegos lived with her aunt.

On the bus, Elder Jensen asked, "So have you thought about what you're going to tell Hermana Gallegos?"

"Flip," replied Elder Heaton, "what can I say? It's kind of tough talking to a woman who's just lost her child."

As he rode the bus, Elder Heaton thought about what he was going to say to her when he saw her. When Elder Heaton was sixteen, his Uncle Orson had died of cancer, and he had walked through the viewing line and looked at him—at his yellowing hands, at his sharp red lips standing out poignantly against his dry plastic face. And then he had walked towards Aunt Edna. Before they had come to the viewing, he had rehearsed with his mother just what it is one says to a dead person's wife, but as he saw her with her eyelids red and gaping loosely around the eyeballs, he had been struck with an emptiness—almost a coldness, and all he could do was hold Aunt Edna and cry. He had been confused and afraid; they lived in Hurricane, and he had only seen his aunt and uncle once or twice on Thanksgiving; but there he had stood, holding Aunt Edna, sobbing with fear.

"I've thought that we'd go by Sister Araneda's place to see if she wants to come and help or something," said Elder Heaton.

"Sounds good to me," Jensen muttered as the bus stopped in Los Obscuros. They walked silently to Aranedas'.

Sister Araneda, a fat Chilean, lived in Los Obscuros about a half a kilometer from where the child had died. She was the president, and the only active member of the Relief Society in the branch. When the elders arrived, she was standing in the back of the one-room home near the kerosene stove, standing underneath the black smoke trail that ran up the red-brick wall and pooled on the ceiling. She stood barefoot on the cement, padding the thick corn paddies of *arepa* flour and laying them in the cast-iron bowl of oil over the kerosene flame.

"Manos!" she exclaimed as the elders came to her open door. "Come in."

Before he sat at the wooden table, Elder Heaton asked, "Have you heard the news?"

"What news?" she asked rubbing her hands on her muslin apron and kicking at a half-bald hen as she approached the elders.

Elder Jensen sat down backwards on his chair and looked out the door at the orange haired children, playing in the yellow dust along the *vereda*. Elder Heaton leaned forward and said, "Pablo came by *Prebol* a while ago and told us that Sister Gallegos' girl had died."

Sister Araneda stood frozen. First her jaw dropped; then her hands came to her fat cheeks till she looked distorted, and she whispered hoarsely, "Sweet Mary, mother of God, what next?" She rambled towards a chair shaking her head and uttering, "No, no, no." After she sat, the color came back to her cheeks, and she asked, "But when—how?"

"Pablo said it was like the others; she got dysentery, couldn't drink enough, and died," said Elder Heaton.

A cock jumped to the door jamb and Elder Jensen stamped his foot, bringing up a cloud of yellow dust and scaring the cock out to the brush alongside the ditch, under the tamarind tree.

"Anyway," continued Elder Heaton, "we were wondering if it would be good for you to go to them with us—maybe to help or something—I don't know." Perspiration dropped into one of Heaton's eyes and made the eye burn.

The three of them walked down the rows of houses, across the aqueduct that the ditches ran into, and down a trail secluded under the long, dried leaves of sugar cane, to *vereda C*, where Sister Gallegos lived with her aunt. The apartment had been dark, the windows had been boarded even under their metal bars, and the door had been closed tight.

Elder Jensen knocked as Sister Araneda stood behind the elders wringing her hands nervously. The door opened, at first only slightly, and then fully, and Sister Gallegos stood in the darkness with her aunt. Both women were dressed in black, the aunt mumbling prayers, counting them one by one on a string of yellowed beads, as if stopping would make her lose her place and her sense of urgency.

"Come in," Sister Gallegos said, swinging her arm back as if it were an imaginary door.

Entering, they saw the girl, She lay on a table to the rear of the house. Along the wall in back of the girl were shelves covered with flickering candles that emitted smoke, stinging the eyes, blurring the vision. The apartment had a rusted tin roof, and was hot anyway, but the candles heated the room more. Heaton felt suffocated when he stepped into the apartment, and the sweat began to pour off his body. He could feel that his shirt stuck to his flesh like a wet rag in the middle of his back, and the rashes in his armpits and crotch were no longer dry and scratchy; they were moist, and they stung where the sweat ran onto them. After shaking Sister Gallegos' hand, he shifted his shirt and scratched at his armpit, but it only made the rash hurt more.

As they came nearer the table where she lay, Elder Heaton could see the silver coins that were laid over her eyes. Her dingy yellow dress reminded Elder Heaton of the dogs in the dust, the dogs that roam the village, rooting in the ditches and panting lazily in the garbage piles. The dead child's prominent ribs reminded him of a dull tan colored puppy he had seen pushing a tin can through the dirt with his nose, licking the dried contents. As the elders had stood watching the puppy outside the door of the shanty that day, three men had appeared, one of them leading a donkey cart upon which was an old machine crate. The youngest man crouched suddenly when he saw the dog, pointing at it and whispering to his companions. Two of them advanced at opposite angles to the dog, and captured him. Elder Heaton had watched as the two men carried the yelping dog to the donkey cart and flopped it into the crate. At the instant they opened the door to the crate, the other dogs within whimpered and barked pathetically. A small woman had appeared at the door of the shanty and Elder Heaton had had to make the contact, so he looked away.

Later, Elder Heaton had seen the younger fellow in the Mercado. He told Elder Heaton that they had sold the dogs to the ranchers who used them to divert the piranhas in the river by cutting the dog's throats and throwing them into the water, and then crossing their herd unmolested downstream while the fish were busy devouring the dogs.

Elder Heaton looked again to the child. Below her protruding ribs, her hands were folded neatly with a golden crucifix and a rosary placed between her tiny fingers. Looking at her, her small, sunken eyes, her dried and wrinkled lips, and her faded face, Elder Heaton felt empty and cold. The house smelled of heat, of candles, of sweat, and of something more, something terrifying. He glanced back at Sister Araneda, her huge arm draped across Sister Gallegos' stooped shoulders. He thought about the doctrine of the Millennium and the idea that women could raise their deceased children during that thousand years. The age-of-accountability doctrine, he thought. No, he thought, he wouldn't be able to tell her—he couldn't feel right doing it. He felt responsible for what he said—he just knew he couldn't tell her. He wondered at times why he'd come on this mission. He disliked things missionaries did. He didn't feel right. he couldn't talk about resurrection or life after death. Death, he thought, was real, while spirits and resurrection were vague, untouchable and unseen. He couldn't; he wouldn't feel right.

"Er, we just wanted to say," stuttered Elder Jensen, "how much we're sorry about Julia, and if it's any comfort to you, Sister Gallegos, I'd like to say that I know that Julia is with our Heavenly Father, and that she's happy, and that you'll be with her again. And I say it in the name of Jesus Christ, Amen." A long silence followed except for the sound of the aunt's prayers, and Elder Jensen looked out the door, as if he had exhausted what he had to say and wished he were elsewhere. Elder Heaton couldn't believe it—Elder Jensen had said it almost as if it were part of the discussions he had memorized in the Language Training Mission; he had said it with almost the same sing-song cadence as the aunt used for her prayers. As he watched Elder Jensen looking stupidly out the door, Elder Heaton wondered if he himself were normal. Maybe I should just quit thinking about what I'm saying, he thought, and just say it, and then look stupidly out the door. Why am I so damned responsible for what I say? He couldn't feel right doing it.

The aunt still muttered prayers on her beads, with the same urgency, rocking in her chair as she went.

"Mano," uttered Sister Gallegos, "did Pablo tell you we want you to do what they do by the graveside?"

"Yes, he did; but I haven't had time to prepare much. He only told me last night. I'm sorry; I really . . . ."

"That's all right," interrupted Sister Gallegos. "We have to bury her soon because of the heat—no?—she already started. My brother, he already made a coffin, and we don't got enough for the priest. All we need is a short graveside talk, sort of."

"What time will it be?" he asked.

"Can you make it at one of the afternoon?" she asked softly as if expecting to be refused.

"Today?—Well yes. No, no: it won't be any problem."

Elder Heaton glanced back at the girl. How, he thought, would this resurrect? The muscles of her face were dry and tight, pulling he lips back, exposing her teeth, like a snarl. Suddenly Sister Gallegos arose and shuffled to the child to scare a fly that lit on her cheek.

Walking back to the Aranedas', Elder Heaton thought and watched the yellow dust.

During the siesta, when the village was dormant, Sister Gallegos, her brother and aunt, Sister Araneda, and the elders stood around the grave. Behind them was the pile of yellow earth and in the depths of the grave was the small box.

Elder Heaton had spent his noon hour studying—studying feverishly, looking for something to say. Ashes to ashes, dust to dust, he had thought; no, he wouldn't be able to do it. He couldn't believe that the bodies of swine, dogs, or people could ever resurrect. He had thought about the rabbits on the highway and the tadpoles in the dried puddles of southern Utah. No, he thought, how could it ever happen? Death had become so real to him—so tangible, ominous; life after death and resurrection, these were the vague, formless objects that stood far off, blurred by the distance. From dust thou art, and to dust thou must return, he thought; good Lord, the child had never left the yellow dust: she was born in it, she played in it, she ate in it, and finally died in it.

During that noon hour Heaton had frantically searched the scriptures for something to say to them, to Sister Gallegos especially. He had spread his books out in front of him, and had looked at them, and finally had realized that he was searching for something for himself, not for anybody else. Then he had laid his head in his sweating palms and cried, cried quietly.

He remembered when he had seen his father cry—his father cried quietly—and the only way anyone knew he was crying was that the tears ran down his sunburned cheeks that day in testimony meeting. And his father had held his worn Book of Mormon in his hand, the blue copy that he always read, the one with the dog-eared edges. And his father had said, "I know that this book is true, and I know that reading this book you can find out 'bout anything you need to know."

During the siesta, when the village was dormant, as Heaton looked into the grave, he still felt a certain despair—a fear. The afternoon was hot and the trees in the distance looked blurry, almost watery through the heat waves that rose off the plains. As he stood in the sun, Heaton started sweating again and the rotting in his armpits and groin started to sting again. The rash made Heaton feel inextricably involved with all he saw around him, as though he too were now a part of it all, caught in it somehow.

Sister Araneda, her arm still over Sister Gallegos' shoulders, looked at Elder Heaton, shook her head and whispered, "It's time."

Elder Heaton held his hands together tightly behind him and started: "Brothers and Sisters, we are gathered this afternoon to give respects to one of our little sisters." He squeezed his hands tighter. His throat started to hurt, and he felt he was going to cry. Why not, he thought, that's what you're supposed to do at funerals. But Elder Heaton knew that he would be crying for himself—not for the dead child, and not for Sister Gallegos—and it bothered him. Why am I so damned responsible—why not cry? he thought.

His eyes clouded and he wept.

"More than any message," he continued in a hoarse voice, "that I could give you, I think that the important thing is that life goes on, and Julia would want you. . . . " He lowered his head. The open grave before him seemed to reach out at him. He was afraid; he didn't want to go on. Oh God, he thought, please God, I don't want to die, I don't want to. Oh grave, he thought, here is thy—no I can't. His whole body shook as he wept.

Looking up suddenly, he realized that they were all watching him, depending on him for strength. "Brothers and Sisters, may we all live in such as way as to return to where Julia is. She's happier now; I know it." He had thought that saying it would make him feel better, but it didn't. He lowered his head again.

"Have you anything to add, Elder Jensen?"

"I just wanted to say," he said, "—how very sorry I am, Sister Gallegos."

They all stood looking into the grave for a time, and finally Elder Heaton said, "Let's pray." The group knelt in the dust. "Would you like to offer the prayer and dedication of the site?" Elder Heaton asked, nodding to Elder Jensen.

Elder Heaton could hear the sing-song prayer above the buzz of the cicadas in the tamarind tree, but he didn't listen. Dear Lord, Elder Heaton prayed to himself, please God, help me; strengthen me. Tell me there's more to it than dying and that's all. Elder Heaton clutched his hands tighter and tensed the muscles in his arms and chest. His rashes still stung, and they terrified him. Tell me there's more to it, he prayed. He still felt the same emptiness, and he still wept in despair.

After Elder Jensen finished, and after they shook everyone's hand, the elders walked towards the *Avenida*. Elder Heaton looked at the yellow dust as he walked. Behind, he heard the buzz of the cicadas and the working of the brother's shovel in the yellow dirt.

At their apartment, Elder Jensen took off his tie and his shoes, and lay in his hammock to sleep like the elders always did. But Elder

Heaton sat on the roof, reading his blue, paper-back Book of Mormon, looking for something in its pages, and listening to the rhythmic pounding of the butcher's cleaver.

Answer to Prayer

Dennis Clark

Ev worked at the farce. They all called it that, joking. Ev nurtured the joke because it was appropriate: superficial. "This place is a farce" one would say, one of the intermittents, new to the place, catching the sounds its initials let one make; forced one to make: **Federal Archives and Records Center**. "Welcome to the work farce" he would answer, then, improvising, test himself: "Just HEW to the line and DOT your IRS and you too can F. C. C."

"A NARS-T FARC" one named Rose, more venturesome than others, once replied, fingering an envelope addressed to **National Archives and Records Service, Region 10**.

"Sort of like Morton's fark" he'd answered; "NOAA to escape. NOAA to go."

"Bacon calls it Morton's crotch" she said, "or crutch. Appropriate for a clerical publican." She'd hardly looked up from THE TWO TOWERS. Like Janet.

"Sorry" he'd answered Rose. "I couldn't help myself. Same impulse that forced the Harvard Lampoon to forge BORED OF THE RINGS."

"Inanition?"

"Farce of hobbit."

She groaned, truly a Tolkienista, over her lunch. "Now I see why we only get a half-hour for lunch" she said, replacing the envelope, her bookmark, and lowering the book, again like his wife, to look at him. "It forces you pun-gent intellects to keep your mouths full."

"We just talk farster."

Sometimes Ev told himself *I don't need to work at farce; I'm living one.* Himself would answer *and although he thinks he's in a play-ay-ay-ay* as he worked, playing to keep his mind off its misery: *Folderol Archives and Reck-herds Center . . . Sintered . . . National Ark-hives and Wreck-word Staplers. Or Serve-worse.* Even his own job title assumed in his mouth the character of farce: "anArchivist, too."

Today the farce was grim. He was pulling Medicare claims, trying to concentrate on the S. S. numbers that indexed them, being continually distracted by other figures, unwanted images rising in his thoughts, the debris of furtive seances with men's magazines whose names formed a litany of reproach in his mind: *Playhouse, OuiPent, Boy.* He tried to squeeze his eyes and shut them out, but they persisted, like the after-image of a light bulb burned in your eyes when you've peeked beneath the shade. *hot-pants, see-through peasant blouse tied above the navel (brown nipples peak through), fine-fleshed white throat, curly locks drift about her face . . . Janis, with shorter hair.* Even the Social Security numbers (if that's what they were — the Blue Cross form listing them called them "HIB #s"), with their dashes and zeroes, distracted him from his searching and retrieval.

Unlike Public Health Service records (marked "DHEW-non-DOD" for civilians), these forms were filed, boxed and submitted to HEW by private companies. Each had its own filing system. They all filed by numbers, usually some variant of the Social Security number, none yet so elaborate as the IRS's Document Locater Number: two digits for the district office, three for type of form, a Julian date, batch-and-item number, list-year digit: 8331117426188. It was written without spaces as a rigid entry for some computer's black box. A complexity of simple-mindedness, ideal for a high-speed enumerator, numbing to Ev's literal mind. In coding people's paper-prints, IRS went beyond SS. Naturally. It was antiSocial and inSecure.

But *that* number worked. He could locate the requested documents. While for Blue Cross of Oregon, in an hour, he had searched for seven of thirty-three forms and found two. Two others were already charged out. *stands by the curb in a shopping center, forearm raised, thumb cocked for a ride: slender, Nefertiti in pink hot-pants, slim muscles in her thighs.* The rest he couldn't find. Each box was filled with folders; each folder was numbered; within each folder 40 or 50 forms were jumbled. He was pulling by patient's name more than number, and that with incredible patience only. Fluorescent tubes flickered and buzzed above his head like an electric migraine. "Mill House!"

He'd fingered the last papers thinking about the lights. "Son of a Rich!"— a curse no one would hear. He stood in an aisle formed by ranges of shelves laid out like the streets of a Utah town on a flat desert floor. They were packed with cardboard boxes. The room was something like 80 by 200 feet under an arching roof. It enclosed around 300,000 cubic feet of air space, which made him feel like a bumblebee loose in a cathedral.

It was once an armory, Walt said. All the air space in this room now held was memories: 100,000 cubic feet of records, each box a cubic foot. Ev was learning to negotiate the maze of numbering by which boxes on the shelves were addressed. It was these *small shapely breasts, leather bag on a long thong over one shoulder, a glint of wildness in her eye,* boxes *she steps in over the door of his Triumph, and he drives* that stymied him. Each box was a cell in the federal data bank and each record an inmate. He was an electrical impulse trying to excite some memory, bring it to attention for someone's instruction or delight.

He stood on a ladder. He rolled along the cell blocks of this vault, tracing the circuits of its memory, on wheeled ladders. Ev checked the name, started through the records again, half of them with a pink cover-sheet, some with a yellow coversheet, several with xeroxed sheets, a few naked (he had to search out the HIB # on those). Graham *By damn. 707-56-3669* it was, between Wilson, Emma, angina pectoris, 541-21-3620, and Crawford, Harold, 493-12-3818, blockage of colon. "Why in the House of Mill won't they just alphabetize?" A charge-out, a xerox of the request with Graham circled on it, supplanted the form in folder 36-38. The open box,

56275, slid from the platform of the ladder to a perch on Ev's left arm and gulped the folder. Retracting flaps, the box closed up, then rotated Ev, nearly felling him as it flew back to its hole. The ladder crept forward in equal but opposite reaction.

"Nix!on it." His head was humming like the tube of light. "Bulldick!" he roared, then started singing

"jail to the thief
he has robbed us of his paycheck
jail to the thief
he has stol'n his salary
bum bum bum
long may our song bang a gong
upon his eardrums
long may he twist in the wind
of our beans."

It didn't relieve his tensions. Needing to relieve himself he started down the ladder, an eleven footer he was using (though only working the middle rows of shelves, 8, 9, and 10) for a plywood plank nailed to the oak braces: a table for his piles of forms. As he walked out of his aisle into the road, no one in either direction, the loudspeaker said "Walt Budger, Walt Budger, 88." He turned right twice into the next aisle north and loped along it to the east wall of the building.

"Walt Budger, Walt Budger, 88." Still not puzzling that one out he slewed left at the wall, toward the pump house, slowed there for a drink from the electric cooler, rounded the corner of the washroom (no sign of sex on the door) and slid inside, unseen, as far as he knew. He rushed into the booth, locked the door, opened his clothes and settled on the seat. *brood, lay an egg . . . a brooding cock? . . . cockatrice. . . . yeah! before the cock crow, thou shalt deny me thrice. . . . Peter turning cottontail and scuttling off.* Persistent images stayed in his mind. . . . Recalling what Pete had said about being a bishop at BYU and counseling students who confessed to masturbating, he was masturbating. *I told one of them 'Don't take it so hard', you know, it's so hard to be grave at such trivial sins, while adultery . . . and I actually said to one guy 'You've got to get a grip on yourself!'.* . . . There were those graffiti, in two hands: "Moby Dick is not a social disease." "N. K. V. D. is!"

Walt and his new intermittent talked by outside, intelligible through two doors, opening and closing others. *flay show? a real tongue lashing . . . Ev's concentration was crumbling under the onslaught of voices, heard and recalled. bicycle pump inflating this vehicle till it sings like a tenor in your thighs. . . . She blows! Thar she blows! Where away?*

He left the stall, toilet roaring from a kick, and washed his hands. He didn't like to look in the mirror at himself, at his square jaw and receding chin, at pinhead scabs tattooing his throat after a lifetime of shaving, at bulging eyes set on, rather than in, his face.

He left the washroom, with its shower no one ever used, stepping into the accessioning area.

"Hey Ev." It was Walt Budger. "This is John Bass . . . uh?"

"Bassett."

"Bassett. This is Ev Cormier, our new reference man.

"Yep, I refer all problems elsewhere." Adroitly, Ev stuck out his left hand. John shifted the box he was carrying to his right hip and shook hands. "Welcome aboard. Don't let Walt forget how to work now."

"I'll tell him everything once," Walt said, "then he's on his own. I've got my drinking to attend to."

"Well, I gotta go fall off a ladder. Seeya later."

"At lunch," Walt said.

"Ciao," John said.

Mounted again on his ladder, working again, he found his anger towards federal authority undiminished, though not so vocal. *Dick Nixon before he dicks you,* as he did in his last election. Things like that, for which any of his friends would blush — he could never keep them down. *banal-retentive . . .*

By noon he had pummeled and battered his way through those BC boxes in the 56000's, moving one aisle north. Blue and cross, he pushed his ladder into the great middle aisle and parked it parallel to the end of a range on the west side (to leave a road for the forklift). That's when he saw the clock and knew it was lunch time.

He had finished requests from Washington Physician's Service and BC, finding 11 records and 3 charge-outs of the 33 BC requests, and 12 of 14 WaPS. Taking the ticked-off requests and the requested forms in two piles, he walked through a gape in the wall about 10 feet by 12 (closed at night by double rolldown fire doors) into the central search room, and slunk to the mailing desk, where he left the proof of his morning's labor, pitiful circled successes in a long string of checked-off frustrations.

Upstairs in the lunchroom everyone else was already eating. That was why Ev was getting a reputation for being anti-social and insecure, although he'd only been working at the FARC two months. He didn't carry a watch, he didn't watch the others, breaks and lunch weren't called over the speakers — but mainly he didn't like to quit working until he had finished a job. For him, time consisted of jobs or songs or tasks. He never had learned to consider work as work. It was always a system to be learned, a method to master. Breaks slowed that all down, unless he was done. He hauled his lunch out of the refrigerator (which didn't cool well, having burned out a few years before) and sat down near Rose, now reading THE RETURN OF THE KING, and John Bass, uh, Bassett, who, both university students, both recently hired (for 800 hours only, both being intermittents), were sitting together.

John was not paying much attention to his food but was earnestly talking. Rose was earnestly eating, spooning in plain yogurt, mixed with herbs and spices and a few raisins. Ev opened a bag of roasted, unsalted peanuts —"that's my wages" he always joked — and poured a cup of apple juice from the bottle he kept in the fridge. Nearly everyone else was concentrating on finishing lunch, the half hour being nearly over. Something slimy, like banana in eggnog, scummed down Ev's throat. He looked at the juice. A cloudy slime floated on top.

Stuart stood up. "Well, back to the salt mines." Stuart Armah was head of Reference Services; Rose and Ev's supervisor, though he'd only worked there two weeks to Ev's two months. Rose jumped up; John arose, a little absently, still chewing; Howard (the other reference intermittent), hurrying, choked. Ev ate on, having twenty or thirty minutes left. Harold Gray, the director of the Center, natty in a wine-dark suit; Will Solomon, head of Accession and Disposal, Stu's counterpart; Walt Budger, chief accessioner—they remained seated, working a crossword puzzle in the PEEEYE (not the one lifted from the NEW YORK TIMES, but a local product).

"Cormier, you're an English teacher. Wasn't Hamlet a Dane?" Will asked. Ev walked over and looked. 9 across (2nd row) was D A R P, defined as Hamlet. The second space held "a" from "rare": "doing this one animal tosses his mane." The others looked right.

Pointing, Ev said "Roar. Like a lion." Hamlet the Dorp? *Better than dork. Or dirk?* "Hamlet the Dorp it is."

Ev sat down, started shelling peanuts in earnest, not drinking the culturing juice. Janis Justis came up the stairs carrying a gothic novel and a can of soup, chicken noodle. She was Archives staff, and they ate on second shift. She was wearing a black jumpsuit. Ev watched the ridges of her panties as she went into the kitchen to pan and heat the soup. She came back and sat at the next table. Ev looked back at her from his peanut husks, trying not to linger too long on her cleavage, or on the edges of a black bra he could see as she settled, looking instead at her eyes, her brow, her hair — swept back from her face like the Bride of Frankenstein's. Her face was not pretty. But with the exposed brow and temples, her hawk nose was not prominent, her eyes not too high in her face nor wide apart, her cheekbones not too high. The result was strikingly reminiscent of Nefertiti. Its effect on Ev was hydraulic.

"Weren't you a teacher before you came here?" she asked him, perhaps because he was staring at her.

He feigned nonchalance. "I was unemployed before I came here. A lexicographer before that."

"As rare as archivists." She wore glistening makeup, not at all matte.

"I was once an English teacher" Ev said. She looked at her book, as if she wanted to read. "Is it any good?" Ev asked. The cover showed a woman in a long dress fleeing a burning hilltop mansion at which she stared in horror over her left shoulder.

"It's about a rather plain young woman of accomplishments who is hired by a mysterious older man to care for his French daughter, a love child. He is stern and she is prim."

"Sounds like *Jane Eyre*."

"It is."

"You gave a very good description of it."

"You English majors are always surprised by literacy in anyone else." She got up to fetch her soup. He walked behind her to the refrigerator, putting his nuts and juice to cool. As he walked past her on the way out he said, "Actually, I took a B. S. in math. It wasn't until graduate school that I became an English major, then a linguist." He was mumbling as he turned toward the stairs.

"With all that study of numbers and words, you must find your work here fairly simple."

"Not when there's another bored boxer at the other end of the calculation," Ev said.

"Maybe you should be a computer programmer?"

"No future in that" he said, starting down the stairs, walking a little awkwardly.

Ev was still working on Medicare, using a three-tiered table on wheels with a spring-loaded, rubber-footed ladder. He had just pulled one form after reading every piece of paper in the folder once and starting through a second time. "Stupid Nixon-loving sons and daughters of Melville Dewey. Self-retarding expletive-deleted blue-penciling skins of blotches." He was composing a letter to BC about private enterprise and public moneys when he jumped at a noise behind him — and, turning, saw Stu swearing a ladder into the aisle across the main corridor.

"Hey, Stu." He ran down the aisle waving Nendel and the request. "There's a leak in aisle 30. I had to shift three of the boxes up on top."

"Tell Jerry about it."

"I did." He paused. Stu turned to push the ladder down the aisle. "You'd think these people would be more careful with their records." Stu stopped. "These medicare idiots must use the forms for poker, then sweep 'em into the boxes. I'm finding about one in five."

"Some people have shitferbrains. Whose files are they?"

"Blue Cross of Oregon. I mean I can't make heads'r tails out of, I mean, I tried the last two numbers, then the first two numbers, the middle two; I tried last name, first name, birthdate, address, disease"

"Oh yeah. That's a terminal digit system" Stu said.

"Oughtta be terminated. Nearly terminated me."

"Kind of an odd one, though. They use the last four digits."

"Really?" Ev looked at the request. Nendel 541-71-7838D. In folder 77-79. The uncircled ones were all like that, too.

"Yep. And then the middle two, and then the first three. Had me puzzled too. I saw all kinds of systems when I was working at SafeCo, but never one like that."

"You mean there *is* some intelligence at work here?"

"Oh, I wouldn't go that far" Stu said. "Maybe some post-intelligence. Most records managers don't know a series from a roll of toilet paper. You academic types have no idea how grim it really is out there in the real world."

Ev had no reply. He didn't feel sarcastic. He despised his

stupidity now, not the filers. They'd done a roar-shock in his brain. Robbed of cynical bullets, he asked "Why not just alphabetically? Everyone knows the alphabet."

"Computers have Brillo for brains. It costs more to program one to translate names into numbers, and anyway, names are non-distinctive."

"Huh?"

"Well, people are sloppy about them, numbers are cleaner. Everyone has one anyway. But if they filed 'em sequentially, you know 1, 2, 3, they'd just keep spiraling and mushrooming. Like the spacing here. Y'know," Stu settled against his ladder, "that's a good example. Ever wonder why they have the lower seven shelves in one run of numbers, then the middle three in another, then the upper four? They moved in putting shelves only seven high. When those filled up they added three shelves. When *they* filled up they put up four more. That's why it spirals. Anyway, yeah, you just start with more boxes and file by terminal digits. Randomly. That gives you more control."

Ev was about to argue that names were randomly distributed through the alphabet till it hit him: he'd been cursing other people all morning. All day. Because he was pissed off at someone else's stupidity. Stupefied, he said, "Gee, thanks."

"It's OK. You've helped me enough. That's how we learn."

"Yeah, but I have been half-crazy, beating my brains out. Like having a skunk in with the chickens. I mean panicked."

"Glad to help."

"Wow! I think I'll finish." Ev plunged across the corridor.

Deep in Blue Cross, having interrupted himself to go back and re-do his morning's work, now almost finished with it all, he heard, high up and a little rumbly, a voice say "Ev Cormier. Ev Cormier. Would you pick up line number one, please. That's line one." Hugh Olson was speaking. He was chief disposer, Walt Budger's counterpart. The phone was on a desk in the accessioning area.

"Cormier here."

"Hi, honey."

"Oh, hi. How's your day been?"

"I've had a really good day" Janet said. "How's"

"Lousy. But enough of small talk, I'll lay it all on you when I get home."

"I called to ask you, would you bring home some fresh spinach for dinner? You could stop by Food Giant on the way home."

"Sounds good to me. Anything else?"

"Yes. Don't buy any Macadamia nuts" Janet said.

"How about some Gouda cheese to go with them?"

"Yes. None of that too."

"Okeh, hun."

"Here, Jenny wants to say hello."

"Hello, Daddy. Guess what?"

"You fed the gerbil in school today?"

"No. I got to do that too, but Daddy I got to lead the line to the bathroom today, and I didn't let *any*one get there first, not any girls."

"That's good. Did you all make it okay today."

"Yep. Nobody wet the floor, either. Not even the boys. Here, Harvey wants to say hello."

"Hi, Daddy."

"Hi. Did you play outside today?"

"Daddy . . . I played horses with Mickey outside but he wouldn't and he took mine away from me. Here's Mommy."

"Say goodbye to Carol. I'll hold the phone up to her ear."

"Good-by Carol; be kind and don't cry too."

"That's all she wanted; as soon as she heard your voice she got down and wandered off."

"Well, I'll seeya later."

"Hun? Don't stop at any bookstores, okay?"

"I won't. Good-by."

He headed back to the stacks and opened the last Blue Cross Box. Forest Service was next.

At 4:30, day worked out, he was unchaining his bike. Janis came out the door. "Is that your bike?"

"I ride it every day." He forced himself to look up, then to keep his eyes on her face.

"It looks like a girl's bike. I had one like that when I was a kid."

"It's not a girl's frame. Or a boy's frame. It's a Mixte frame."

"Sounds all mixed up. You must call it Hermie."

"Who?" Ev said.

"Hermaphrobike," Janis said, walking down the stairs. It was a pun worthy of him on his finest days. Even Rose couldn't match it, even Jan. He watched as Janis crossed the parking yard to her car, a black Datsun Z-80. A living playmate. Only now she didn't fold right.

He locked the chain about his waist, mounted morpheobike, drifted down the ramp from the porch and began pumping furiously, making shift to catch her car. He did manage to dodge the puddles, but she was faster.

When he reached home with a bouquet of spinach for his wife, with no nuts nor cheese nor books in hand, Jenny and Harvey and Carol were on the porch waiting for him.

"Daddy, Daddy, Daddy," Jenny yelled, running down the walk, arms out, working a big smile across her face.

"Daddy, Daddy," cried Harvey, bouncing alongside Jenny, running faster just to keep up.

"Hi Dada!" Carol called from the porch. She was playing with a pounding bench, cobbling shoes; wouldn't leave it. Ev loved her for that.

"Daddy, Daddy," Jenny was now grabbing for his legs, and he swung off the bike rather than break her arms.

"Daddy, give me a ride on your bike," Harvey asked.

"Me too, me too," Jenny said.

"Hi, kids." He swung Harvey and Jenny through the air, then hugged and kissed each one. He had a hard time prying Jenny off. She hugged him about the neck with her arms and about the waist with her legs, sitting on the chain.

"Hey, you little octopus. Sit on the seat here and I'll give you a ride. You too, Harvey," he added, proleptic of controversy. "You sit on the rumble seat. Hold on. Here, Jenny hold on to my arm." He unparked the bike. Jenny clung like cloth, a very concerned gravity pulling her smile into a slight frown. Her eyes, lids retracted, darting, expressed her fear more clearly. Harvey sat secure on the luggage rack, laughing as Ev wheeled them around the house to the garage.

Wobbling, wheeled, the bike came to rest in the garage. Restless on its kickstand, the bike suffered its riders to dismount. Unladen, it rolled surely to an eyebolt in one of the studs. Chained there, it set itself to graze on the pebbles and sawdust of the garage floor, content, at rest. Ev climbed the steps of the back porch, escorted by Harvey on his left hand, announced by Jenny before him, his right hand holding spinach behind his back. Jan met him in the back hall, coming up from the cellar. "Hi, honey," he said, "I'm home." She hugged him, grinning. "I brung ya flowers," he said, producing the spinach, presenting it as a nosegay.

"Oh, honey, ya shouldn't've." She smiled and kissed him. He kissed her. Jenny sat on his left foot and wrapped herself around his leg. Arf was hanging from his right hand. Walking in to the kitchen he felt like a victim of elephantiasis. "Where's Carol? Would you go find her?"

"Yeah, if I can get shed of these Strange Creatures from the City Park." He shook his left leg vigorously, like a dog; too vigorously for, overbalanced by his Arf hand, weak of leg from the long pedal home, foiled by Jenny's clasp and grasp, slowly, thrashing and shouting warnings, he toppled to the floor, striking hard with his right knee and left elbow, sprawling in the crumbs and dirt of a day's traffic. He landed near the fridge, seeing under it momentarily a fork and a truck and a paper airplane among the crud and dust.

"Daddy," said Harvey, bending over to look at him, "do me upside-down around in a circle."

"Me too," said Jenny, letting go of his leg. "Do me too, daddy," He started crawling for the door instead. "Horsey-back ride," she said, climbing on. Harvey climbed on too, over his rump.

"Piggy back, you mean. Hi Yo Slobber, haWaaay." He reared briefly, almost dumped the boy, cantered through the dining room, loped through the living room, galloped into the front hall, where Jen opened the door. "Hey, Carrie."

"Hah, dada."

"Want a ride? Ride?"

"Yah, dada."

"Bring in the toy." She stooped, picking up the pounding board and said "Bench." Bracing himself against the door post with his head, he lifted her onto his neck. He crawled back into the living room, then loped over to the couch, leaped a footstool, lumbered through the dining room — shifting and clutching in fantastic patterns to keep the kids on his back, hunching muscles, leaning now left, now right — to the stairs and clambered up, on hands and feet, legs stiffened to keep his back level, to the bedroom, where he collapsed on the floor, spilling kids on the rug. His head was pounding where Caroline's bench had pounded it. One of the kids was crying. No, all the kids were laughing. Jennifer was already jumping on her parents' bed, calling for another ride.

"Honey, would you check on Benny" Jan called. "I think he's awake." Keeping low to the floor, Ev crawled into the nursery.

After dinner, during pajamas, Ev sneaked away downstairs where Jan was washing dishes. He carried Ben on his right hip. "Hi honey," he said, coming up behind her, and kissed her on the neck. Her neck wrinkled as she lifted her head and hunched her shoulders.

"Hi, dear."

He patted her bums, each several times, *steady, old girl,* then rubbed each cheek, fingers lingering in his favorite curves, never quite pinching. "Good old wife," he said.

"I wish you wouldn't do that," she said. "It makes me feel like a whore."

"But honey, I love you." He stepped back a little.

"Just no respect, feeling of me from behind."

"I'm sorry, dear."

"You always say that, too. I hate to feel like a horrible witch because I can't stand to be felt up all the time."

"I'm sorry," he repeated, kissing her neck again.

She turned around, her rubber gloves dripping on his foot. "Ev," she said, "Hi, Benny," and stripped off the gloves. Laying them on the sink she took her son and sat down on a stool. "Hun, I've told you before I don't like that. When you kiss the back of my neck it feels . . . all prickles and cockles, like a burr up under my hair."

"Sorry, just trying to add a couple of years to our marriage."

"If you really wanted to add years to our marriage, you'd do the dishes, and feed the children and feed this monster — he bit me today, he's cutting teeth — and get Jenny off to school in the morning and take the kids to work with you and do the shopping and clean the house and keep the yard up and let me get some rest!"

"I'll be glad to do the dishes tonight."

"I just haven't had *any* rest since I was seven months pregnant, and if I don't get some soon you're going to be married to a witty jello salad."

"I'm sorry. I shouldn't forget. I was just trying to be friendly."

"We're not dating anymore. We don't have to make out. We're married. I'll be 29 in April. Can't you treat me like a woman?" Ev came over to her and began to comb her hair with his fingers.

"I'm sorry, honey. I guess I just can't believe you don't like a little affection."

"Not when you know it irritates me like this. When you kiss me on the neck it's like you were announcing the suave seducer straight from *Playboy*, here to transmogrify the fat ugly frog of a housewife with one kiss from his magic lips."

"You're *not* fat. And I'm uglier than you" Ev said.

"I know I sound like a Beehive teacher, doing the old stick of gum bit, but I can't believe you respect me."

"I bit the gum once, when the bishop tried that with the Explorers."

"As long as you don't bite *me*," Jan said.

"Honey, I'll do the dishes tonight. I'd rather do that than put the kids in bed. I've really got a headache," Ev said.

"I don't mind getting the kids in bed. They're kinda cute. Until they start stalling."

"And now that I don't have to read sources every night I can do the shopping with you. Like we did when I was still in school."

"I know you don't *like* the records center, Ev. If the levy passes, you could get back into teaching."

"I've already given up one great job. . . . " He didn't add "back east."

"I'm sorry I blew up."

"You shouldn't be" he said, pulling on the glove. "You gotta right to. I just love you so much. . . ."

"You're just horny."

"Hi, horny, I'm home."

As he was finishing the dishes, Carol came downstairs, naked, for a drink of milk. Filling a glass of milk, he had a moment's painful vision of her as a foldout, thumbtacked to the wall in a back room in some office building, or littering the wall of a shop somewhere, a few scraps of black lace mocking her like a penciled-on mustache and goatee. As he refilled the glass for the other kids she went back upstairs. As he closed the fridge door Jan was calling him to come look at Carol, cute. As he rounded the stair wall at the bottom, carrying the glass, she ascended the last step. "It was so cute, honey. She was walking up the stairs with a hand on each bum, saying 'ba-bum, ba-bum.' It was really cute. I know it sounds dumb but"

"Bums feel nice, walking," he said, walking upstairs.

"Some aren't all flab and flop." As he sat on the bed, Jen came into their room, hands on hips, leading Harvey and Carol in a strophe of "Ba-bum ba-bum's." Jan grabbed bare Carol and started to diaper her as the antistrophe began back to the kids' bedroom.

"It's not as funny when it's planned," Jan said. "Cute enough to puke a buzzard. That's the way I feel about Jenny now. Most of the time. She's driving me crazy." The chorus came back in for another round of bums and applause, and left.

"I mean she's so silly," Jan said.

"Hey, that's pretty good. Who said that?"

"All the time; I don't *like* her. I mean, I still love her, but"

"About the buzzard" Ev said.

"Doesn't it bug you?"

"Yeah," said Ev, "always performing." Jen whispered to Harvey.

"But it's so silly." The kids came back in, holding their stomachs. "Belly, belly, belly" they chanted. Carol, clad, slid off the bed and joined them, parading around the room, up one side of the bed, bounding off the top, barely missing Benjamin, down the other side and out. Ev was laughing through his frown.

"But doesn't it bother *you*? I mean, she's six years old now. Arf is still cute. You know what he did today? After Jenny left for school he went around singing 'Jimmy crap corn, Jimmy crap corn, Jimmy crap corn.' I told him the words were 'Jimmy crack corn,' and he went into a corner and dumped."

"He did what?" Ev asked.

"You know, curled up and sulked. So to comfort him I told him the whole song. After a few minutes he came back to me and said 'Why mustard, mom?"

"Wow!"

"Can't you just imagine what must have been going on in his head? As if he wouldn't have to eat the corn without mustard."

"Oh, wow, that's great," Ev said, laughing. The chorus came in for an ode and episode of "Jimmy crap corn."

"He must have really been worrying about that. I mean, even I don't understand the song. It's kind of nonsense," Jan said.

"Oh," said Ev. "It's a chorus from an old slave song. Jimmy was a common name for a house nigger, as opposed to a field nigger —

that's what they called themselves. The slaves. It's a defiance song. The master's gone for the day, and one of the men is out in the barn, brewing corn likker. That's what it means to crack corn. You know, distilling and all that. And the singer doesn't care, because the master's gone away."

"I like Harvey's version better. Yours sounds like an explication by Cleanth Brooks."

"I just made it up."

"Not one of your trashures of truth?" As they were still grinning the kid came in for a second go-round. "All right, that's enough. Let's get in bed now."

"Honey" Ev said.

"They've had a book and brushed their teeth and heard a Book of Mormon story and I've had them up to here all day. Get in bed kids and Dad will tell you a story." Ev followed them into their room.

"Tell us a Bible story, Dad," Jenny said, climbing to the top bunk.

"Tell us a Matilda story, Daddy" Harvey said, hanging back.

"Tell us a Bible story *and* a Matilda story, Daddy," Jenny said.

"Just one story tonight, kids. I have a headache. Get in bed, Harvey." Jan put Carol in her crib. The older kids all slept in one room. The other room upstairs was their playroom.

"Milk. I want milk."

"Give her milk, honey."

"I want some milk too, Daddy."

"Arf a minute, son."

"Mull!" Carol was yelling for the glass. When it silenced her, Ev began:

> There was once a little girl named Matilda, who lived with her mother and her father and a little brother named Archibald and a baby brother named Grumblebum in the Sound Paint housing project in Skedaddle. One day

"In Sloshingbum, Daddy." Details mattered to Harvey. "Skedaddle Sloshingbum."

> Sloshingbum. One day Matilda and Archibald and Grumblebum were outside

"Whose name is Grover, Daddy,"

and Grumblebum, whose name was really Grover, were standing outside on the porch. Skedaddle is a city much swollen and wrinkled by rainfall, and today it was *still* raining while they waited for Daddy to come home from school. They were under the porch roof looking way down the sidewalk. All over sodden, they saw a bicycle. It was a yellow bicycle, very pale, washed out like lemonade. It wasn't a boy's bike or a girl's bike, it was a mixed-up bike.

"But yours is a man's bike, isn't it, Daddy."

No Arf; mine is a rider's bike, a dreamer's bike. And this was just like mine, except that the color was all washed out. Like your Big Wheel got before we had a garage. Now this was an unusual bike for Matilda to see, because . . . uh, it didn't have a rider. It was rolling up the sidewalk all by itself. It was even pedaling itself, like Matilda did on her bike. Matilda even thought she could see something on it, but maybe it was just the rain.

Then Archibald said 'Look, Matilda, there's daddy's briefcase.' And it was! Daddy's briefcase was on the luggage rack over the front wheel. And Grumblebum, who really wasn't a Grover yet, said 'Dada coat!' Now Daddy's raincoat was grey, like bad weather, and Matilda and Archibald were not sure they could see it. But as the bike came closer, they saw daddy's rubbers, which leaked, in the toe clips. And when the bike reached their porch, it stopped. 'Hi, Matilda,' it said. 'Hi, Archibald and Grumblebum.' Its voice was like bath water going down the drain. 'I'm home.'

'Daddy?' said Matilda.

'Yes, honey. Let me put the bike away,' the voice said (but no one was crowding around). It rolled over to an eyebolt in the wall of the building, where it was chained and covered with a sheet of plastic Mommy had sewn up like an envelope. Then the rubbers, which were sloshing and squelching, walked over, and it looked like daddy's raincoat was there, almost holding onto his briefcase. The coat bent over and each child was wetly kissed.

Matilda ran into the house, screaming and calling for Mommy. Archibald backed away. Grumblebum said 'Dada?' Then the briefcase herded the two boys into the apartment and closed the door and sat on the floor.

'I'm home, Darling,' said the voice, which now sounded like a shaken shower curtain. Mommy came into the room and looked around. Then she started for the rubbers.

'Who left these wet' she said, then Mommy almost screamed, then she almost cried.

'Are you feeling all right?' asked the coat, sounding like a dishrag being wrung out. Mommy started laughing then, until she did cry.

'Is that you, Wilbur?' she said.

'You were expecting maybe the milkman?' burbled a blur above the coat, which shrugged and fell halfway to the floor. The coat swung around by its collar and shook itself and flung itself onto the couch. The rubbers flopped and curled and flew into the coat closet. 'I really feel washed out,' said the rocker, and started rocking. Matilda turned on the light in the living room, because it was evening. 'Come here, Matilda,' babbled the rocking chair, 'and sit on my lap.'

'Daddy,' said Matilda, 'You're not there.' Archibald came over and touched the arm of the rocking chair. Grumblebum came and crawled up on the chair. He was not afraid of a wet seat or a sloshing bum. 'Hah, dada.'

'It's true,' said Mommy. 'You are washed out.'

'I guess I'm all wet too, huh?' the chair sighed.

'I can't tell, dear,' Mommy said, and she bent over the chair. 'Kiss me.' She got a big wet kiss moistly on her throat. 'You are all wet. Just look at you.'

'I can see myself perfectly clear,' said Daddy. And he was.

'I can see right through you, dear.'

'Hmm,' said Daddy. He *was* hard to see. He was even more faded than his jeans. 'What can we do about this? I'd like to feel all here.'

'I know, Daddy,' said Matilda. 'Let's get out my painting set and we can paint you.' She ran upstairs to get her paint set. By now Daddy's clothes were drying out, and his white tee-shirt was almost as visible as his blue jeans. Even his sweat sox and tennis shoes showed. Only his hands and arms and neck and head were not there.

'Take your clothes off, dear,' said Mommy, helping him get out of them. Then she stood him by the sewing table and stood Grumblebum on the table and Archibald on the floor.

'Here's the water colors, Mommy,' said Matilda. Then Mommy stood Matilda on a hassock and divided Daddy up.

'Grumblebum will paint your head, and Matilda you paint Daddy's chest and back, and Archibald will you paint Daddy's legs. I'll paint Daddy's arms.' They all set to work, and before long Daddy was done. He had orange and green hair, and a black face with yellow eyes and a purple throat, and a red and blue chest, and a brown back, and green and yellow and red and blue and white and orange legs with black feet—and a few clear spots. 'There,' said his wife. 'You look quite handsome.'

'Daddy looks like J. Pooh Peaches,' said Matilda; he was a TV clown.

'Daddy doesn't have a penis,' said Archibald, and started to laugh.

'I'll take care of that,' said Mommy, and she led him into the bathroom, where she powdered him with Johnson's Baby Powder until his penis was all white. Daddy took one look at himself in the mirror and flushed himself down the toilet, and that's

THE END.

Ev left their room quickly, closing the door behind him. "Don't close the door, Daddy," they said, so he opened it a crack.

"That was pretty good," said Janet. "One of your better efforts."

"Yeah, I thought it was pretty good myself once it got started."

"You ought to write it down in your journal."

"Yeah." He wasn't enthusiastic.

"Except that the ending's kind of flat."

"Watered down?"

"I was thinking, maybe you could have Matilda suggest that Daddy go out and run around in the rain. You know, to mix the colors."

"Hey, that's a fantastic idea."

"Don't be sarcastic."

"No, I mean it." Ev rushed back into the kids' room. "Hey, kids, that wasn't the end really. Daddy didn't really flush himself down the toilet. After he saw how funny he looked, like a pile of dirty clothes, he started to cry. Matilda said, 'Don't cry, Daddy.' And then she watched a tear run down his face, and she said 'Daddy, maybe if it rained on you, you would be all the same color.' So Daddy went outside and ran in the rain, and turned cartwheels and somersets and slid down the hill on the grass, and rooted in the bushes and jumped in all the puddles until he was back to his normal color. And he would have stayed out all night playing in the rain if Mommy hadn't said 'Come in here before the neighbors see you,' and took him to bed. And that's *really* THE END."

Ev kissed and tucked in each of his children and went out the door.

When Jan was ready for bed, she came down to the study and sewing room to get him. "I'll be up as soon as I finish my journal," he said, pleased with the story. After she left; after he finished writing; after the light was out and the house was quiet; Ev knelt by the desk chair and folded his arms on its left arm, clad only in his temple garments, a second skin against the world and all its clothes, and said

"God, I'm such a prick," shocking himself, because it was what he meant. After a minute he added "Father forgive me . . . but you lived through this once, you had to learn discipline, maybe it wasn't easy for you to grow out of a sire into a father. And you, my Mother: you couldn't've had an easy life of time. Maybe your marriage was like ours. I'm glad for the kids, and for Jan; she's a good wife, and kind" . . . the picture of Carol on his desk, a few hours born, fiercely gasping in air and shutting out light — he recalled more than saw it in the street light. "I'm sorry for jacking off." He was blushing now. "I can't blame Satan, wasn't his handiwork; I'm afraid he didn't need to tempt me — maybe the tension of not being able to figure out those medicare requests. I hope you don't keep records like that." *'Cormier, Everard / 31 March 1975 : one manual emission. — motive : lust ; judgment : voluntary, mitigated by frustration in inserting charge-outs' . . . coded by master Alpha and occasional Theta waves and Julian date.*

"My God, don't strike me down tonight. Both of you: you were parents, and you were kids. Now I seem to be both at once. I don't want Jennifer and Harvey and Caroline and Benjamin to be praying this way to you, at my age, trying to raise kids while they grow up too. . . . They'll have enough to learn and do and change without having to unlearn and forget my ways of sinning. Let me show them love that doesn't size-up tits. How can I teach them about passion? Show them that it's not a function of variety? That it's the square root of knowledge, not novelty cubed. How can I teach *me* that? Or help them to see that it's the love you've ordained to teach us to cleave to spouse?

"O God, it must disturb you to see all the sex sold between covers, wasted in volume. I'm glad we could plan our family, I think that's a real luxury, a benefit. Don't let me stop planning. They're not weeds. Or goats. How can I learn to live with them as friends, neighbors, brothers, sisters — not just children taking up time and room?" He looked slowly around the room, at the stereo and records lovingly arranged, shelved, protected against sun and dust, the books carefully classified and laid on their shelves. It was easy to care for things that could only wait to be used, even if they held the love of a brother or sister dead or distant, an author. "Help me to live as one having authority and not as a scribe. I don't want to bribe my children for their affection, without love, without care. What will I do? Can we play ball without making a balls of it?" After several minutes of waiting for a reply he added "and without being caught red-handed, red-faced, spanking? Thank you for the ears, God. I know Jesus can understand these questions, and I believe you have answers. In the name of Christ, my brother, help me, father, mother."

Jan was asleep, and the children were asleep, when he slipped into bed. Lying in bed, he started to cry. His tears ran into his ears. Crying in bed, he fell asleep. Sleeping in bed, he dreamed. He was suffering his Ph. D. exams again and somewhere a baby was crying. "It's your turn to bring Benny," said Janet, and rolled him out of bed.

When he slept again, he was standing with Janet and their kids in the warm water of a shallow lake, trying to launch a sailboat. The lake looked like one of those *LIFE* magazine drawings of earth in the Jurassic. They were at a resort in jagged mountains, at the bottom left hand edge of the lake, and were going sailing again. They shoved the boat into the lake, to launch it, they kept shoving it into the lake, but the water kept receding from it. "Look, Daddy," said Matilda. Across the lake a cliff at the shore had opened its mouth and was drinking the lake; water surged and ebbed with each swallow, with each swallow receding, revealing the bottom of the lake cobbled with white stones. Something clicks. Out of the mouth shapes are walking, morpheotic. Snatching up the kids we flee into the cottage, and stand in the dark room, praying for invisibility. Animals come across the lake into the cottage: a hippopotamus, a giant ground sloth, a megatherium, alive. These are our judges, and they are laughing. One is humming, one is buzzing and the room is growing lighter. The roof is burning, the kids rise up through the flame—

Slapped, the alarm stopped. He found the plunger and pushed it home. Jan reached behind her and pulled him against her. "Morning." Then she patted and rolled and petted him. "Would you like to make love, honey?" Ev didn't say anything for a minute; then fearing she would take rigidity for consent, because it always was, he said,

"I have a confession to make. This will probably sound mildly repellent, I mean kind of disgusting, anyway, but,"

"I'll still love you."

"I've been masturbating." He gulped. "Since we were married. Not all the time, I mean. I didn't the first year, back at the Y. But when you were carrying Jenny — and it's been worse with the other pregnancies. I think about it every time I pass a magazine rack, even at Food Giant. And I'm sorry honey. At least I don't think of you when I do it."

"Not good enough for ya, huh?" They lay molded together for a minute. She reached back and rubbed his back awkwardly. "I did that when I was a girl."

"Really?" Still tired, Ev yawned.

"Even a couple of times after we were married. Then I decided it was wrong. But I didn't have to think of anyone. It just felt good."

"I didn't know that. I mean I knew girls could do it, I mean. Why?"

"I married you." She dozed off, then startled awake.

"Why did you start?"

"I found out it felt good. One day, I think it was back in junior high school." Both were quiet then, lying together. Not thinking, Ev was drifting to sleep and snapping awake, twitching each time along his legs.

Then children were stirring. Jan turned over and kissed him. "Remember Hamlet the Dorp? I looked it up after dinner. A dorp is a fishing village. A dorf."

"That Hamlet was crazier than he knew."

"It shows up in place names as thorp."

"I would have to marry an English major."

"No, you didn't have to."

"Didn't Daddy marry you, Mommy?"

"Yes, Jenny," she said to the girl climbing into their bed. "But he wanted to."

By the time Ev was ready for work, rain was bucketing down the wind. Each night as he parked his bike beside the Rambler he vowed to drive to work tomorrow. Each morning as he mounted and pedaled away, he told himself Jan would need the car. When it furiously rained he walked to the bus stop and rode to work. By the time he reached the bus this morning, rain was sweeping in curtains down the spine of the city. He transferred during a drizzle, but by the time he got off on Sand Point Way and ran for the FARC, white and immense across the street, he was running through the aerial equivalent of the Mariana Trench. He had dried to dampness by nine o'clock, aided by warmth of spirit he generated composing a stiff reprimand to the Bureau of Land Management, Fairbanks. They'd asked for a record without sending numbers.

His next request was for a court case, from the district court in Spokane. Accession number indicated it would be in Archives. The Archives stacks were in an enclosed room with a controlled atmosphere, its temperature and humidity differing from the Center at large. He could enter by passing through the offices and reception area of the Record Center and the Archives and into the Archives reading room, walls lined with microfilm readers, where there was a locked door into the stacks. This he did, since it was close to the mailing desk where he had written the letter. Janis, as it turned out, was the only staffer who had a key — the rest were lost, or mislaid, or left home. She pulled it from her pocket and handed it to Ev.

"Won't be but a minute," he said, "I only have one request" as he opened the door, and putting the key, still warm, into his pocket, passed through, closing it behind him. The area around the door was clotted with boxes. Side stepping, he ran down the Eastern Washington aisle, looking for his box, and spotted it at the end of the aisle, at the end of the Eastern Washington stacks, up on the top shelf. You could only get a ladder into these aisles at the far end, where the access was clogged, near the door. Ev glanced around, then climbed up the shelves, which on one side were filled with large docket books, pushed back from the edge. He'd reached the top hoping he was alone, and opened the box, straddling the aisle, leaning to his right, when the speaker said, "Would you open the archives door please?" Janis was the speaker. Startled, he dropped the request. It floated and flapped fourteen feet to the floor. Guilty, he swung down the shelves, banging a knee and twisting a wrist. Picking up the court request, scuttling down the aisle, opening the door, he apologized.

"Here's your key. I should've brought it back."

"That's all right. I don't know your name."

"Ev."

"Everett?"

"Everard. I'm not from around here."

"What?"

"I'm from Utah."

"Everard what? from Utah.

"Oh. Cormier."

"Everard O. Cormier. I'll try to remember. I'm Janis Justus."

"So I hear." He turned to go back down the aisle and smashed into a streamliner stacked with boxes, knocking one off. He caught it, falling, by reaching over it, nearly ripping a finger out of his left hand.

"This place is really congested," she said. "I wish you people would take these boxes out of here."

"What are they?" he asked. There were two streamliners. Each was half full. Two hand-trucks stood there also, one stacked four high, one three high. Two odd stacks of boxes cluttered the floor randomly.

"Customs boxes. Customs officers have been searching them for misfiled manifests. Some kind of a kickback case."

"Are the officers done with these?"

"Yes." She sounded perturbed, as if any idiot could tell they were done with them.

"Fine. I'll take'm back when I leave. Get'm out of your way."

"Please do. It should have been done last week."

"I couldn't even get a ladder past them for this aisle."

"There's a thing back there, a big platform thing, that you can get around the other end."

"Hm. Thanks. I'll use it."

"Do." She pirouetted, and flowed through the door.

Ev started back down the aisle. He didn't know what she was wearing. He pictured some kind of skirt and blouse, or shirt and slacks, or a combination of them, or a dress. He wasn't sure. He nearly skipped down the aisle. He hadn't looked! He didn't remember! He ran back to the south wall seeing the platform somewhere, remembering gym dances in junior high and a fight over a girl he didn't know. He found a blank space in the wall of boxes, turned his request over and began writing on the back, trying to capture the memories and ideas flashing and rumbling in his head. He wrote:

> When I was in junior high, my friends defined flirting for me: any kind of talking with girls, especially attractive girls. They also told me, these friends, "Don't talk to Melody" — she was like a pretty girl — "she's Glenn's. There's plenty of other wahines around. That's Hawaiian, you know." This was a warning, not information. If I talked with girls, I was flirting.
>
> Now it seems equally simple: interject, state, comment, reply, listen, hear and speak. That's conversation. Not flirting. No more lust just because a woman is friendly to me. Or ignores me. I should respect anyone I deal with, as well as myself, because I won't be always laying plans and planning lays, singing hymns to drive off cuckoos, scratching to get their droppings off my head. No longer need dandruff be a metaphor for evil thoughts. Dry scalp, not dry rot. All I have to live with now is all I have, not everything I have to stifle. I have sense, I have sensation, I can share or spare either one; my conversation can beseem my life. The continental drift unseaming Jan and me just ground to a halt. We have new grounds for love. And all because of Janis Justus. (Good journal entry. Expand.)

After pulling the court case and removing the Customs boxes, Ev headed for the lunchroom. It was 9:40 and the Records Center staff were already upstairs on break. As he ascended into the lunchroom Rose stood up. "It's worktime" she said. Janis was sitting at Rose's table, drinking coffee.

"It's always worktime" he said. "That's why anytime is breaktime."

"Paradox again." Rose grimaced. "No wonder you like that hermaphrobike of yours."

"What?"

"Hermie. That's what I'd call it" Rose said.

"You're too much like Dawn."

"I won't bite."

"Neither did she" Ev said.

"Who?"

"Rosey-fingered Dawn. Best masseuse I ever met. Ease any muscle with a few light touches." Rose groaned down the stairs.

Ev was pouring himself a glass of juice when Janis spoke.

"Hi, Cormier. Didn't see your bike this morning."

"No, I took the bus. I always do, when it rains."

"Have a seat." She pointed across the table. "Where do you live?"

"Over in Wallingford. A little bit south of Food Giant, on Bagley."

"Would you like a ride home tonight? I go that way."

"Oh." He sipped in silence, lost in visions.

"Thanks for hauling those boxes away" she said. "I didn't mean to be quite so bitchy."

"De nada."

"I go across 40th every night. Every morning, too." A woman of regular habits, even if none were nun's. Hell, she was as fussy about order as he, and as bothered by clutter. She picked up her cup and drained it, something he'd never seen her do.

"It's okeh about the boxes. We shoulda got 'em." He drank some juice. "I'd like a ride. I usually ride a bike, but"

"Beats waiting for the bus in the rain. If it's still raining."

"Thanks. Jan, she's my wife, Janet, will be pleased to see me home early."

She smiled, almost nervously, and left.

Jesse and Louise

Sibyl Johnston

Jesse took Louise to the hot springs last week. It was a big occasion; she'd cornered him several weeks in advance to set it up. Jesse and Louise go back a long way, but lately, she's been pretty sweet on him. She was in the bathroom all day, steaming up the mirror, fixing her face and singing *Tonight.* I spent twenty minutes that afternoon untangling a pink foam curler from behind her ear, and a lot longer the next day listening to the details. Louise talks about her love life like other people eat hot fudge sundaes. I hear all about each romance after the fact—and a whole lot before, too, while I'm combing and curling and messing with curlers. That night, after an hour of romantic confessions, Louise's hair stood out in yellow waves around her face. It's like her to want to set her hair for a steambath.

A lot of people are beginning to wonder why Jesse puts up with Louise—she's been calling him a lot lately, and she's always here and waiting when he comes by, always asking for love songs on our old piano. And Jesse always sings for her. I guess it's his way of being nice. Jesse isn't always very nice.

*Song lyrics by Lee Charles Kelley

Jesse met Louise at Vriner's Lunch, one day when he was the noon-hour entertainment there. Vriner's is your basic greasy spoon—red vinyl barstools, Merle Haggard on the jukebox. "The touch of Americana," Jesse says. Louise likes the chicken fried steak. Anyway, they met there one Tuesday. Louise was sitting in a booth wearing her pink beaded sweater, and Jesse was singing the blues. He writes his own songs and sings around town a lot of places, always in overalls, cowboy boots, and a brown sweater. A lot of people think he's a little strange; Louise was very taken by him. After lunch, he took her for a drive in his DeSoto and she brought him home for a root beer float. He's been coming by between romances ever since. I guess Louise is kind of like home base, someone to sing for when he's lonely. "You've got that touch of Americana, Louise," he told her once. "You're all right." But, she sighed that night in the bathroom, "that's as close as he's come to making a pass."

So it was Louise's move and she took him to the hot springs, this little shack with a pool of water inside. There is something, as Jesse would say, very funky about the hot springs. It's a dangerous place to go alone; they say a drunk cowboy murdered someone there last year. Moonlight—you have to go there at night—hits the water through a hole in the ceiling, and if you squat down and float your chin you can see steam rising. People go there to kill each other, or themselves—or, in Louise's case, to declare love. It's a great spot for a showdown.

"Rachel!" Louise took both my arms and told me tonight was the night. They would be alone. "'Despite their separate origin'"—Louise quoted a critic's description of her favorite painting, Millais's *Ophelia*—"'landscape and figure fuse flawlessly to represent Ophelia's consummation with the element, her fainting ecstasy!'" Ophelia, sinking in the black water, her gown covered with wildflowers and her lips parted, reminds Louise of the hot springs.

So they went out there in Jesse's old DeSoto. Jesse goes for anything funky: old cars, 1940s movies, Louise in her pink sweater. Give him a little atmosphere and he's in his prime. But the car is great—all black and white, with a plain brown interior, a couple of capos hanging from the dash. I think even if he could afford a Porsche, Jesse'd keep his DeSoto. "The car and I," he says often, "we go back a long way. We're almost friends." The DeSoto's a classic, like all those old movies he watches. And it gets him where he's going. He didn't clean it for the occasion, though, and when Jesse's out of love—as he has been for some time—the right front seat becomes a garbage dump. So Louise must have been knee deep in Oreo wrappers, TV Guides, and old Dorito bags.

I was here when they left. Louise looked great, eccentric as always in her terrycloth bath jacket with a petticoat ruffle hanging out below. "What do you have to wear that old slip for?" Jesse griped when she opened the door. Jesse doesn't necessarily mean to be rude; Louise just gets on his nerves sometimes. Louise adjusted her glasses. She's pretty nearsighted. She smiled at him. "Oh, there's something so sensual about it," she said in her shy voice, that business she puts on when she's flirting. "All this filmy white cotton floating up around you. . . . " She lifted her petticoat with two fingers, and waltzed a few steps. It was her favorite petticoat, embroidered with small flowers on the ruffle. *"There with fantastic garlands did she come,"* sang Louise, and she danced like Ophelia around Jesse, *"Of crowflowers, nettles, daisies, and long purples, That liberal shepherds give a grosser name."* I could tell Jesse wasn't too thrilled that night. "Why does she want to change a good thing?" he asked me later, when he had figured out the situation. Louise fluttered white fingers. *"There's rue for you and here's some for me, Oh you must wear your rue with a difference. Eidelweiss, eidelweiss. . . . "* Her tune changed suddenly.

"Oh, get off it, will you?" Jesse isn't much on Julie Andrews, and he's never wanted Louise thinking he was too much on her, either. He hadn't shaved, showered, or changed overalls in a while. I could tell he didn't want to laugh. He touched her. "Come on, let's go."

"Oh—wait—" She ran back inside and stuffed a candle into her knapsack.

"Louise, do you have to bring all that garbage along?" He slammed the front door behind them and I parted the curtains to watch. He was helping her into the car.

Jesse told me he had to sing at the top of his lungs blues from his album in production, all the way to the hot springs. "Man, she just would not knock it off with that *Sound of Music* crap," he said. *The Sound of Music* is Louise's favorite musical, and she sings it loudly at moments of particular ecstasy. I guess Jesse just wasn't up for raindrops on roses at the time. Louise likes any kind of music, though, especially when Jesse sings. I'm sure she got her fill of barstools and beerglasses that night.

So they drove down the freeway like always, Louise's hair blowing wild and Jesse, with his elbow out the window, breaking all the short silences with his songs. It's a long way to the hot springs, south on Fifteen by way of Springville, and then up through the mountains. Jesse leans back, on those mountain roads, and rests one hand lightly on the wheel. And this time he sang *Shakespeare Avenue Blues.* "This one's for a friend of mine," he said the first night he ever played it, and he winked at Louise. That first night she was pretty quiet, just smiled and held his hand awhile before we left Vriner's. Jesse didn't seem to mind.

"I'm not one of those rosebud Romeos you chose to play the part,"—I know Louise just listened to the sound of his voice in the car, always a little like a whisper, and thought about that night at Vriner's—*"Of the somewhat mad but doting lover who can't quite captivate your heart."*

There's a train track following the freeway into town, and you can see the freight's light coming toward you by the black mountains. There's nothing much in Springville at midnight—just pink strobe street lamps and a 7-11 at the edge of town, where Jesse stops for Pepsi Light and the comics. "Spiderman!" he told me. "Fantastic Four, Howard the Duck—you name it—best damn comic books in the state of Utah!" So they dragged Main all alone a couple of times. Jesse always drags Main, any Main. Touch of Americana, I guess. And you can almost hear the cars in Jesse's mind, grinding gears alongside his DeSoto: Mustangs and jacked-up Camaros, ready for action underneath the street lamps. All kinds of dragons Jesse fights in his mind. After a couple of turns around the median, he pulled into the 7-11 parking lot and left Louise in the car in her petticoat.

Nights are cool and sort of quiet in Springville. You can rest the side of your face out the car window, look up and listen to the cottonwoods. Pink lamps over the lot draw moths and Junebugs, flatten and shadow every crack in the asphalt and all those flecks and smears on the windshield. The glass leaves a line on your skin. Louise watches the stars a lot when she's with Jesse, likes to tell him all about the constellations. She really wants to love him. And that makes him mean. "The trouble with Louise," he's told me before, "is, she comes too close. Man, I always feel like we're nose to nose!" Coming nose to nose with Jesse can be a dangerous business, a good way to get burned, I hear. But Louise doesn't see it that way; she's always looking close at things she likes. "Oh, Rachel!" she whispered, while I curled her hair. "Do you think maybe, after I tell him, we'll make out?"

Jesse kept on singing: *I've seen you all alone and lonely, From your makeup to your shoes, in Shakespeare Avenue Blues.*

She likes to hang one arm out the window as he drives, feel the wind on her fingers, and watch the mountains. At night outside Springville the Rockies are flat, black, with a line of moonlight along the top. There's a long, lonely stretch out of Springville, nothing but rocks and wire fences and, later on, those iridescent signs: *Warning: Sheer Drop*. And it's dead quiet out there, blue, just the sounds of the car on the highway.

The turnoff for the springs is pretty sharp, and I guess Louise was half asleep by then. She fell over close to him. "Are you pulling over, Jesse?"

"We're *here,*" he told her, and they followed the gravel lane that runs along the mountain to the hot springs. Jesse's car rattles and squeaks on that road, the ceiling light blinks on and off. "Damn light," he generally mutters, and unscrews it. No doubt that night Louise began to get ideas. "Well, get out," Jesse said, at last. "We're here."

"And then she just *sat* there, stared at me all moon-eyed," he told me. "So I got out and ran around the car and opened her door for her." He sounded pretty disgusted. "Then I went to take a piss."

Louise gathered up her knapsack and wandered over to the shack. It's a ritual for her, every time; with one hand she unties her ratty bath jacket, slips it off and leaves it in a heap on the ground. "There is nothing," she tells me, "as sensual as clothing on the ground!" Then she takes out her candle and sets it on the ground right by the water, and steps in.

By the time Jesse got undressed, Louise said, she lay back in the water, floating and feeling the steam rise all around her face. "Jesse," she whispered when she saw him, or I guess his shadow in the doorway, "will you light my candle?" And somehow Jesse found a match and wandered over to the candle, and he tripped over Louise's bath jacket and kicked it into the springs.

"Damn!" He fished it out and hung it over the door. "You ought to put your stuff away," he muttered, and he stepped in the water.

The springs are hot, and if you stand still you feel tiny bubbles rising now and then. Jesse grunts when he gets in the water. Louise sighs, she always sighs and breathes a lot in the hot springs. "I like the way you grunt, Jesse," she said, after a moment.

"I mean, what do you say to a woman who likes the way you *grunt?*" he asked me later, waving his arms. "Man, she is difficult!"

"So then he started to sing. Oh, Rachel, he's *so* erotic! His voice echoes in the hot springs!" By candlelight, she could have seen the outline of the pool, and small ripples around him catching light. Jesse sits a lot on a rough wooden beam at the far end of the pool—we call it the Throne. So I guess that's probably where he was, on the Throne. And Louise sighed and floated while Jesse sang on the Throne:

She's a wild rose, livin' on numbers and beaux, Takin' off secondhand clothes, everybody knows. . . .

Louise loves the hot water and the feeling of her petticoat floating around her legs. She swam slowly back and forth from one end of the pool to the other, sometimes backing up a little so the skirt would float up around her waist, and never quite nearing the Throne. In the candlelight Jesse looks like a satyr, water streaming from his beard and shadows all around his eyes. Louise's glasses steamed over about then, and she took them off. Only Louise wears glasses in the hot springs. "Jesse . . . "

He sang to the hole in the ceiling, his eyes closed. *You can't hold on to dreams, they're like wind and water, They keep movin' on just as your fingers close. . . .* And he kept singing, so she couldn't get personal. He never lets her in too close. Jesse has a lot of class; someone else would play right along. She swam a little nearer to the Throne and he turned his back, still singing. She likes the sound of his voice, soft, in the water, and she lay back in the springs and listened. The petticoat billowed, brushed against Jesse's thigh.

"Damn it, Louise!" He stood up straight. "Look, I didn't want to have to say this. But the thought has not occurred to me, and it does not occur to me now. So cool it!"

Louise sat very still for a moment, water dripping down her neck, goosebumps on her shoulders. She moved her hands a little, back and forth, and made ripples. "It feels just like a bath," she said. "Warm all over. Oh, Jesse, look—you can see the moon through the ceiling, oh, Jesse, it's a full moon." She pointed, her arm blue in the dark. It was a gibbous moon.

"Louise," said Jesse.

I heard them drive up around two-thirty, and I pretended to be asleep on the couch. I knew Jesse hadn't made any moves; I knew he never would. You know I think Louise would die if he did. But somehow it seemed like the decent thing for me to act like there was something not to see.

The TV was on low, some old movie, and all the lights were out; Jesse would be in his element. I had the swamp cooler on and the damp air rushed and whistled. Louise walked across the room, kind of flat-footed. She smelled like sulphur. She sat on one end of the other couch and slowly pulled her knees up close to one side. Louise has skinny legs, you can see blue veins on the backs of her knees. She held her bath jacket in one hand, all grey and wet, and her hair hung in strings. She looked like a ten-year-old boy. She leaned her head against the back of the couch like Judy Garland, her eyes closed. Jesse sat down on the opposite arm of the couch and after a minute the jacket slipped from Louise's fingers. She was asleep.

"Was it a rare affair?" I asked, finally.

Jesse smiled. "Touch of Americana," he said. "Louise and I, we go back a long way." He leaned over slowly and picked up Louise's bath jacket from the floor. "She dropped it in the hot springs," he said. He looked tired. After a minute he went to the piano, stood there and vamped. It was something familiar, I thought; oh, *Raindrops on Roses*. But the melody sounded minor and the vamp was in the wrong key, the rhythm staggered. He stopped. He leaned over, switched keys, and began a song. *Rain, rain, rain. . . .* Jesse sound hoarse late at night. *I get the blues, sometime, in the afternoon*. He straightened, turned, and looked at me. "Well," he said. "Later."

"Later, Jesse," I said.

The Hawk

David L. Wright

"You can't do everything you want in life," Dad said, and took the milk bucket from my hand. I dreaded in my heart he was going to tell me more about the differences between boys and girls and I already knew more about girls than he did and it hurt me to see him thinking he was teaching me something new because it was so painful for him to speak about certain things like that.

I started to let the rails down but he said, "Don't turn them out yet," so I walked back to the milk can and watched him snap the lid on tight with just a quick snap of his wrists. "So," he said, lifting me with one hand up to the top rail. "So you won, did you? How high did you jump?"

I'd been wondering when he was going to talk about the pentathlon or if he ever would so I told him four-foot-three but four-three wasn't very high because he could almost *step* over a fence that high. Then he walked over to the rail gate and let the rails down and started turning the cows out, like that was all the talking he was going to do today. So I hurried over and told him I scored nearly

4,000 points which was more than any of the other district winners I'd read about in *The Deseret News,* even those kids in Nevada and Arizona and Utah.

"Four thousand?" he said. "How could you score all that many points?" He didn't have to say I was no bigger than a peanut because I knew he was thinking it, so I told him about my low coefficient.

"Well," he said, "that gives the little feller a chance anyhow." He dug his very strong fingers into where my biceps were supposed to be and hoisted me on down from the fence. Then he grabbed the milk can with one hand and started packing it to the springs. I grabbed the other handle but he said, "Just hold your horses. You might hurt yourself." And I wondered if I'd ever be strong enough to carry a filled-up milk can with just one hand.

While he was setting the can in the water he motioned with his head to the upper pasture. "See that hawk?" he said. And sure enough there was a hawk just getting into the mountain skyline from the upper-pasture willow bushes. "Maybe you think that hawk is free an as angel," he said. "But he don't get far from home."

Not that a hawk has got a darn thing to do with *The Deseret News Junior Pentathlon,* but I answered him respectful. "No, I guess he don't," I said.

Dad leaned his elbow on the top rail and pitched his eyes down on me until I looked up. Then his eyes turned back to the upper pasture, the mountains, and the hawk.

"Mr. Burns tells me the winners from each county gets to go to Salt Lake for the finals. That right?"

So I told him that more than a hundred winners from all the Western states would go to Salt Lake and that the name of the meet was *The Deseret News Junior Pentathlon* and the three big winners would get trophies and the winners of each event would get a medal—like for instance if I jumped four-three again I'd get 900 points but even if a bigger kid went four-six he'd get maybe only 500 points. That's because *The Deseret News* had a system worked out according to size and age and I also explained that anybody who could get 4,000 points was almost sure to win and . . . but Dad wasn't listening very much.

"I see" he said. "How come you didn't tell me all this before?" So I told him about everybody had to pay their own way to Salt Lake. "Mmmm," he said and tucked and folded his hands inside his Lee Overall bib and looked down at his toes just like when Mother told him she had to have a new washing machine. Then he commenced staring into the upper pasture again where the big hawk was coasting high and easy.

Our cows weren't much interested either and they wandered over to the spring and started to drink. According to *The Deseret News* they'd sell for about $75 a head.

"Salt Lake City," Dad said, just like he always said "ah" when he came in from the hayfield and Mother poured him a glass of homemade root beer. And then, just as if he was telling the story for the first time, he told me about when him and Mother were married in the Salt Lake City Temple. And how for more than two weeks his folks and Mom's folks had planned for the trip and it took three days to get there and when they got almost to Uncle Rhen's place in Brigham City one of the horses got a nail in her foot and they had to borrow one of Uncle Rhen's horses before they could go on. But the part I liked no matter how many times I heard it was how they camped in Logan and Sardine Canyons and built a big bonfire and Mother played the guitar and everybody sang and Grandpa Simmons made everybody sing for the last song *Our Mountain Home So Dear, Where Crystal Waters Clear* . . . and then everybody knelt by the fire and prayed. It made funny listening when Dad told about Mama's guitar string breaking because he liked to kid her that it was the "G" string that broke, but he didn't start telling this story until after the war when Oren Prescott came home and told him what a "G" string was.

"Your Mother won't let on about it," Dad said with a twinkle in his eye, "but it was the 'G' string that broke." And it was okay for me to laugh too because he didn't think I knew what a "G" string was. So we laughed together in our wide pasture, and suddenly the sun broke out of the sundown clouds and splashed greeny bright all over the east mountains.

Then he told me things about Salt Lake City I'd never heard him say before. He said Salt Lake was a big city—so big that even though it was the headquarters of the Church it was a very sinful place. He said he knew it was even bigger and more sinful now than when him and Mother were there because so many gentiles had moved in and set up business and intermarried with the Saints. He said Brigham Young had brought the Saints to Salt Lake to escape from the persecutions of the gentiles and President Young once said he wished he could put his arms around the whole Salt Lake Valley and keep all the gentiles out. All the West would have been better off, Dad said, if Brigham Young could have done this because the West was a sacred land where God chose to build His land of Zion.

Then he told about the chokecherry jam somebody stole from their wagon right while they were in the temple getting married and how Grandpa Simmons had come near to swearing when they walked down one of the streets right off Temple Square and seen the cheap hotels and the bars and people drinking and some even begging which was worst of all, and Grandpa had said he didn't care if none of his family ever set foot in Salt Lake City again. And Dad remembered that advice and him and Mother have done all their temple work in the Logan temple from that day to this.

So I promised him right then and there that I'd stay right with Mr. Burns and wouldn't go down that street. "I know you wouldn't," he said, and started putting up the rails. Suddenly he popped his hands and shouted: "Scoot, Peanut!" and I lowered my head and ran like the wind. "Like a deer!" he laughed from behind me. And by the time he got to the car I had already stacked the Bible, the Book of Mormon and *Famous American Athletes of Today* underneath me and was ready to go—sitting in the driver's seat.

As I pulled myself up from last year's manure pile, I saw Dad walking toward me from the corner of the barn. He handed me the box he had in his hand. "Maybe you'll make forty-five hundred points now," he said. I was going to say thanks or something but he'd already turned around and was walking back to the house before I could even get my brain to working. I opened the box and inside was a pair of real track shoes. Brand new.

The next morning he let me take the car alone for the first time and milk alone, almost for the first time. When I got back I saw him softening up the hardened manure pile with a shovel and in front were two new two-by-fours, set solid as posts, and with new nails driven solid in them. "I guess a champion has at least got a right to have some decent equipment to practice with," he said. But when I tried to put my eyes into his, he gathered up the tools and a sack of nails and commenced to leave. "Pick up the pieces," he said. "We can use them for kindling." So I gathered up the pieces of my old tree limb standards and carried them to the garage.

The rest of the week I hardly ever saw him because I was very busy teaching myself a fast start with the new track shoes, the first choppy strides, the arms pumping close to my sides and keeping my head down; and high jumping, which I knew how to do best of all; and broad jumping, keeping my legs far back in midair, then at the last second kicking them forward and rolling ahead. And I got the keys to the gym from Mr. Burns and shot baskets until I could make at least 32 in two minutes, which was more than anyone had ever made in any of the district meets. The only event I wasn't so good at was the shot-put and that's because it's pretty hard to practice right with only a big rock.

But all the practicing came to nothing anyway because just the day before the meet a terrible thing happened. If I'd have known Mother was in the house I wouldn't even have went in. Sure enough she started preaching just like I knew she would, saying how awfully mysterious I hadn't seen that nail before and how even more mysterious that a fool thing like this would happen the very day before the trip. Then she finally came right out and said my accident was a sure warning that I wasn't supposed to go to that wicked city after all. She took my shoe off and put my foot in hot salt water and was going to phone Mr. Burns, but I begged her please and double please not to, anyhow not till Dad came home.

I was in my room still soaking my foot when Dad came in the kitchen and I heard them talking. He wasn't exactly mad at her but when she said this bad luck was just what we all deserved for not paying our tithing this month, he told her pretty sharp that she talked too blamed much about signs from heaven. Which kind of surprised me because Dad was always talking about things like that himself.

When he came into my room I couldn't even try to put my eyes into his. He knelt down and took my foot in both hands, frowned, then touched the tender spot. "Let's see you walk," he said, so I walked best I could across the room. He shook his head. "Well, Peanut, I'm afraid you won't make no four thousand points," he said. He went into the living room and called Mr. Burns, explained what had happened and told him to call by our house at 4 a.m., just as planned.

A little later when I was in bed and Mother had left for choir practice, I decided I had to do something even though I was afraid to do it. But I knew it was a good thing to do so I put the words in my mind over and over again while I listened for Dad's big sigh which would tell me he was settled in bed. When I heard the signal, I got up and stood in the door frame of his room and called to him. I heard him reaching for the lamp switch.

"No, don't turn the lights on," I said. "I just want to say something. I want . . . I want to do something. You know . . . for you . . . in Salt Lake . . . buy you something, maybe . . . well, you just tell me and I'll do it."

I heard his body shuffle and he cleared his throat a couple of times. "Come here, son," he said, I felt kind of nervous but I walked up beside the bed. As he put his big muscled arm around my waist I almost thanked the Lord he couldn't see me.

"All right," he said, "I guess maybe there is something you can do for me."

I felt his eyes burning into my eyes and a very small quiver entered his voice. "After Mr. Burns takes you to Temple Square," he said, "tell him to let you walk down Second West Street. Go alone, and don't you be afraid. Don't you say anything or think anything bad about the people you see. And if someone comes up to you and asks you for a quarter, I want you to give him a dollar. Promise me right now you'll give him a dollar."

I lay awake a long time that night before I suddenly remembered the first day in the pasture and what he had said . . . I mean about the hawk that looked free as an angel.

Original Sin

Lynne Larson

It was to be remembered as a summer of excesses. Up and down the long valley colors quickened early, brazenly, under a sun more familiar with the August that would be than with the April that was. Sap dripped finally, bees droned, ripening fruit bulged and burst and fell heavy with the season and the surfeit. And Susan Scott, smooth and lean and blonde, confronted guilt at seventeen.

He was firm of jaw, hard of muscle, splendidly youthful, which is to say slim and strong, and warmly impulsive in a way that is at nineteen not only forgivable but attractive. Kisses wet and warm seemed inevitably in season just then, and burning restless hands simply a natural progression from there.

Raised as she was, born in this valley, surrounded all her life by towering mountains and traditional morality, Susan Scott sensed a psychological crossroads. Still, she observed, this guilt wasn't a sudden, awesome burden, dark and overwhelming, but much instead like the deed itself: a touch, a whisper, a breath. Not tormenting, it merely teased, darting on tip-toe through her dreams.

She would have talked to her mother, bustling carefree and oblivious around the kitchen, if she had not been so certain of the response. Something trite and time-worn about "bruised petals." The metaphor had never appealed to her. She was flesh not flower and did not place a high premium on fragility. Besides, her mother was possessed of a placid faith and Susan did not feel herself sufficiently sinful to necessitate disturbing it. Indeed, during quiet moments away from Chris she found it difficult to believe that she had ever "slipped" at all. During heady moments with him, however, she found it difficult to stop sliding.

But stop she had, short of anything "drastic." There were strong religious ties, to be sure, countless "standards nights" and chastity celebrations, all geared to eternal motivation. But her youth had been framed by another more specific theme: "I will never be a cliche." No one, she vowed, would ever say, "Poor Susie Scott... got herself into trouble with some boy. Isn't it all such a shame!" The Relief Society would never cluck its collective tongue on her account. Heaven forbid that she would ever *have* to marry anyone!

It was vulnerability she feared and vulnerability she regretted that summer as desire and indulgence grew and she even felt called upon to assure Chris that she was not promiscuous. "I've always been straight-arrow before," she told him, and was a little surprised at his response, "Me, too," and wondered within whether to be excited or frightened.

They were standing at that moment at the end of a high riding trail, warm and dusty, exhilarated from their wild race to the top. The panting horses lingered behind them as they spoke, and Susan felt exceedingly glowing and youthful, teasing confidently with a purposely wicked twinkle. "You too?" she answered. "Do you mean to say, Chris Ballard, that throughout all eternity *I* will be your symbol of initiation . . . loss of innocence?" She spoke lightly and with general exaggeration, as was her custom with serious subjects.

He pondered her for a moment, playfully toying as she was with phrases and feelings and the single straw-colored braid on her shoulder. "Loss of innocence?" he finally replied in dead earnest. "Oh, Susie, I hope so . . . I wish . . . just once. I'd be careful, I promise."

She accepted the remark as a compliment but raised a polite eyebrow just the same, relieved that he had posed the question at a peak in his excitement rather than hers. There had been times when. . . . Now she shook her head "no" and stepped back slightly. He sighed and his hands slid nervously up and down her arms from shoulder to elbow and back again as he apologized, "I'm . . . I'm sorry, Susie."

"We're only human," she shrugged, anxious to excuse the moment.

"I wasn't quite, before this summer," he replied, exhaling again as he turned from her to face the broad expanse of velvet valley which lay below them.

"I know . . . straight-arrow."

"Now a pretty girl's made a mortal of me," he finally laughed, adding self-consciously, "I read that somewhere."

"Yes, and written by a villainous male, no doubt," Susan beamed, glad for his change of tone, though fully aware of the meaning of his words.

"And you know what they say about mortality," he continued, lightly now. "It's just a matter of time."

It was her brother Michael in whom she finally confided—indirectly. He was absently scribbling on the plaster cast that held his right leg straight and stiff over the front porch railing, and as she sat near him in the swing wondering what to say, he commented on the weather, adding as an afterthought that he had never seen Chris Ballard show so much blond and brawn this early in July. "He'll be getting the women come September," he observed without looking up from his work. Was that a warning? An invitation to confidence? She wasn't sure.

She adored Michael as one given like herself to a great number of glorious excesses. He was twenty-five and not ordinarily at home, but his leg, this summer, had made him accessible. Vulnerable?

She had listened with enthusiasm at his telling and retelling of the skiing accident, excited because he was, even in the face of injury. He had broken the leg in early spring when the hills around them were still white. The set had been wrong, and the bone had to be re-broken. It was pinned and plastered now again with the hope of better results. And it was July. Still, with husky charm and considerable relish Michael would recount the tale, until Susan, herself a skier, could feel the blast of air, the ache and thrill of fear and flight, and the crush of snow and ski and finally bone in a bumping, tumbling climax.

"The drop jumps up at you like the devil," he began at her

request, pointing earnestly to a distant peak as if he could still see every detail in rugged retrospect. "Sheer rock for what seems like forever. A perfect vertical. Your eyes bug out and your brain won't work, and you fall half way maybe before you realize that the lump in your throat is your stomach and all that's in it, and you've left your breath somewhere behind you in another world.

"I knew it would be that way, too," he continued. "A hundred times comin' down that hill I'd tempt myself with that cliff, and every time I'd have to turn and twist like a willow in a windstorm to miss it at all. Until the last time. Then it got me."

Susan nodded. "You lost control."

Michael put his arms behind his head and leaned back to look at the sky. "No, not really," he mused. "I think I could have missed again. I knew that mountain like a map. I would have had to pull like a demon, but I think I could have done it. But I got to a certain point and said, 'What the hell' and over I went. I was gone. I didn't even try, and that's the truth of it. Now there's your story, and I still say Chris Ballard's something to behold, ain't he?" Michael was smooth, but serious, and looked at her with clear, bright eyes that tracked her own with precision.

"You should take that story to church, Mike," she said, avoiding his glance. "Temptation, surrender," she gestured toward the leg, "punishment. You'd be a big hit the next time they talk about bruised petals."

"Yeah, I might stir some souls," he answered, straightening in his chair. "Only thing, though, it wouldn't be completely honest. I'm still looking at that mountain. It's still my mistress. It's part of me. I haven't repented."

He paused then as if to change the subject, but didn't quite. "You shouldn't take a fellow to church when he's eight years old and make him promise never to kiss the girls." He smiled. "Somebody else said that. Browning or somebody. So I guess it makes sense." He looked at her in a tender, empathetic way. "Nature is a hard thing to repent of, Susie," he said.

Hearing her mother's voice just then from inside the house, she moved from the swing. In the doorway she paused, thumbs in her pockets, to shrug self-consciously and give Michael an appreciative smile. "Try not to break your leg," he said as she turned to go.

She purposely saw less of Chris in August, and though he initially seemed a little frantic, she sensed in herself a certain relief at having regained some cherished independence. She felt better then. She went riding in braids and a checked shirt and felt slim and brown and youthful. She viewed the panorama of splendid nature around her and felt simply a part of it. Wild, spontaneous, beautiful. Definitely flesh not flower, and glad of it.

When Chris began squiring Debbie Cowley around town, Susan found the transition quite painless, blond and brawn notwithstanding, for she had never really been in love. The summer, however, was still there, and she saw it now in the same way she believed Michael saw his mountain. She had tasted the honey, played in the heat, and with both freedom and virtue still intact, she had proven she was strong enough to survive.

She knew Debbie Cowley, though they were not particularly friends. The girl was pretty in an active and enthusiastic way, but more a favorite with the valley's mothers than its daughters. Susan regarded her now only while contemplating rather absently whether Chris would still go away to school in September or be persuaded by Debbie and her steadfast family that a church mission would be in order.

September came with no announcements of either, and then something Susan's mother said made it all seem academic anyway. It came one day while they were stocking the pantry shelf together after a trip to town.

"Debbie Cowley was in Nelson's today when I stopped there," said Mrs. Scott, sliding a sack of flour to the far end of the shelf.

"Debbie Cowley?" Susan yawned. "Cute as ever, I suppose."

"Now that you mention it, I thought she looked a little wilted."

"Wilted?" Susan looked up. The word seemed to her an odd choice.

Her mother raised her chin as if she were contemplating the bottled peaches on the top shelf. "Yes, 'wilted.' I think that's a good word for it. Now where did I put that corn relish?"

"A good word for what?" Susan pressed.

"Oh, I don't know. Debbie's always been such a nice girl, so eager and friendly. You know what I mean. But the last couple of times, and Marybeth Cutler was with me once and said the same thing, she's seemed kind of tired, indifferent . . . wilted," she concluded. She stopped to fan a fly away with her hand. "Maybe the heat's gotten to her," she sighed. "I've never seen such a summer!" The sentence came floating out from between the apricot preserves and the bottled string beans, but it cut cleanly, invisibly, like an edge of thin paper, through Susan Scott's better self.

The value she placed on self-determination prevented Susan from long acknowledging any surging renewal of guilt, especially on supposition. People, even the fragile ones, were responsible for their own actions, were they not? So after a tender and troubled thought or two about villains and vulnerability, Debbie Cowley simply became another fragment of this summer of initiation. And it was only a day or so later, while on a long solitary ride, that Susan stopped by a cluster of tiny yellow sage blossoms and wept alone in a bitter way, as the petals beside her trembled with the first breezes of fall.

Biographical Notes

Wayne Carver grew up in Plain City, Utah. He graduated from Weber Junior College, served as a combat engineer in western Europe, attended Brigham Young University, and graduated from Kenyon College in 1950. He has since spent his life teaching, mostly at Carleton College in Northfield, Minnesota. "Teaching," he says, "is my vocation, my calling, and writing my hobby, perhaps too casual a one. But I do not like writers who look upon teaching positions as sinecures, their schools and the foundations as their Patrons, while their hearts and minds play at being Left Bank or Sausalito artists." In 1969 he received the Danforth Foundation's Harbison Award for Distinguished Teaching. He has published many essays, stories, and reviews, and for seventeen years he was either editor or associate editor of the *Carleton Miscellany*. His present literary project is an oral history of Plain City, which, he says, "used to grab its sons and daughters hard and clench deep."

Kevin Cassity claims Anchorage, Alaska, as his home town. He has worked in a variety of jobs—as firefighter, oil rig roustabout, construction worker, banjo and guitar instructor, youth home counselor, copywriter, and editor. His interests are music, writing, outdoor recreation, and history. He attended Brigham Young University and graduated with a B. A. in English from the University of Oregon in 1980. He has been published in *Alaska Magazine* and has essays and stories in the process of submission. His senior thesis, a collection of short stories, received the 1980 President's Award at the University of Oregon. One of his stories won first prize in the fiction category and editor's choice award in the 1982 University of Alaska-*Anchorage News* creative writing contest.

R. A. Christmas (Robert Alan Christmas, born 1939, Pasadena) was educated at Stanford, the University of California at Berkeley, and the University of Southern California, where he received a Ph. D. in English in 1968. He has taught English and creative writing at Idaho State University, the University of Southern California, San Jose State, and Southern Utah State College. He is married to Olivia Lara and is the father of seven children, ages one to twenty. He is currently employed as an order desk clerk by ABC Products in South El Monte, California, an aluminum window and sliding glass door manufacturer. He also teaches part-time at Pasadena City College. His fiction has appeared in *Stories Southwest* and *Dialogue*. His poetry and criticism have appeared in *The Southern Review*, *Western Humanities Review*, *Sunstone*, *Dialogue* and other little magazines. His story "Another Angel" received an award from the Association for Mormon Letters as the best Mormon fiction published in 1981.

Dennis Clark is a native of Los Angeles and a long time resident of Seattle. Now he lives, as he says, "face-to-face with the Wasatch Front (would it were back-to-back), along which I work as a librarian." He holds a bachelor's degree from Brigham Young University and master's degrees in creative writing, the teaching of English, and library science from the University of Washington. He resides in Orem with his wife Valerie and their six children. He serves as poetry editor of *Sunstone*. He has published poetry in *Dialogue*, *Ensign*, *Poetry Northwest*, *Exponent II*, and Cracoft and Lambert's *A Believing People*.

Kent Farnsworth, a native of Orem, Utah, now makes his home in Muscatine, Iowa, where he is dean of students at the local community college and is completing a doctorate in mass communication at the nearby University of Iowa. Following a mission to England, he graduated from Brigham Young University with a B. A. in political science, then served five years as an Air Force pilot before completing graduate degrees in international relations and counseling. As an undergraduate at BYU, he took first place in the J. Marinus Jensen contest with a story which was later published in *Twenty-two Young Mormon Writers*. A poem written during his service in the Air Force won the George Washington Medal of the National Freedom Foundation. He is an active free-lancer whose articles have appeared in a number of national, regional, and church publications.

Sibyl Johnston comes from Champaign, Illinois. She completed a B. A. in English at Brigham Young University where she served as managing editor of *Century II*, the student literary magazine. She has published a number of poems, stories, and articles and is currently working on a novella. She is enrolled in Boston University's writers' program and plans later to attend Iowa's Writers' Workshop.

Bruce W. Jorgensen, born in Salina, Utah, graduated *cum laude* in English from BYU in 1966, attended Cornell on Woodrow Wilson and Danforth fellowships, and received an M. A. in English (1969) and a Ph. D. in American literature (1978). He is now associate professor of English and co-ordinator of creative writing at BYU, is married to Donna June Dutro, and has eight children. He has published criticism, poetry, and fiction in *Carolina Quarterly, Dialogue, Encyclia, Ensign, Exponent II, Sunstone, Literature and Belief*, and *Modern Fiction Studies*. He has studied writing with Eileen Kump (BYU, 1964), James McConkey (Cornell, 1971), George P. Elliott (Syracuse, 1979), and John Hawkes (Duke, summer 1982). He hopes that if good writers become recording angels, Chekhov is assigned to his story.

Eileen Gibbons Kump was born in St. Johns, Arizona, and grew up in Logan, Utah. She received a B. S. in journalism from Utah State University and an M. A. in creative writing from Brigham Young University; she also studied for two years in the Creative Writing Center at Stanford University. At USU, she was editor of the student literary magazine; afterward she worked as a newspaper reporter. She also spent two years as manuscript editor on the *Improvement Era* and for six years taught writing courses at BYU. She presently lives in St. Joseph, Missouri, with her four children and her husband, Ferrell, who is a college professor. Her articles and stories have been published in a variety of magazines. Her book, *Bread and Milk and Other Stories*, was published in 1980. Her story "The Ladder" received first prize in the 1981 Sunstone fiction contest.

Lynne Larson lives in Burley, Idaho, with her husband, Kent, and their three children. She has a B. A. in English from Brigham Young University and will finish an M. A. degree at Idaho State University in 1983. She teaches school in Declo, Idaho, (English and social studies) and also teaches night classes in English for the College of Southern Idaho. Her articles and stories have appeared in

Ensign, New Era, Mountainwest, and a number of educational magazines. In 1982 she was awarded second prize in the annual D. K. Brown Memorial Fiction Contest sponsored through *Sunstone,* in which her winning story "Bawdy and Soul" subsequently appeared. Her husband, a media center administrator and photographer, has illustrated the setting of some of her stories visually through his lens; they enjoy working on creative projects together.

Donald R. Marshall grew up in Panguitch, Utah. He received a B. A. in art and an M. A. in English at BYU and a Ph. D. in American literature in the University of Connecticut. He has lived in Paris, Madrid, London, Tahiti, and Hawaii, and has worked as a writer, painter, composer, and free-lance photographer. A professor of humanities at BYU, he has recently been on leave studying the foreign film and interviewing filmmakers around the world. Two novels are presently in the process of publication, and he is at work on a third. He is author of two published collections of short stories, *The Rummage Sale* (1972) and *Frost in the Orchard* (1977). He has also written a play, a musical, and an Emmy-award-winning TV special, "Christmas Snows, Christmas Winds."

Joseph Peterson was born in Monticello, Utah and reared in various parts of the state. Following a mission to Venezuela, he received a B. A. and an M. A. in English at BYU. Currently he lives with his wife, Rebecca, and daughter, Annie, in Roosevelt, Utah, where he is resident English instructor at Utah State University's Uintah Basin extension center. His fiction has won various honors, including first places in BYU's Mayhew contest and English Department contest, and a first place in *Sunstone's* D. K. Brown contest. His short stories have appeared in *Century II, Sunstone,* and *Dialogue.*

Levi S. Peterson grew up in Snowflake, Arizona, and served as a missionary in French-speaking Switzerland and Belgium. He lives in Ogden, Utah, with his wife, Althea Sand, and daughter, Karrin. He holds degrees from BYU (B. A., M. A.) and from the University of Utah (Ph. D.) and teaches English at Weber State College. His articles, essays, and stories have appeared in a number of publications; a collection of his stories on Mormon themes, *The Canyons of Grace* (1982), was published by the University of Illinois Press. His stories have received awards from the Utah Arts Council (first place for a collection, 1978); the Association for Mormon Letters (first place for Mormon fiction published in 1978); and the BYU Center for the Study of Christian Values in Literature (first place for "The Gift," 1981).

Karen Rosenbaum received a B. A. in English from the University of Utah and an M. A. in English from Stanford University. She lives in Albany, California, and teaches at Ohlone Junior College in Fremont. She says of her commitment to the writing of fiction: "I work slowly, squeezing out stories between the other parts of my life, and I revise continually, recycling the backsides of discarded drafts, hammering away on a small Adler that skids across my desk, and whispering to myself during the whole process. I feel writing is work and pleasure and obligation, and I feel mildly guilty most of the time because I do not write as much as I would like to. I am indebted to many people, many experiences, many books and two gently supportive writing teachers—Margaret Moffit, who saw talent in an eighth grader with a proclivity towards maudlin tales, and Wallace Stegner, who aimed me towards excellence in western—and Mormon—art."

Linda Sillitoe is a native of Salt Lake City and a graduate of the University of Utah. She is employed as a reporter and feature writer for the *Deseret News*, and in 1983 was awarded its annual recognition for excellence in writing. She has free-lanced investigative articles, short stories, poetry, essays and book reviews, which have appeared in *Utah Holiday, Network, Sunstone, Dialogue, BYU Studies, Exponent II* and elsewhere. She is poetry editor for *Exponent II*, and a former member of the advisory council of the Association for Mormon Letters, and has also published poetry and songs for children.

David Lane Wright was born in Benningto, Idaho, in 1929. Although he served in the United States Air Force most of his life, he was first and foremost a writer—a fact verified both by the numerous publications to his credit and the quantity of unpublished works he left behind when he died in 1967, at the age of 38. His poetry was published in such places as *Golden Quill Anthology, National Anthology of Poetry*, and *Poetry Public Quarterly*; his fiction in such places as *The Humanist, Mutiny, Arizona Quarterly,* and *Best Articles and Short Stories*; and his play "Still the Mountain Wind" was produced by Utah State University, the University of Minnesota, The Poet's Theatre of Cambridge, and just recently by Brigham Young University. His unpublished letters, poems, stories, journals and novels are housed in the Special Collections Library at Utah State University.

Acknowledgements and Copyrights

"A Song for One Still Voice." © 1979 Bruce W. Jorgensen. First published in *The Ensign*, IX, 3, 1979.

"The Age-Old Problem of Who." © 1983 Kevin Cassity.

"With Voice of Joy and Praise." © 1965 *The Western Humanities Review*. First published in *The Western Humanities Review*, XIX, 4, 1965. Reprinted by permission.

"Four Walls and An Empty Door." © 1983 Linda Sillitoe.

"Low Tide." © 1980 Karen Rosenbaum. First published in *Sunstone*, V, 5, 1980.

"Another Angel." © 1981 R. A. Christmas. First published in *Dialogue: A Journal of Mormon Thought*, XIV, 2, 1981.

"Counterpoint." © 1983 Kent A. Farnsworth.

"The Gift." © 1981 Levi S. Peterson. First published in *Dialogue: A Journal of Mormon Thought*, XV, 2, 1982.

"Everncere." © 1979 Eileen Gibbons Kump. First published in *The Ensign*, IX, 8, 1979.

"Lavender Blue." © 1981 Donald R. Marshall. First published in *Sunstone*, VI, 2, 1981.

"Yellow Dust." © 1979 Joseph Peterson. First published in *Century II: A Brigham Young University Student Journal*, IV, 1, 1979. Republished in *Sunstone*, IV, 5-6, 1979.

"Answer to Prayer." © 1983 Dennis M. Clark.

"Jessie and Louise." © 1980 Sibyl Johnston. First published in *Century II: A Brigham Young University Student Journal*, V, 2, 1980. Acknowledgement is made to Lee Charles Kelley for the song lyrics in this story.

"The Hawk." © 1960 *The Arizona Quarterly*. First published in *The Arizona Quarterly*, XVI, 4, 1960. Reprinted by permission. Gratitude is also expressed to Charlotte M. Wright, daughter of the author, for her endorsement of the republication of this story in this collection.

"Original Sin." © 1978 Lynne Larson. First published in *Mountainwest*, May, 1978.

"Introduction." © 1983 Levi S. Peterson.